SAVED BY THE BANG

SAVED BY THE BANG

M. J. NEARY

A DYSTOPIAN NOVEL

www.penmorepress.com

ISBN-13: 978-1-942756-54-5(Paperback)
ISBN   :-978-1-942756-55-2   (e-book)

BISAC Subject Headings:

FIC052000FICTION / Satire
HIS032000HISTORY / Europe / Russia & the Former Soviet Union
FIC055000FICTION / Dystopian

Cover design by Dawné Dominique
Cover Illustration by Christine Horner

Address all correspondence to:

Penmore Press LLC
920 N Javelina Pl
Tucson AZ 85748

Dedication

To my beloved mother, the queen of cats, whose elegance and sarcasm continue to intimidate and inspire those around her. Your soft paw with sharp claws continues to guide your students towards excellence. The world is your scratching post! It's a privilege to be your kitten.

Endorsements

Neary's wry narrative, sharply delineated characters, acerbic dialogue and descriptive detail vividly evoke a dysfunctional late Soviet era Belarus. "Saved by the Bang" should appeal to readers who like their fiction laced with wickedly funny, politically incorrect satire that goes down like a stiff shot of moonshine vodka with a nuclear chaser.
—Gary Inbinder, author of *The Devil in Montmartre*

A hilarious romp that bounces between post-Chernobyl Belarus and Connecticut, this novel is a witty, clever, and sexy must-read!
—Shifra Hochberg, author of *The Lost Catacomb*

Neary's "nuclear comedy" proves an explosive delight. Readers will tingle from the sparks that fly from her deftly developed conflagration. Her hot cast of characters includes survivors from the Chernobyl disaster, rivals in love, musicians, and Afghan veterans. At story's end, you'll feel yourself glowing.
—Mary Sharnick, author of *Thirst: a Novel*

Saved by the Bang is an intimate and often shocking portrait of a family and nation in turmoil. Told with M.J. Neary's distinctive dark humor, the novel is an eye-opener to life behind the Iron Curtain and a story of resilience in the face of hatred, violence, corruption, and a nuclear catastrophe.

– Kim Rendfeld, author of *The Cross and the Dragon* and *The Ashes of Heaven's Pillar*

Marina Neary's *SAVED BY THE BANG* is hilarious, provocative, shocking,at times horrifying, deeply moving, thought-provoking, absurd, and real as can be! From the heart and not for the timid.

—Bill Bowler, Coordinating Editor, Bewildering Stories

Chapter One

Midday Hookups in the Coat Room

Regional Music Academy, Gomel, Belarus – April 25, 1986

If Vladimir Ivanych had any hair left, he would be pulling it out right about now. With the spring showcase less than a month away, the rehearsal was not going well at all. The star tenor and the female accompanist were too busy playing footsy under the grand piano. After twenty-some years of grooming and herding musicians, Vladimir Ivanych knew better than to expect discretion in the workplace. But these two were really butchering the piece! And it was a marvelous piece, really, a gypsy-themed romance to the lyrics of Pushkin, and it suited them perfectly. When Nicholas and Antonia were on stage together, the audience wept, and the shabby walls of the auditorium crumbled away. It was just the two of them, betrothed in music.

Alas, that day they were just not on top of their game, and they could not have picked a worse time to slack off. The chairman of the vocal department of the Moscow Conservatory was coming to the showcase. It was a chance for Vladimir Ivanych to prove to that snooty pig-faced Muscovite that Belarusian musicians were no chopped liver. It was critical that he put the best of the best in the limelight. He had exactly four minutes to make an impression. Those would be arguably the most important four minutes of his career. And now his two golden children, to whom he had entrusted his reputation, were goofing off in the most vulgar way.

"By God, woman, have you forgotten how to sight-read?" he roared at the accompanist. "If I were hearing you for the first time, I'd think you were drunk."

Antonia Olenski, age thirty-two, five-foot three, one hundred pounds, blood pressure one hundred over sixty, boasted a modest yet noble lineage. Her maternal great-grandfather, a member of untitled Russian gentry, had been named a distinguished citizen for his efforts to contain a cholera outbreak in Kolomna. After the Bolshevik revolution, he was forced to relinquish his czar-bestowed honors and denounce his Orthodox faith. Antonia's paternal ancestors were German Jews who had fled eastward to escape the holocaust, morose aesthetes, as proficient with watercolors as they were with interest rates. There was nothing blaringly Semitic in Antonia's features except for the slight curvature of the dorsum and the sultry shape of the eyelids. Not that she looked distinctly Slavic either. She was a transcendent creature without a nationality, more feline than human. She did not speak—she meowed, hissed, purred and growled. Her hair was bobbed, frosted and teased to look like the mane on a Siberian tabby. Nicholas Nichenko was wild about her. And who could resist this taciturn kitten? In the world of crude, large-boned Belarusian women with ruddy faces and deep bosomy voices, she was a rare gem of fragility, haughtiness and subtle sarcasm. The director's reprimand stirred most fervent protective sentiments in Nicholas.

"Vladimir Ivanych," he implored, "don't be cross with Antonia."

"Why shouldn't I be cross with her? She's falling a good measure behind. Her fingers are tripping over each other."

"It's not that she's playing too slowly. It's me singing too fast. I had too much coffee this morning. That's why we sound off sync."

Vladimir Ivanych threw the score across the rehearsal room. "Get out, both of you! Good God, you'll drive me into an early grave."

* * * *

"Looks like we're officially off the hook." Nicholas took Antonia by the elbow and dragged her into the coat room. "In all fairness, you owe me one kiss, for rescuing you from that bald ogre."

"Silly man," she chided him. "You know perfectly well that I don't kiss tenors, only baritones."

But Nicholas was not your typical tenor, all chubby, soft and effeminate. He was tall, strapping, and hyper-masculine, and had one hell of a stage presence, especially in a tailcoat. The only man who could rival him in the masculinity department was Antonia's Polish-born husband Joseph—a baritone, naturally—who was currently out of town on yet another folkloric expedition through the countryside, gathering and transcribing folk tunes. His trek started in the misty marshes of his native Grodno and continued eastward into the legendary White Tower Forest. Rumor had it Joseph was collaborating with the lead singer of the Bards, a famous folk-rock band from Minsk. On the day of the showcase he was going to knock everyone's socks off with a totally obscure Belarusian peasant song in rock arrangement. Wouldn't that be a royal fuck-you to Evil Stepmother Russia! The director of the Moscow Conservatory would have a heart attack in his plush front row seat. Once again, Joseph Olenski would emerge a hero. You would not expect any less from a former child laureate who at the age of twelve had harvested all the trophies available in his age category.

Another unspoken reason behind Joseph's prolonged business trip was to visit a certain young lady to whom he referred as "destitute kinswoman"—a euphemism for *bastard* in polite circles. He had fathered that girl in his late teens, while treating tuberculosis at a sanatorium in the Carpathians. His fleeting flame, Tatiana, was an anemic childless widow some twenty years his senior, a compassionate soul who had kept the comely youngster warm in her bed for two weeks, no questions asked. The pregnancy that followed was the reward for her kindness. Having no desire to complicate the young prodigy's life, Tatiana had kept the sweet secret to herself. Tragically, premenopausal childbirth had triggered a relapse in her tuberculosis. Gasping on her stiff hospice cot, Tatiana had finally summoned Joseph, her only request being that he should occasionally visit little Anastasia at the orphanage. It was not too much to ask, and Joseph was far from a heartless monster.

Looking into the fading eyes of the woman who still stirred giddy warm fondness in him, he had made a solemn promise. Yes, Anastasia would have warm socks in winter, and no, her teeth would not rot away from lack of vitamins. He, Joseph Olenski, would see to that. The only thing he would not let the girl have was his last name. That would make the weird situation a little weirder and a little more real. His own family wouldn't care, but his conservatory professors would probably think it rather gauche that their star pupil was a father at eighteen. It just wouldn't be good for his public image. Every few months he would come to the orphanage and bring jars with homemade raspberry jam and bundles of home-spun socks from his mother's house. The administration believed him to be the Anastasia's distant cousin. Several times he sang old Polish and Lithuanian carols at New Year's parties. He flirted with all the nurses and the caregivers, kissing their chlorine-soaked hands and pinching their soggy breasts. The glow on their broad faces gave him a profound sense of fulfillment. He knew he was put on this earth to make unattractive women feel desired, if even for a few minutes.

Essentially, there are two kinds of people—those who use power to get sex, and those who use sex to get power. While in Minsk Conservatory, Joseph had prostituted his dewy pimply youth to middle-aged altos to get plum roles, which in turn gave him access to twenty-five year old sopranos. For a few years, he was stuck in the draining circle of fame and carnal indulgences. One way to break the circle was to get married, to a penniless virgin. Antonia Rosenberg, an engineer's kid, was a perfect candidate, living in clean, dignified poverty that obliged her to impeccable behavior.

Saved By The Bang

Her uterus was not scarred from venereal diseases and frequent abortions, which was a major attraction for Joseph. Soon he had another daughter, a legitimate one this time, whom he did not need to hide. Maryana had inherited her mother's small frame, so he could proudly carry her on his shoulders through the riverside park. He would buy her an ice-cream cone, and she would eat half of it and let the rest of it melt and drip on top of his head. Such exaggerated paternal devotion solicited gasps from Antonia's colleagues.

"With a husband like that, you should have five children!"

But Antonia had no desire to continue procreating. The four of them were crammed in her mother's one-bedroom apartment. To make room for another baby crib Antonia would have to get rid of the piano. Another argument was that she had a mild heart defect, and doctors did not recommend another pregnancy. When Maryana was four months old, Antonia popped in an intrauterine device and returned to the music academy, where the boys greeted her with howls of adoration. The glowing young mother looked womanly without being matronly. The smell of breast milk mixing with the smell of Baltic perfume drove them wild. During the rehearsals you could cut the testosterone with a knife. The moment Antonia Olenski would walk into the hall, clicking her heels, the tenors would rush towards the piano, pushing each other aside, to pull out the bench for her. Nicholas Nichenko, the tallest and the strongest of them all, quickly established his supremacy as the alpha-tenor. One scowl from him, and the boys would back off with grunts of resignation. On stage Antonia belonged to him. For the past eight years they had been enjoying a chaste romance worthy of Guinivere and Lancelot, star-crossed lovers doomed to necking in the coatroom.

"Just one kiss," Nicholas begged, pressing her into the corner of the dark coatroom. "Nobody will know."

Antonia gave him a swat across the mouth and then collapsed into his embrace, not in a sexy take-me-now, but in a troubling call-the-ambulance sort of way.

"Take me home, Cole," she whispered. "It's been a long day."

"What are you talking about? We've only been playing for forty minutes. It's not even three o'clock."

"But it feels so much later."

Nicholas patted her on the cheeks. "Your skin feels clammy. Maybe I should take you to the doctor instead?"

"Just give me a ride home, Cole. No more questions, please. If you want to be useful, do as I ask you for once."

Nicholas threw her over his shoulder, carried her out the back door and laid her on the back seat of his black Volga.

"Are you sure you don't want to go to the hospital?" he asked one last time as he fixed his rear view mirror. "It's just a few blocks away."

Antonia did not answer. He took it as a no.

Chapter Two
ASPIRIN COCKTAIL

Telman Street, the Olenski residence – 3 pm

The elevator of the luxurious Kruschev era apartment complex was broken again, which meant that Maryana Olenski had to hobble up to the third floor. Barely eight, she was intimately acquainted with pain. Slings, braces and crutches had become integral parts of her anatomy. At any given time one of her limbs was either broken or sprained. Ah, the price a young gymnast has to pay for getting bronze in the regionals!

The ache in her bandaged ankle kept Maryana from dwelling on the idea that she was returning to an empty apartment. Earlier in the week she had seen a story on the news about a burglar masquerading as a plumber who would butcher his victims and use their meat to make sausages and sell them on the market. Maryana found comfort in the fact that she did not have enough flesh on her bones and to make her sufficiently attractive to the psycho butcher. He liked his meat juicy and laced in lard. She was mostly sinew and scar tissue.

Leaving her backpack and shoes in the hallway, Maryana went to inspect her miniature zoo in the kitchen. The water in the fish bowl was turning yellow and murky, with three more guppies floating belly up. It would probably be a good idea to flush them down the toilet, but Maryana decided to wait for her father's return. After all, he was the master of burial ceremonies. The female Syrian hamster was still rustling in its beach bucket. Maryana reached down to scratch its bobbing striped head only to get nipped. The albino parakeet, sadly, was not looking too robust with its eyes half-shut and crusty. The empty perch was covered in runny droppings with loose, brittle feathers stuck to it. When Maryana ran her fingers over the metallic bars of the cage, the bird shook up and pulled its head deeper into its neck.

Never buy pets at a farmer's market, her grandmother would say. You never know if that so-called Syrian hamster is just an ordinary rat with its tail cut off. Never marry a guy you met at a bar, even if he claims to be an engineering student.

Point taken, Grandma Lily. No more buying birds and hamsters from the same old ladies who sold neon lipstick and stonewashed jeans with a fake Levi label. As for marrying an alcoholic engineer, or any guy at all for that matter, it was not in the cards for someone like Maryana. She knew she was ugly, and no male specimen would ever look at her with romantic longing. All her teammates said so. Boys just didn't like short girls with frizzy dark hair, slanted eyes, and big crooked noses.

Luckily, even ugly girls had an opportunity for redemption. Nature was not so cruel as to shut all doors at once. At the age of eight, Maryana was the star of the Yuri

Saved By The Bang

Gagarin Magnet School famous for its accelerated English program. There were several video salons in Gomel that showed American horror flicks. Maryana could watch them without subtitles. With any luck, she would gain the status of a "good friend," the kind that would allow her classmates to copy her homework. In addition to a lively brain, Maryana had a compassionate heart and took pity on the delinquents whose vibrant social lives outside school left no time for studying. By letting others peek into her notebook, she was putting herself in great danger. Contributing to the delinquency of fellow students was the gravest offense an A-student could commit. If caught, Maryana would face a public reprimand by the school principal. The authorities would expel her from the Children of October party and take away her shiny red star. For an eight-year-old, it was the worst kind of humiliation imaginable. Still, Maryana continued letting her classmates cheat from her notes and plagiarize from her compositions. The class hooligans secretly admired her subtle rebellious streak. In other words, this girl had everything except for a pretty face.

Being ugly had its benefits, according to Grandma Lily, who had been pretty her whole life and knew all the annoying liabilities that came with it. Ugly girls who had come to terms with their plight did not waste time on all that lyrical bullshit about white lace and rose petals. No, they focused on becoming astronauts and nuclear physicists. A woman who was not distracted by marriage and back-to-back maternity leaves could easily obtain her doctorate by age twenty-six and become tremendously valuable to the State. The State in turn rewarded its loyal servants with medals, certificates of appreciation and vacation packages to the Crimea. The State was the girl's most loyal boyfriend.

As much as Maryana admired her maternal grandmother, she was not crazy about the idea of serving the State, at least not the one she lived in. She did not really love Grandpa Lenin, not in the way all good children were supposed to love him. If anything, she thought he looked kind of silly with his bald head and pointy beard. The whole communism doctrine struck her as a bunch of baloney. The sentiment grew stronger with each trip to the October parade. Watching those ugly floats with red flags and pine wreaths move down the main street, listening to the brass bands that played the same cheesy march tunes, she cringed. It looked more like a freak show than a celebration of workers' triumph. At times her embarrassment would reach a point where she would wish she had been born in some other country. It didn't have to be the dreaded United States of America, the home of the infamous Mister Twister from the classic children's book. She would settle for Northern Ireland, or Honduras, or even Somalia.

Gosh, there are so many nice places in the world. Why did she have to be born underneath the red star? How did the song go? *I know no other country where a man can breathe so freely.* Yeah, right. Keep telling yourself that, comrade, especially when they ship you to Afghanistan to spread socialism. When you come back with your legs missing—if you're lucky to come back in the first place—they'll give you a spot on the float at the next year's October parade.

Of course, if Maryana said it out loud, the homeroom teacher would pillory her in front of the class. A first-grader yapping against the government would probably land the rest of her family in hot water. Maryana shuddered as she pictured her mother being called on the carpet and interrogated about her parenting style. Nah...a public execution could wait. Sincerity was overrated. In a way, life would be so much easier if she just believed what other kids her age believed. Or did they? What if...what if there were a few renegade souls in her school who fantasized about setting those tacky floats on fire? If only they'd speak up. Of course, they wouldn't! They were cowards, just like her. Seriously, you're better off telling people what they want to hear. When your social studies teacher asked you where you see yourself in ten years, you told her that your highest aspiration is to build an underground bunker in case Reagan dropped an atomic bomb on us. That's an easy A right there. Your essay would be put on display in the hall of honor, even if it had tons of misspellings in it. Your grade was based on the depth of your persuasion, not grammatical accuracy. In this school and in this country you got rewarded for lies, for saying that the novel *The Young Guard* depicting the Nazi occupation of Eastern Ukraine was the most goddamn moving piece of literature you've ever read, even if you haven't read a single page from it. Hell, it didn't have to be *The Young Guard*. It can be any other novel set during World War II featuring a tomboyish heroine named Zoya or Uliana who dies in the hands of German tormentors. The last word escaping from the virginal martyr's lips is invariably "Motherland!"

Maryana had no desire to end up like Zoya or Uliana, even if it meant having a whole book written about her. Having your teeth and your nails pulled out, all in the name of the State? Totally not worth it! Screw Grandpa Lenin and his whacky ideas about the inherent dignity of the proletariat. Maryana was yet to meet one factory worker who did not smell like rotting bologna or spit through the gap between his gold-plated teeth. There were plenty of those beauties hanging out at the trolley stop. Sometimes, while on her way to gymnastics practice, she would have to share a seat with them and listen to their conversations—if that's what you call that symphony of grunts, belches, farts and profanities. Who knows, maybe the proletariat was different when Grandpa Lenin was around. Or maybe had never actually met a factory worker. Or he had a really sick sense of humor if he thought that these guys could run the country instead of the czar and his ministers. Grandpa Lenin, really?

However, there was a certain guy whose ideas Maryana sort of liked, a guy she would actually not mind serving. His name was Jesus. Yeah, *that* Jesus! From the New Testament, you know. That thought of joining a convent had been planted in her head by her father, a closet Catholic. Joseph wasn't crazy about following the moral code with the long list of the sexual restrictions, and turned a deaf ear to the sermons on chastity. As for the esthetic component of the faith, the architecture, the ritual, the organ music, he was totally enraptured by it. When Maryana was four, Joseph had her secretly baptized during a trip to western Belarus, where Christianity had not been completely stamped out. From him she had picked up bits and pieces of the Catholic faith. Nuns get to wear those super cool habits that come in white, blue or brown, depending on the order. They bake bread and gather honey all day long. Best of all, they don't have obnoxious relatives pestering them. Hey, it beats being married to some onion-eating, moonshine-drinking asshole and paying monthly dues to the Communist Party. If given the opportunity, Maryana would gladly trade her school uniform for the habit and her red star pin for the silver crucifix.

There was one Catholic icon in the entire house, tucked away behind the bronze bust of Alexander Pushkin on the desk where Joseph wrote his music. It was Maryana's secret altar. On those rare occasions when she found herself alone in the apartment, she would rehearse for her future career as a nun. She would tie a linen towel around her head like a veil and kneel in front of the icon. Having only been to a Catholic mass twice in her life, she tried to reconstruct the litany from memory. She could not remember the exact words, but she did a pretty good job mimicking the pathos in the priest's voice.

"Almighty Father, take that parakeet already. End its suffering, before Papa Josey comes home and wrings its neck."

Joseph was totally capable of doing something like that, jokes aside. His pastoral childhood on the farm had made him callous and unceremonious when it came to animals. He had put many ailing creatures of various sizes out of their misery. Neck-twisting, throat-slitting, skull-breaking—he was a pro! Whenever his daughter's pets showed signs of organ failure, he would dispose of them efficiently, seamlessly and discretely. Well, most of the time. One morning Maryana found the carcass of her calico guinea pig wrapped in a paper bag and stuffed in the trash bucket. The animal had been suffering from intestinal parasites and Joseph had hastened its demise by giving it rat poison. Maryana figured out the cause of death from the chunks of dry vomit caked on the fur. Moving forward, Joseph was more thorough about hiding the dead bodies.

After saying the obligatory prayer for another creature, Maryana could focus on her own selfish interests. She adjusted the pillow under her knees. "I also pray that Grandma Lily doesn't find out that I messed up on my math test. Please don't let her look in my backpack when she returns from Kiev. Cloud her memory, oh God. Send us some disaster to make her forget about the math test. And while you're at it, oh Lord, please burn down the gymnasium. I'm sick of that place!"

* * * *

When she heard the front door creak, Maryana jumped to her feet, pulled the towel off her head and stuffed it under the pillow. She could not afford being caught in a state of spiritual nakedness.

"Cotton Paw!" she heard her mother's voice. "How many times have I asked you not to drop your junk by the door? I nearly tripped."

"Sorry, Mama Cat," Maryana whined from the living room.

"No, you're not." Antonia tossed her keys on the telephone stand. "You're not sorry one bit. You can memorize Pushkin's epic poems, yet you cannot remember a simple request to keep your smelly shoes and your backpack out of my way. It's your way of aggravating me."

Maryana found it a little odd that her mother, instead of rushing to the piano as she would normally do, collapsed on the sofa with her shoes still on, breathing rapidly, just like the sickly parakeet in the kitchen.

"You're home early," Maryana said, sitting down at her mother's feet. "I wasn't expecting you until after dark."

Antonia flicked her hand weakly. "Vladimir Ivanych was in a pissy mood, so he cut the rehearsal short. The man is a walking powder keg. Cole and I took a royal whipping earlier today. I'm getting fed up with that place."

Maryana examined the tiny scratches on her mother's lacquered shoes. "If it's any consolation, Mama Cat, my day wasn't any better. I also got yelled at by the coach. Irina Petrovna said if I fall off the beam again, she'll kick me off the team."

Antonia made eye contact with her daughter for the first time and tried to prop herself up. "That will never happen, Cotton Paw."

"How do you know?"

"There's a pact between our families. Last year your father placed Irina Petrovna's son, a tone-deaf retard as far as I'm concerned, into the accelerated program. The boy has zero musical talent, and his intellect is that of a kindergartener. So now your coach is eternally indebted to us. She promised to turn you into a champion gymnast. The day she kicks you off the team, her son will land in the remedial class where he belongs, among other thumb-suckers. See how this works, Cotton Paw? Parents have to trade favors sometimes, in the interests of their children. Your coach will put you on that podium, even if she has to break you."

"She's already broken me." Maryana stared down at her braced ankle. "I don't want to go back. I hate that place.

Everyone on the team is laughing at me. Nobody wants to share a locker with me."

Antonia squeezed her daughter's hand. "As your mother, I won't tolerate this...this *defeatist* talk."

"But it hurts, Mama Cat! It hurts everywhere, all the time."

"I got news for you, sweetie. Life hurts, from start to finish." Antonia huffed and fell back against the cushions. "I was born weighing two kilos, with a gaping hole in my heart and another one in my palate, plus a deviated septum. For the first five years of my life I was a runt with a nasal voice who suffered from frequent ear infections. Still, it never occurred to me to milk my ailments as an excuse for not succeeding in life. My mother would make me take icy-cold showers and run in the snow to strengthen my immune system. Basically, she told all those pessimistic doctors to go screw themselves, especially the cardiologist. When I started school, I was the shortest and skinniest in my class, yet nobody messed with me. And you were born perfect, with every advantage that I didn't have. So don't dare telling me that you're broken."

"I'm sorry, Mama Cat," Maryana pleaded in desperation. "I'll go back to the gym. I'll never complain again. Just please, don't be mad."

"Stop crying, for God's sake. You look pathetic when you do. The tip of your nose swells and looks like a red light bulb and your eyes turn into little chinks. Not very dignified."

"What do you need me to do, Mama Cat? I'll do it."

"Bring me an aspirin and a glass of water." Admitting she needed help was very taxing on Antonia's pride. "It's in the kitchen cabinet. You may need to climb on a chair to reach it.”

Inspired by the prospect of doing at least one thing right and winning her mother's approval, Maryana rushed to fill in the order. It took her a few minutes to find the little plastic bottle with a red lid.

“These pills expired four years ago,” Antonia muttered, examining the label. “Painkillers lose strength as they age. Perhaps I should triple the dose just to be sure they kick in.” She opened the bottle and found a mixture of colorful pills of all shapes and sizes, from round powder tablets to oval gel caps. “What's all this? Don't tell me your father put all the loose pills in the same bottle. How in the world am I supposed to figure out which ones are aspirin?”

“I think it's the ones with the letter ‘A’ stamped on them,” Maryana suggested.

Antonia scratched her daughter on the head. “You are so clever, Cotton Paw. And if I was harsh on you earlier, it's only because I want to raise you the way Grandma Lily raised me. Thanks to her, I became such a productive and well-adjusted member of society. I trample over my rivals. And some day you will too.”

Wincing, Antonia shoved three aspirins in her mouth. The powdery pills resisted going down her throat, even with water. “No, don't swallow us!” they seemed to protest.

“You know what would make me the happiest girl in the world?” Maryana asked suddenly.

“What?”

“If we could go to the market and buy some animal print fabric and make matching dresses. Then we'd look like mama cat and her kitten.” Maryana pulled at her mother's limp clammy hand. "Please! It's been my dream ever since I saw that pattern in the *Burda* magazine."

"You know it's not possible. Your Grandma Lily would never allow it. Only whores and circus performers wear animal print."

"But Grandma Lily isn't here now. She'll be at a conference in Kiev until the end of the month. We have plenty of time to make the dresses and take some pictures."

"We'll never get away with it. One day, when we least expect it, Grandma Lily will find a tiny strip of spotty fabric under the sewing machine. Her eyesight is excellent. Remember that time you tried to hide your report card from her? Trust me. She'll know that we misbehaved in her absence. Then we'll be in major trouble, both of us. She'll box our ears."

Maryana crossed her arms. "Why do you always listen to Grandma Lily? Why do we always have to play by her rules?"

Antonia did not like when her daughter asked her questions that she already knew the answers to. "Because," she said in a tone of exasperation, "we live in her apartment, and she can kick us out at any given moment. There's a housing crisis in the country. Don't you ever watch the news? It's next to impossible for a young family to get a place to live. Grandma Lily was generous enough to give us a bedroom, but she likes things a certain way. We mustn't irritate her."

"Why can't Grandma Lily marry a man with a nice big apartment and move there? This way we could have this apartment all to ourselves and do whatever we wanted. We could get a Saint Bernard puppy and play German rock at full volume. You could have parties with friends every weekend and not worry about asking her permission."

Antonia shook her head with an air of regretful skepticism. "I don't think Grandma Lily is in the market for marriage. She likes her independence too much. Ever since Grandpa Eli died, she hasn't had to pick up anyone's dirty socks or check anyone's shirt collar for traces of lipstick. Grandma hasn't had to do any of that in sixteen years. Once you get used to that sort of freedom, it's hard to give it up."

"But Papa Josey says she needs a man," Maryana insisted. "He says Grandma is still full of juice, which quickly turns to venom. If she got married again, maybe she she'd loosen up a bit. Papa knows a few nice men at work who'd be all too happy to marry Grandma."

Antonia wagged her index finger. "Papa Josey shouldn't be discussing such things with you. Anxious as he is to get Grandma's apartment, he shouldn't be playing matchmaker. An engineer and a musician wouldn't make a good pair. One day you'll find out."

Maryana sensed it would be better to get off the topic. Her mother's face looked pale, and her voice sounded weak.

"Mama Cat," the girl asked timidly, "may I take a nap next to you?"

"Whatever," Antonia replied half-audibly and covered her eyes with her hand. "Just don't make any noise."

Chapter Three
White Linens and Dark Chocolates

Midnight express, April 25-26

On the train from Minsk to Gomel, Joseph kept banging his forehead against the window, hoping to dislodge the tune for "White Linens". It was an awesome song, and he could not wait to play it for his colleagues at the academy, but it had been stuck in his head for the past fourteen hours. The same "La-la-la-la-mmmm" swirled and swirled in his brain, making him dizzy. Oh, the sufferings a man must endure for his art!

A few years earlier Joseph had embarked on a mission that was nothing short of apostolic. He had always felt sympathy for the smaller republics of the union, especially Belarus, whose children, robbed of their cultural identity by the oppressive Soviet beast, would gulp cheesy western pop. It wasn't even good stuff, the kind he had gotten stoned to on hashish while in conservatory. It certainly wasn't Led Zeppelin, or Pink Floyd, or Genesis. No, it was toxic rubbish that American recording studios ejaculated each month. The streets of Gomel were littered with shady looking kiosks where teenagers would go to get abysmal quality recordings of Cindy Lauper's greatest hits. For as little as ten rubles you could drop off a blank cassette and pick it up a few hours later. Hey, Belarusian girls wanna have fun too!

Now, Joseph had no beef with Cindy Lauper or America, for that matter. Those Yankee clowns struck him as sufficiently benign, in spite of the atomic bomb hype. He had a beef with the Moscow-centered government that sought to stifle the spirit of national pride in the annexed republics, to sever their indigenous subjects from their roots and turn them into sterile slaves of the State. The Moscow tyrants were encountering some resistance from the people of Ukraine and the Baltics. In Vilnius and Riga, Russians were being thrown off the trams. In Belarus, however, the situation was rather dire. The Russian cancer had metastasized through the republic. The native language was still taught in schools, but on a very primitive level, bare grammar without the flavor. The students, raised on Moscow-controlled television, would recite the epic poems of Jakub Kolas out of mere obligation, without any intention of practicing the language outside the classroom. Those deep soulful vowels that often resembled an owl's hoot simply did not sound fashionable. The only people who spoke the old language on daily basis were the elderly living in the countryside. That was how Belarusian came to be known as the language of senile peasants. Every time Joseph thought of that, saliva would start boiling in his cheeks. How he would love to spit at the red union flag, at the hammer and the sickle. No, he would not grant Moscow this victory. Somehow, with help from God and like-minded nationalists, he would manage to persuade the world that Belarusian was the language of valiant ancient warriors, the closest to the Old Slavonic. Yes, it takes a Pole to resurrect Belarus.

He was bringing home a song that would be used as a weapon against the Russian oppression. "White Linens" in the Bards' pseudo-rock rendition was guaranteed to become a sensation, first on the republican radio, then on the national. The best talent in Belarus had been pulled to collaborate on this two-minute masterpiece. Who could resist the song about a milkmaid and a shepherd boy kissing under the willows? Sex sells. Joseph knew it better than anyone. Take a folk song about two villagers having an illicit tryst, dress it up in rock, and you got yourself an international hit. Joseph Olenski was going to do for the Belarusian folk music what Ian Anderson of Jethro Tull had done for the English. He was going to wed the ancient dulcimer to the electric guitar, and the final product was going to be fucking awesome. And he was going to stick it to the damned communists. One song was going to start a revolution!

All those artistic and patriotic thoughts gave Joseph a painful boner. Righteous indignation always led to sexual arousal. Yet he was stuck on the train with four other people in the compartment, so he could not even jerk off. The three adults were asleep, but the eight-year old girl was very much awake, munching on a stale bagel and washing it down with pear-flavored soda. She kept burrowing Joseph with her beady cornflower eyes, as if she could read his thoughts. It suddenly occurred to him that the girl was fascinated by the bulge in his pants.

"What have you got in there?" she asked him.

"Nothing special, just a tennis ball."

"Oooh, I like balls. Can I see?"

"It's a present for my wife," he said with a smile. "Little girl, haven't you been taught not to talk to strangers?"

"But you're not a stranger. I know who you are. I've seen you on TV."

"Did you really?"

"My Mommy watches *Belarusian Hour* every Saturday morning. She gets up early just for that. It's the highlight of her week. We saw your interview with the Bards."

Joseph perked up and fixed his collar. "Oh, yeah?"

"Mommy thinks you're pretty amazing."

"Well, your Mommy has exquisite taste in music."

"Not just music, art and poetry too."

"A Renaissance woman, huh?"

"Totally! She's a professor of early twentieth century Belarusian literature. She did her thesis on Janka Kupala. Last year she made me memorize chunks of *The Little Flute*."

Joseph nodded at the bloated middle-aged woman snoring in the corner. "Is that your Mommy?"

"Nope, that's my great-auntie. She's taking me to Gomel for a funeral." The girl pulled out a photograph of a stunning blonde in her late twenties with high cheekbones. "*This* is my Mommy. She couldn't come to the funeral because she was moderating a poetry workshop. It wouldn't be right to cancel an event like this last minute. She thinks it's time we kicked Russia's ass."

In his life, Joseph had encountered many sharp, precocious children, but the last phrase knocked the breath out of him for a few seconds.

"Say, little one, you're a real spitfire. I like that."

"I take after Mommy." The girl looked down coyly. "She's such a fan of yours. My God! She says you're her kindred spirit. She'd give anything to meet you in person."

Joseph had to pinch himself to make sure he was not hallucinating. Perhaps, it was that dose of hashish he had taken with the lead singer of the Bards.

"Perhaps, we can do something about it. What's your Mommy's name?"

"Ilona."

The name was not a typical for Eastern Belarus, which led Joseph to conclude that the woman came from the west, like him. She probably had some Polish and Lithuanian in her. Baltic genes don't lie. Assuming that blonde hair was natural, of course. You just could not get such perfect flaxen gloss from a bottle.

"Tell you what." Joseph leaned in. "I have a message for your Mommy. She can come and see me at the studio any time. I'm going to be in Minsk again in two months to film a choir performance. I can easily get her a studio pass. It'll be like a private audience. Tell her I'll take her out for coffee and pastries, and afterwards...she can play with my balls. How about that?"

* * * *

On the way to the bathroom Joseph groped the bosomy train conductor. The quick sloppy tryst did not ease his tension. If anything, it only inflamed his desire for Antonia. He could not wait to get home and give his wife a royal shagging. Antonia's puritanical mother was out of town, so he knew they could make some noise. His erection carried him through the dark streets of the slumbering city.

By the time he reached his apartment on Telman Street, it was eleven o'clock at night. As soon as he crossed the threshold, the song evaporated from his head, and his erection went down. He sensed something was terribly amiss. The lights were off, and there was a weird pungent smell coming from the living room, a mixture of blood, piss and vomit.

Without taking his shoes off, Joseph stormed into the living room and flipped the lights on only to see Antonia on the floor in a puddle of red mucus. Her beautiful custom-tailored dress was soaked. Maryana was sleeping on the couch with her back turned to her mother. The girl's ribbon-tied pigtail was sticking from under the blanket.

Joseph pulled his daughter off the couch and shook her. "Christ Almighty! What happened here? Answer me!"

Maryana blinked a few times. "Papa Josey? Back already?"

Joseph gave her a hearty whack over the head. "You dumb little bitch! You troll! Your mother is bleeding to death, and you didn't call the ambulance."

Still reeling from the blow, Maryana crawled into the corner, a blanket over her head. Through the layers of plaid wool she could hear her father's trembling voice.

"Send an ambulance. My wife is dying. Telman Street, building number two. Yes, the brick one. They're all brick, you idiots! What? How am I supposed to know if she has a pulse? I didn't take it. I just came in, and she was on the floor. It's your fucking job to take her pulse, you cock-suckers!"

Saved By The Bang

* * * *

Gomel Central Hospital—April 26, 1986

"They should make chocolates shaped like embryos," Dr. Peter Mihalych muttered, tossing a golden wrapper into the half-empty box.

Dear God, he was so sick of chocolates! He was the best obstetric surgeon in Gomel, and his eternally grateful patients seemed determined to give him diabetes. Always, always candy. Why couldn't those women bring him more imaginative gifts? He wouldn't mind getting a cassette player, or a hand-knit sweater, or even a set of Polish soaps. Anything to break that cocoa and sugar monotony! The most popular thank-you gift for a successfully installed contraceptive device or a late-term abortion was a box of candies from the Spartacus factory. It was always the same deluxe assortment called "White Tower Forest" featuring chocolates in the shapes of various animals from Belarus' famous national park that had inspired so many local painters, historians and composers. After being in practice for fifteen years, Peter Mihalych could not stand the very look of milk chocolate squirrels filled with strawberry jam. What if confectioners used the same ingredients to make human embryos? About time people started appreciating the hard work of Soviet abortionists. Yeah, right! Like that was going to happen.

Peter Mihalych chuckled at his own thoughts. It was past midnight, and he could barely think straight. He had another hour until the end of his shift, and he was hoping that no emergencies would arise. There was one fifteen-year old on the third floor having a late-term miscarriage, but the nurses would handle her. He had no patience for those underage screamers.

At one o'clock Peter Mihalych removed his scrubs and put on his raincoat, ready to leave. The night sky looked misty. He tried to remember if he had brought his umbrella. Suddenly, the alley leading to the hospital entrance became illuminated by the flashers of the ambulance van.

"Oh, man," he moaned. "Not another bleeder."

It did not look like he was going home early after all. The ambulance driver would not put the flashers on without a good reason. It meant the patient was near death and would need an operation immediately. Peter Milalych's fingers were already stained in chocolate. He was hoping he would not have to scrub his hands again.

A few seconds later a disheveled man in his early thirties charged through the door. The doctor recognized the local celebrity, Joseph Olenski, the folkloric revivalist whose gorgeous Western Slavic features graced the cover of the season program at the music academy.

Joseph fell on his knees and grabbed the doctor's leg.

"I implore you, please save my Antonia. She's bleeding badly. She is a national treasure. I'll do anything to repay you. I'll teach your grandchildren music for free. I'll turn them into opera stars. They don't call me a miracle maker for nothing."

Peter Mihalych wiggled his leg out of Joseph's grip. "Husband," he barked, "stand aside."

Joseph fell back with a whimper.

Saved By The Bang

Dear God, please let Antonia live! I swear I won't touch another woman for the rest of my life.

The paramedics wheeled the patient through the hall into the examination room. The idea of performing emergency surgery at one o'clock in the morning did not appeal to Peter Mihalych. The elegance and the fragility of the patient could not soften his heart. In his practice he had seen many pretty women in distress. They always came to him begging him to dislodge an IUD or finish a home-induced abortion. The frequent flyers would bring thank-you gifts. The most popular gift would be a box of candies from the Spartacus chocolate factory.

He yawned and pulled on a pair of rubber gloves.

"Woman," he said with the austerity of a Pharisee about to stone a harlot. "How long have you had this pain?"

"For three days?"

"And have you been taking anything for it?"

"Just aspirin."

Peter Mihalych looked away and chuckled. "Brilliant, fucking brilliant..." He then turned back to his patient and roared. "Woman! You have blood in your abdominal cavity."

"Dear me...Do I really?"

"Yes, woman! You had an embryo lodged in your right fallopian tube. Do you know what that means?"

"I'm afraid I don't."

Peter Mihalych remembered that he was dealing with a musician, and musicians are removed from such vulgar subjects as biology.

"You have an ectopic pregnancy, woman. The embryo caused the tube to burst. By taking aspirin you made matters worse. Aspirin thins your blood. Now we have a royal mess on our hands. We have to operate immediately. I'm not at my best after midnight, but we can't wait until morning."

"Is it dangerous?"

"I'll say, yeah."

"Can I die from this?"

"It's a distinct possibility."

"Well, doctor, that's just not acceptable. I have an eight-year-old at home."

"You should've thought of that before you devoured a bottle of aspirin." Peter Mihalych did not appreciate this accusatory tone of voice. Like it was his problem that the silly woman had a kid at home! "Haven't you been told, woman? You never, ever take painkillers for abdominal pain. It's the first thing they teach you in health class."

"If something happens to me," Antonia thought out loud, "my mother will go mad with grief, which will leave Maryana an orphan."

"The girl has a father, doesn't she? What about that jolly chap who was licking my shoes minutes ago?"

"You don't understand. Joseph Olenski cannot be trusted. He'll dump her in an orphanage. That's what he did with his other daughter. It's the most distasteful thing, I swear. He wouldn't want a whining brat encumbering him as he hunts for a new wife. In fact, there's a plum cellist he's been eyeing for some time now."

"Then it's a good thing there's a contingency plan. Our government provides for its minors. I hear those establishments have come a long way since the postwar era."

"You know they don't have strong musical programs there. All those private piano lessons will go out the window.

Saved By The Bang

Not to mention, they don't have good gymnastics equipment. And Maryana has been making such progress on the beam."

Antonia kept on babbling even as they wheeled her into the operating room. She ranted to the bright lights above her head until the anesthesiologist placed a rubber mask over her face.

"Scal-pel!" howled the Abortion King.

The procedure could have been done laparoscopically, but Peter Mihalych did not feel like tinkering with tubes and needles. He simply did not trust himself to blindly locate the embryo at such a late hour. So he slashed the patient open from the navel down to her pubic bone.

"What a shame," he mumbled, spreading the layers of tissue. "She has such nice abdominal muscles. I can see why she was the lead cock tease at the academy. Bye-bye flat tummy. Bye-bye bikini body. Hello scars and flabby skin."

* * * *

Antonia awakened to the sound of blood-curdling bawling. Her throat was parched and her vision still blurry from the anesthesia. In the glare from the streetlight she saw a human form thrashing under the sheets. The first thought that crossed her mind was that she had died on the operating table and gone to hell. But why? God's admissions officer must have made a clerical error. She did not belong in a place of eternal torment. Had she not been a virtuous girl? Had she not resisted Cole's advances?

That haphazard spiritual self-analysis lasted exactly two seconds. The smell of rubbing alcohol brought her back to reality. She was not in hell, not exactly. She was in a Soviet hospital. Close enough. The figure thrashing and screaming just a few meters away was a teenage patient with an impressive set of lungs and an even more impressive arsenal of profanities.

Antonia kicked off the blankets, crawled out of bed and started making her way down the chilly white hall, her hand against the wall, ignoring the pain.

"Help!" she cried hoarsely. "Anyone?"

She stood in the doorway of the supply room, her gown open and exposing her freshly operated and bandaged abdomen.

The elderly nurse on duty who was busy rolling up gauze strips turned around her massive trunk and eyed the delirious patient. "Olenski! What are you doing out of bed?"

"The woman next to me is screaming bloody murder."

The nurse shrugged and resumed rolling the bandages. "So? She's in labor. She's twenty weeks along. She'll pass the fetus and that'll be it. Now go back to your bed, before your stitches pop."

"Oh no, I'm not going back in there. How am I supposed to sleep with those ungodly screams?"

"Gee, I don't know. Just put a pillow over your head or something."

"Why don't you put a pillow over your own fascist head?"

The nurse raised her crayon-drawn eyebrow. In the thirty years of work she had been called worse names. She suddenly remembered that she was dealing with Antonia Olenski, an ethereal flower with rather convoluted ideas about human dignity. "Fine, stand all night in the hall if you want to. Just don't bother calling me if you start hemorrhaging."

Saved By The Bang

Antonia crossed her arms with an air of juvenile petulance. "Then my husband will sue the hospital, and you'll all go to jail." She knew that the threat was rather far-fetched. In the three decades of the hospital's existence there had not been a single lawsuit that resulted in a patient victory. Numerous fatalities had been swept under a rug. "A callous creature like you should be plucking decapitated chickens on the market. You shouldn't be allowed to work with human beings."

The bawling suddenly stopped, as if a fire alarm had been turned off.

"It's over, Olenski," the nurse said. "It's safe for you to go back."

"No, you go first. I'm not going in there. You don't suppose..." Antonia's voice suddenly faltered and her belligerence cooled. In the thirty-two years of her life she had never seen a corpse, not even her father's; Officer Rosenberg was ushered off in a closed casket. "She wouldn't just *die*, would she?"

"Good question, Olenski. What do you think? It's a hospital, for crying out loud. People die here all the time. They don't exactly ask for permission. It's not a sanatorium or anything like that."

Antonia was hoping that the hospital workers would have enough courtesy to at least pull the sheet over the dead patient before wheeling her off to the morgue, though her intuition told her that they probably would not. All concepts of delicacy and good taste were clearly foreign to these people who handled dead meat all day long. Had they always been so nonchalant, or had their occupation made them that way? Antonia shivered under her hospital gown, as spiking terror unleashed another emotion—curiosity. The urge to cover her eyes was rivaled by an equally strong urge to peek. This was her opportunity to finally see a breathless body. Hey, it very well could have been her exiting feet first.

* * * *

The fifteen-year old patient was sitting on the bed, legs spread apart, panting and staring down. Peeking over the nurse's shoulder, Antonia caught a glimpse of something red and glistening between the patient's knobby knees. With expert dexterity, the nurse scooped up the red mass into a towel and stuffed it into a cellophane bag.

"Now, dearie, what exactly did you do to bring on contractions?" she asked. "I'll need to tell Peter Mihalych the truth in case he needs to go inside and patch up any additional damage."

"Nothing, I swear. Oh, please, don't stare at me like that!"

"Look, dearie, I don't have time for these bullshit games. Seriously, what did you use? Come on, spill it. Was it a coat hanger? A knitting needle?"

The girl fell back against the pillows, abdicating. "A crocheting hook. Satisfied now?"

Indeed, the nurse was satisfied. Extracting this sort of confession from an underage patient usually took more time. "Now that was a stupid thing to do," she said, patting the girl on the head. "Never try that at home. Next time come to Peter Mihalych. He'll give you a nice jolt of saline solution. Did you at least dip the crocheting hook in alcohol before you stuck it inside you?"

Saved By The Bang

The girl's face contorted, and the gulping sobs spilled forth. "I kept on believing...until the bitter end...that he'd come back to me. He promised he'd marry me after the army. But then...then he stopped responding to my letters. I was afraid...my stepmother would...kick me out of the house, aaaaah! There was nobody in the village I could turn to."

Antonia stood at the foot of the girl's bed. "Shame on you! Sleeping with boys at your age? When I was in ninth grade, I was playing Tchaikovsky's concerto and rock-climbing in the Caucasus. I have ribbons and medals to prove it. And what do you have to show for yourself, except for a hole in your uterus? You've disgraced your school, your family, your entire generation. Little sluts like you, who open their legs for everyone, contribute to the moral decay of the society. That's right. Men aren't the ones to blame. They're only as rotten as women allow them to be. Why should any man bother wooing a lady of quality, when there's an indiscriminating semen receptacle right in front of him? By the time my daughter is old enough to hunt for a husband there won't be any decent men left."

Chapter Four

STALINIST–VICTORIAN

Telman Street, April 26, 9 am—

Maryana dreamt that she was inside the Trinity Cathedral in Gervyaty, marching through a cloud of incense, leading a procession of other little girls in white lace dresses and gauze veils, carrying the heart of Jesus made of red glass on a hand-embroidered pillow. Gradually, the smell of candle wax started waning, giving way to a stronger, sweeter smell of Red Moscow perfume. The Latin anthem turned into a patriotic march. When she glanced over her shoulder, she saw the entire gymnastics team behind her back. The ethereal girls in white were gone. She was standing in the middle of a sports arena. Her coach, her homeroom teacher and the school principal were there, all three sporting navy-blue suits with boxy jackets and pencil skirts.

A chilling seizure ran through her body as she awoke with sweaty feet and a parched throat. It puzzled her that she was lying on the floor and not the couch. The ache on the side of her head brought back the events of the night. Maryana remembered the long philosophical discussion that ended in her mother's request for aspirin. She remembered trying to do her science homework but then giving up and then curling into a ball at Antonia's feet. Then the memories got a little fuzzy. Her father stormed into the apartment in the middle of the night, turned a few chairs upside down, called the ambulance and whacked her on the head. She was pretty sure things happened in that order. Mama Cat was nowhere in sight. The smelly red stain on the carpet was still there. Was that puddle of bloody mucus the only thing left of her mother?

The messy living room started spinning. Maryana squeezed her throbbing head to slow down the carousel. Suddenly, her eyes fell upon a lacquered black purse on the desk. The radio in the kitchen was playing Shostakovich.

Grandma Lily is back from Kiev! I'm dead meat.

Maryana ran into the bathroom and stuck her head under a stream of icy water. She could not let her grandmother see her like that, disheveled and with yellow crust in her eyes.

"Your father called me from the hospital in the middle of the night," Lily said when her granddaughter reported to her. Hugs and greetings seemed like unnecessary frivolities under the circumstances. "I caught the first train out of Kiev. What a mess, Cotton Paw! Your mother behaves like a wild animal. Don't you know? Wounded animals always hide their symptoms until the bitter end, so other members of the pack wouldn't sense their weakness."

In Lily's book, the worst thing anyone could do was to show weakness. It was almost as embarrassing as appearing in public in torn pantyhose. She belonged to the delightful breed of women that could be described as Stalinist-Victorian. These female specimens, born between 1920 and the beginning of World War II could look Hitler in the eye but then screech at the sight of a spider. They were self-professed unbelievers, yet their speech abounded in religious imagery. Lily had the signature high cheekbones, a button nose, large hazel eyes and perfect teeth. She always sported two rows of pearls—one in her mouth and one on her neck. This way her bosom was always smiling, even when her face was not. As a teenager she had posed for a fashion magazine cover in Austria where her military father was stationed after the war. That was the only vainglorious episode in her life. Every pretty girl is entitled to her five seconds of glamorous nonsense. Shortly after, Lily enrolled in an engineering program, as expected by her parents. She spoke German fluently, sang nineteenth century romantic ballads and could add an entire row of numbers in her head in a matter of seconds. She firmly believed in the intellectual and moral superiority of women and swooned at the very mention of sex.

Joseph knew of his mother-in-law's aversion to anything that had to do with flesh and made it a point to make love to Antonia frequently and loudly. He was secretly hoping that Lily would have a heart attack from disgust and he would finally have her apartment at his disposal. He felt he deserved it, after all the humiliation he had endured there. He would get rid of all the World War II memorabilia that Lily's father had left behind and replace it with an ample records collection. Lily suspected that her son-in-law was planning her demise and resolved not to give him that satisfaction. The dirty lascivious Pollack was not going to squeeze her out of her apartment. It was bad enough that he was already banging her daughter. Antonia was weak and susceptible, always succumbing to his carnal onslaught. Of course, the poor innocent thing had nothing to compare to. Alas, that's the flip side of waiting until the official exchange of vows. Lily found herself to be torn on the subject of premarital sex. Perhaps, minimal amount of experience would not automatically turn a good girl into a slut. It irked Lily to see her professionally accomplished yet sexually clueless daughter taken advantage of by a man who was not even a year older yet eons ahead of her in worldly matters. Antonia, dominant in every other aspect of their marriage, assumed the submissive role in bed. Joseph did not like to have his manhood constrained by various barrier devices, so naturally he cajoled Antonia to obtain that horrid intrauterine trinket that looked like a crossbow and increased her chances of an ectopic pregnancy. Maybe this trip to the operating room would teach the foolish girl a lesson. Maybe now the rosy fog before her eyes would scatter, and Antonia would finally see her husband for the hedonistic savage that he was. Maybe she would even impart some wisdom to her own daughter. There would be one exploited female fewer in this world.

Sensing a swelling grudge in the air, Maryana was desperate to get on her grandmother's good side. She quickly got dressed and brushed a wet comb over her hair.

"Grandma Lily, do you need help unpacking?" She looked like a puppy eager to perform a trick. "I hope you had a nice train ride."

"Bah! Don't get me started. The train was overrun by gypsies. They trawled through the cars with their mud-colored children, asking for spare change. I didn't get a minute of sleep. I had to keep my hand on my purse at all times. Of course, all the good seats were sold out. I need at least three hours of shuteye to function." Lily poured a spoonful of freeze-dried coffee into a cup of boiling water. "Cotton Paw, we need to have a serious talk."

"I'm listening, Grandma Lily."

"As you're well aware, Antonia is my most precious possession. I went through great pains to give her proper upbringing, without much external help. Her father died when she was sixteen. Last night her life was in great danger, and your father is to blame for it. That's a fact. Of course, he'll try to deny it, but I wanted you to know the truth."

"Of course."

"Splendid." Lily gave her granddaughter a terrifying warm smile. "Your father is a selfish, impudent beast, who only thinks of his own pleasure. He may claim to love your mother, but the only person he truly loves is himself."

"Oh..."

"Deplorably, his savage blood runs through your veins. That makes you half-beast, my poor Cotton Paw. Sad but true. The only way you can redeem yourself and justify your existence is by trying to be a little bit more like your mother, daunting as the task may sound, given her talent, intelligence and poise. Do try, Cotton Paw."

"I will, Grandma Lily."

"That would mean the world to me. You know, your mother was born with a hole in her heart. She's very fragile and susceptible. A slightest upset can be detrimental to her recovery. Therefore, you mustn't upset her, under any circumstances. Not another word about wanting to quit gymnastics or struggling with math. I don't want the whole engineering community discussing my granddaughter's failures."

Maryana sighed. She truly did not have a good explanation for her failures, other than half of her genes being from a lascivious Polish beast.

"What's a kike?" she asked suddenly in hopes to reroute her grandmother's wrath.

Lily took a few seconds to process the question.

"Where did you hear that word, Cotton Paw?"

"In school."

"From another first-grader?"

"No, a teacher. I was passing by the principal's lounge, and I heard my classroom teacher say that Edward Moiseich, the chemistry teacher, is one scheming kike. So I wondered what that word meant."

"Well..." Lily swallowed. "It's a compliment of sort. But you shouldn't repeat it, ever. Your late grandfather had been called that name by his detractors. Eli was a Jew, and it showed. Top notch engineer, always one step ahead of his Russian colleagues. They couldn't live with this knowledge, so they arranged for an accident at a construction site. They pushed him off the scaffolding. He broke his neck and died instantly. His fall was well-calculated. I'm pretty sure that's what happened."

"Did they go to jail for it?"

"Of course, they didn't, silly girl! These cowards always cover for each other, ganging up on one man. I tell you, Russians are dumb cattle."

"Aren't you Russian, Grandma Lily?"

"A different sort of Russian, Cotton Paw! My family has aristocratic roots. We, the Maximovs of Kolomna, pride ourselves on being enlightened and unprejudiced. To people of our intellectual caliber nationality does not exist at all. Being a Jew isn't easy in this world. But it surely beats being a flamboyant Pollack like your father." Lily straightened Maryana's collar. "We must thank the good doctor for saving your mother's life. I brought a delicious merengue from Kiev, and I want you to be the one to give it to the doctor."

* * * *

Gomel Central Hospital, April 26—

When Lily and Maryana walked into Antonia's hospital room, they found her in the company of the two men who allegedly loved her more than life. Joseph was holding a mirror in front of his wife as she was attempting to reconstruct her ruff, which proved next to impossible without her favorite shampoo and hairspray. Nicholas was smoking by the open window, releasing long gauzy ribbons through his nostrils. It seemed as if his very soul was burning inside. He could not bear the sight of his muse sitting face to face with her undeserving husband.

"Cole, you'll ruin your divine voice!" Lily scolded the long-suffering tenor. "Throw away that vile thing at once. If Vladimir Ivanych were to see you now, he'd have a heart attack. Remember, your voice is not your own. It's the property of the state, like the rest of your gorgeous self."

Nicholas found it difficult to disobey Antonia's mother. He threw the cigarette out the window. The stern elegant widow awakened the schoolboy in him. Besides, he hated the taste of the cheap Belamor tobacco. Only teenagers and criminals could settle for those nicotine missiles.

"Aunt Lily," he said, squeezing her hands, "what a frightening night it was. I was so worried about your daughter. Yesterday afternoon she wasn't looking too good. I offered to take her to the hospital, but she refused, so I drove her straight home instead."

"It's awfully chivalrous of you." Lily batted her mascara-crusted eyelashes. Under certain circumstances, she could be quite coquettish. "Selfless men are hard to come by these days."

"I'm sure any man in my shoes would've done the same. Our beloved Antonia is a national treasure. I'm sure the entire musical community will rejoice upon hearing that a major tragedy was averted."

* * * *

While Nicholas was busy scattering platitudes in front of Lily, Joseph furtively pulled Maryana outside and slipped a giant lemon lollipop in her hand.

"Is this also for the doctor?" she asked him.

"No, stupid, it's for you."

"What for?" Maryana knew the answer but she wanted her father to say it out loud. "I don't understand, Papa Josey. What did I do to deserve a treat?"

Joseph squatted to be on his daughter's level and wrapped his arm around her neck. "Don't tell your mother what I did to you last night. Got it? All those words I said, they aren't to be repeated. I'm not sure if she heard any of it, but if she brings it up, just deny the whole thing. Tell her she was hallucinating. Can I count on you to do that?"

Maryana rubbed the fresh bruise on the side of her head. "I don't know, Papa Josey. It still hurts. I think I need a doctor to take a look at it."

"Don't look at me like that. I'm not exactly proud of how I acted, but sometimes you leave me no choice. Have pity on your mother. Think of the sacrifices she's done for you. Last night she nearly died. She's still not out of the woods. This is not a good time to upset her by snitching on me. Can you for once put someone else's wellbeing first? Just tell me what it will take to make you keep your mouth shut?"

Ordinarily Maryana would simply nod and accept the bribe, but this time around she could not bring herself to get excited over a chocolate bar. She already had three of them sitting at the bottom of her desk drawer. All of them were given by her father on various occasions to buy her silence. Contrary to the medical report, Maryana's last elbow injury did not happen during a gymnastics practice. It actually happened on the way home, after the coach had told Joseph that his daughter was not applying herself enough on the balance beam. The dislocation of the elbow was the direct result of the girl being grabbed by the wrist and spun around her by her father. It was dark, and there were no witnesses around. The next day she had to skip school and go to the trauma center instead. Antonia and Lily did not suspect a thing. The girl and her father made sure to cover the traces. Impossible as it seemed to keep secrets in a one-bedroom apartment, Maryana and Joseph had sealed a clandestine pact between them. The father would periodically lose his temper in front of his daughter and then bribe her into silence. This time, however, she was not so eager to accept compensation.

"I don't know about this lollipop," she whined, knowing how much that tone of voice aggravated Joseph. "Candy isn't good for me. My coach says it makes me fat."

"The stupid bitch is on crack, and I'm gonna have a heart to heart with her. You're not fat. Just take the goddamn lollipop and forget what happened last night."

Maryana rubbed her wrist and raised her dark eyes at her father. "I was really hoping to get that Mickey Mouse watch we saw at the kiosk across the street. Every popular girl in school has one."

Joseph pushed his daughter away, feeling another onslaught of dizziness coming on. "You scheming, manipulative troll!"

Maryana smiled, agreeing. Joseph noticed that she had a few loose baby teeth in the front. If they fell out at the same time, they would create a perfectly symmetrical little gap. It would take nothing short of a portable video game to buy her silence, which would mean he would have no money left for a gift for the "destitute kinswoman," the one who demanded nothing.

* * * *

Nicholas desperately needed another cigarette. Being in Antonia's hospital room with her mother and husband present was more than his delicate nervous system could handle.

"I'll be right back," he growled.

Nobody noticed his departure.

As he was passing by Peter Mihalych's office, something forced him to halt and listen. The Abortion King was on the phone. Nicholas could see the surgeon's slouching back and the folds on his neck that appeared unusually red and sweaty. Peter Mihalych kept shifting the weight of his body from one leg to another, rocking to soothe himself.

"For Chrissake, slow down, Igor. Exactly how bad is it? Uh-huh...When you say catastrophic, are you sure you're not exaggerating? Because that's what you said when your favorite soccer team lost the gold cup. I remember your exact words. You said it was 'the end of the world'. If this is another apocalypse according to Igor...So it's really that bad, huh? Yeah...No way...The whole thing blew? Reactor four... You're kidding. Someone screwed up royally. Someone's ass will be on fire, big time. Last night? When do they plan on releasing the report? Which way is the cloud heading? To the north? How about that...No, they are not going to evacuate. I'll tell my daughter to take her kids to skip town. I'll put them on a train to Moscow. Is that far enough? No, I don't keep iodine pills in the house. Jesus Christ, this shit is unreal...Right before the May Day demonstrations too! You think they're going to cancel the parade? Of course, I'll keep mum. You can count on that. The last thing I need is mass panic."

Peter Mihalych turned around and saw Nicholas standing in the doorway, arms crossed. The surgeon blanched and covered the receiver. "Can I help you?"

"Why, yes," Nicholas replied, stepping into the office. "You can let me listen in on the call. It sounds awfully interesting. I promise to be quiet."

Peter Mihalych muttered into the phone, "Igor, I'll call you later. I can't talk now. There's no privacy in this goddam place."

"You want privacy?" Nicholas continued, closing in on the doctor. "This is a hospital, not a KGB interrogation chamber. Now, I'm just a dumb musician, far removed from the world of nuclear physics. As a man of science, you tell me what the hell you were talking about a minute ago."

The surgeon glanced behind looking for anything that could be used as a defense tool, but the sharpest object he could find was a ruler. "Look, Nichenko, I don't have time for this."

"I'm not asking for three hours of your precious time. It will take no more than three minutes to paraphrase what your chum on the other side has just told you."

"Nichenko, it's nothing."

"This is why you're putting your daughter and grandkids on a train to Moscow?"

"It's just a precaution." The doctor shook his balding head. "There's no reason to panic."

"Meaning, the authorities haven't given us their official permission to scream and run? You realize you can get imprisoned for withholding this sort of information?"

"You are more likely to get committed to an institution for paranoia if you start spreading rumors about a nuclear apocalypse. Even if there was cause for alarm, there's nothing anyone can do. You can't evacuate hundreds of thousands of people all at once. We're talking of an entire nation being displaced here."

"The fate of the nation doesn't concern me any more than it concerns you. But in that room there's a woman without which my life has no meaning. It also happens that she has a child by a man I despise. They are both in that room. It's a tragic technicality that Maryana should have an egotistic buffoon for a father. It's not the child's fault. I'm as eager to protect her as I am to protect her mother. They are one flesh, and I shall see to their safety. Now talk."

* * * *

When Nicholas returned to Antonia's room, he found her cuddling on the bed with her husband who was humming some bawdy Polish ditty into her ear. The sharp smell of aged musk permeated the air. Joseph had brought a flask of Scythian Gold perfume from Minsk for Antonia's upcoming birthday in June, but in light of her recent brush with death, he had decided to give her the present early. That scent was hugely popular among entry-level courtesans who were sleeping with provincial officials, but respectable women like Antonia used it also without any detriment to their image. Musk is universal. Whores and wives of KGB agents alike turned into goddesses when they applied a drop of Scythian Gold to their necks. Apparently, the perfume contained a hefty dose of aphrodisiac, because Joseph was all over Antonia, his hand squeezing her breast through the faded hospital gown. Her toes peeking from under the blanket were wiggling and curling, signaling arousal.

Lily was fanning herself with the medical chart, her posture communicating resigned disapproval of such lascivious displays. Clearly, the surgery had not affected her daughter's libido. Antonia had just had her reproductive parts nipped, clicked, rinsed out and reassembled, and she was already eager to resume her usual sexual activities. If given the opportunity, the shameless hussy would probably do the dirty deed right there in the hospital bed, in front her own child. Not that Maryana was paying any attention to her parents' necking. She was too busy playing with her new Mickey Mouse watch. She would bring the wrist to her ear, listening to the faint ticking, and grin triumphantly. While Nicholas had been trying to beat the information out of the old abortionist, she had cajoled her father into buying the watch from the kiosk across the street from the hospital. The plastic trinket was not expected to last more than a week, but to her it symbolized victory over Joseph. Sometimes nagging and blackmailing worked.

Mad laughter expanded Nicholas' chest. He surveyed the people in the room—four self-absorbed fools, oblivious of their doom. "You shouldn't keep the windows open," he said hoarsely and slammed the fragile frames shut. "There, much better."

"But it's gorgeous outside," Lily protested. "I cannot stand this stale hospital air."

Nicholas turned to his would-be mother-in-law. "Woman, you have no idea what you're inhaling this very moment."

His tone perplexed Lily. She stopped fanning herself for a second. Did Nicholas Nichenko just call her a woman? In the past he had never resorted to such familiarities. Ordinarily such form of address was reserved for the slovenly vegetable peddlers.

"Oh, what's the matter with you, Cole? Why are you panting? You look like you've seen a ghost."

Nicholas nodded. "I did...I did see a ghost—that of Hiroshima."

"Can you stop with figurative speech and get to the point?"

The tormented tenor turned to Antonia. "I have dreadful news for you. Apparently, your fallopian tube was not the only thing leaking last night. So was reactor number four in Chernobyl."

"Where's that?" Antonia inquired, not in the least embarrassed by her ignorance of geography. "Not the fallopian tube—the reactor."

"Just across the Ukrainian border, in Pripyat. There was a power surge, and the core exploded. They were testing some cooling feature." Nicholas paused, realizing he could not regurgitate the exact terminology. "I don't know what exactly happened there. Nobody has the facts straight, but it doesn't look good. Fires broke out. Radiation is leaking everywhere. Raw radiation, penetrating the soil, the air, the water. People are fleeing—the ones who know what's happening. It's the worst nuclear disaster in the history of mankind."

Lily walked over to Nicholas and pinched the scruff of his neck. This pacifying tactic had worked with the German shepherd puppies her late father used to breed. "Cole, I understand that you are an artistic soul and need a steady supply of drama to fuel your creative process, but there are healthy boundaries to be set. You shouldn't be saying such outrageous things in front of my daughter. Her mind is still a little fuzzy from the anesthesia, and you dump all that science fiction on her. This isn't some apocalyptic novella by Boris Strugatsky."

Nicholas shook off her hand and jumped to his feet. "It's quite real, I'm afraid."

"For goodness' sake, have some faith in the system." The sight of a terrified male disconcerted Lily. "If something was truly wrong, don't you think the authorities would've informed us?"

"Huh?" Sometimes Nicholas could not tell if Lily was being earnest or sarcastic. "You expect that from our authorities? You expect full transparency and a timely response?"

"Of course, I do!" Lily's voice went up a pitch. The boy had now crossed the line between artistic paranoia and downright blasphemy. "We have the privilege of living in one of the most advanced and civilized societies, where the human dignity of every citizen is held in high esteem. Thanks to the unflinching solidarity of our people and the unparalleled fortitude of our leaders, we singlehandedly won the war with Germany."

Nicholas let out a sigh of defeat. He would not have expected a different answer from a military officer's daughter. To question the integrity of the government system was one way to get on her bad side, and Nicholas did not want to prematurely antagonize the mother of the woman he loved.

Chapter Five
PEACEFUL ATOM

Pripyat, Ukraine – April 27, 1986

The glorious city of Pripyat, named after the nearby river, boasted a whooping fifteen-year history and served as a masterpiece of the late Soviet era urban development, something one would see in a futuristic cartoon. The city was founded in 1970 to house the workers of the Chernobyl Nuclear Power Plant. The original plan had been to build the plant some twenty kilometers from Kiev, but the Ukrainian Academy of Science balked at the idea of the nuclear monstrosity sitting so close to the capitol, so the power station was moved farther north towards the Belarusian border.

By 1986 the population had grown to nearly fifty thousand. The new city had a unique triangular layout, designed by Moscow architects. The plan featured five-story buildings and high-rises, arranged in perfectly symmetrical blocks, with the horizon visible from almost every corner, so different from the old cities with their narrow windy streets. Pripyat had a defined downtown with the council hall, the

Saved By The Bang

Polyssia hotel to house officials and delegates, a cluster of shops and restaurants and the Palace of Culture. The map of the city was speckled with traditional ideological names such as Lenin Avenue and Heroes of Stalingrad Street. One street was named after Igor Kurchatov, the Father of the Soviet Atomic Bomb. With the Cold War winding down, "peaceful atom" was the buzzword du jour.

The newest landmark in Pripyat was the amusement park featuring a giant Ferris wheel, bumper cars, swing boats and a paratrooper ride was scheduled for grand opening on the first of May in time for the May Day celebrations. Colorful streamers and banners fluttered in the tepid spring air. The people of Pripyat got a pleasant surprise when the gates of the park opened early on April 27th. Hundreds of children and their parents lined up in queues for the rides. Spirits were high as ever, in spite of the talk of some mysterious illness striking dozens of people, causing severe headaches, nausea and uncontrollable cough. Local doctors did not seem particularly alarmed and attributed the symptoms to a flare-up of influenza left over from the winter season and the unusually high pollen level. The freshly oiled gears moved with a squeak, and the Ferris wheel went for its maiden spin.

The festivities were cut short by an evacuation announcement. A deep female voice poured over the loudspeakers.

For the attention of the residents of Pripyat! The City Council informs you that due to the accident at Chernobyl Power Station in the city of Pripyat the radioactive conditions in the vicinity are deteriorating. The Communist Party, its officials and the armed forces are taking necessary steps to combat this.

* * * *

The evacuations started at two pm. Each apartment block was served a bus, supervised by the police and the city officials. The residents were advised to bring their documents and vital personal belongings. The general atmosphere was of mirth rather than of alarm. It felt as if the city was going on a spur of the moment field trip to Kiev. An explosion? Way cool. Radiation? Far out. A spontaneous change of scenery, a random chance to escape the drudgery of the daily routine. They were all extras in a direct-to-video, end-of-the-world movie. Cheese sandwiches, bottles of juice and cans of condensed milk were being passed around. Who doesn't like free food? The children visibly rejoiced over the school year ending one month early. In a way, they felt sorry for those few who were mandated to staying behind to maintain the facilities in order.

The euphoria started wearing off when the first symptoms of radiation poisoning set in, with vomiting, nosebleeds, fainting spells and episodes of blindness. The half-eaten cheese sandwiches started coming up in foul-smelling mush. The sentiment went from "Free food—yay!" to "Holy shit, we're screwed!"

* * * *

Smolensk, Russia – April 28

The general public learned about the disaster only two days after the explosion. After radiation levels set off alarms at the Forsmark Nuclear Plant in Sweden, some one thousand kilometers from Chernobyl, the Soviet officials had no choice but to admit that an accident had occurred. That day all major radio stations in the Soviet Union had been playing classical music instead of airing their regular broadcasts—a common way to prepare the listeners for an announcement of a tragedy. At nine o'clock in the evening, the news program Time ran a twenty-second blurb.

Antonia was watching the broadcast from the safety of her aunt's spacious Stalin era flat in Smolensk where she and Maryana had taken refuge. They were almost four hundred kilometers away from the epicenter of the disaster.

Only two days after the surgery, Antonia felt like her abdomen was a warzone. The twenty-centimeter wound was burning and leaking through the bandages. She was dying for an honest-to-God, full body hot shower, but she was not sure if she was allowed to get the incision wet. Before getting discharged from the hospital, she signed a waiver stating she would not hold the doctors accountable in case of complications. They gave her some painkillers and antibiotics, but she had lost them at the train station. She pulled out a mirror to apply some gloss to her lips, and the bottles with medicine must have slipped right out of her purse. How in the world did she survive the six-hour ride? It was a bumpy ride too, with countless stops and jolts. Their compartment was right next to the toilet. A few times she had come close to fainting. Now she was running a low-grade fever. Was it a sign of sepsis setting in? Luckily, her aunt was a doctor and could procure an emergency serving of penicillin.

Before going to bed that evening, Antonia telephoned her boss back in Gomel.

"Vladimir Ivanych, I would've called you earlier, but I wanted to give you a chance to calm down. I hope you aren't mad at me anymore."

The director of the academy growled on the other end. "Why in God's name would I be mad at you, Olenski? Because you abandoned me and your colleagues when we needed you the most?"

"I haven't abandoned you. For Christ's sake, don't make it sound so dramatic. All I asked for was a sabbatical. Is that an unreasonable request?"

"Well, your timing really stinks. The showcase is three weeks away! Olenski, have I not been sympathetic to your lot? You were so young when you lost your father. For the past nine years I've been trying to take his place, to provide you with the guidance and protection you've been missing."

"And you have been that and so much more, Vladimir Ivanych. I couldn't have achieved as much as I have without you."

"Have I not paired you with the best vocalists in the city?"

"I'll never forget your kindness."

"Then why are you doing this to me? Who's going to play in the showcase?"

"I'm sure you can find a replacement. There are so many talented girls."

"Just like that, huh? I swear to God, Olenski, anesthesia must've damaged your brain. Do you realize what you're asking me to do? You think it's easy to find a replacement? Nicholas won't sing with any of them. Only you can make him sing."

"Yes, he will sing. Nicholas was the one who urged me to leave. He said it wasn't safe to stay in Gomel."

"And of course, you listened to him. What is he, a scientist? He planted this whacky idea in your head that we're all about to cook. God, I could kill him for that."

"Please, don't kill him, Vladimir Ivanych. You can't afford to kill your top tenor. He only did what he did because he loves me so much."

"He loves you, eh? Well then, he can have Galina as his accompanist."

"Excellent choice! Galina is a great musician."

"Galina can't play worth a damn. She can't tell right from left, major from minor, Schubert from Schumann. That girl claims to have German blood in her, but I don't believe her. Germans are supposed to have great technique and a vast ocean of theory. Let that be Nicholas' punishment. He'll perform with that horse-faced klutz and embarrass himself on stage. Let the audience laugh. What do I care?"

Antonia could picture her boss throwing his arms up and grasping at what was left of his hair. She gave him a few minutes to fume.

"Vladimir Ivanych," she said in a very calm unapologetic voice. "One last thing. Would you mind terribly wiring me an advance? I hope you don't interpret my request as presumptuous. I'll earn back every single kopeck when I come back in the fall."

Click.

At first Antonia could not believe that her boss actually hung up on her. She whispered "hello" a few times into the receiver, hoping that the yelling on the other end would resume. To her dismay, the only sound that came out was the flat dial tone. It was pretty obvious that the conversation was over, and the much-counted-on advance was not coming.

Then Antonia heard a tiny voice behind her back. "Mama Cat, is there anything else on TV? I'm tired of watching the news."

She turned around with a gasp and saw Maryana standing in the doorway. It suddenly occurred to her that she would be spending a great deal of time with her daughter. Antonia was almost four hundred kilometers away from her colleagues, and Maryana was away from her homeroom teacher, piano instructor and gymnastics coach. For the first time in eight years the mother and daughter were left completely alone with each other. Aunt Eugenia did not count, as she had made it clear that she wished to be left out of the equation. The idea of being tête-à-tête with her own child was making Antonia a little nervous. She had no idea whether the girl would be obedient and cooperative. She did not even know what sort of interests an eight-year-old would have.

"Have you practiced your calligraphy, Cotton Paw?"

"I think I left the workbook on the train," Maryana replied without any hint of apology in her voice.

"How convenient. Just for that you'll do an hour of math, and an hour of geography. And if you don't get all the answers right, I'll make you memorize thirty pages of Pushkin's *King Saltan.*"

"Do we really have to do this, Mama Cat? I thought we were on vacation."

"We aren't on vacation, stupid girl. We're in evacuation. Do you understand what that means?"

"Mr. Reagan dropped a bomb on us?"

Saved By The Bang

"It's ten times worse than that. This disaster was caused by our very own countrymen. However, that doesn't excuse you from your academics. You can ask Aunt Genie how she studied for her chemistry exams with bombs bursting over her head."

Dr. Eugenia Kuzmin, a widow with two grown children, split her days between the hospital and the laboratory. It was not unusual for her to fall asleep in her armchair with her clinical white coat and rubber gloves on. Like her younger sister Lily, Eugenia boasted an hourglass figure and satin skin, attributing her youthful looks to a line of Baltic cosmetics. She adorned herself generously with amethysts and perfumed her cleavage with Red Moscow. Her most impressive skill was eating an entire ice-cream cone without smudging her red lipstick. Undoubtedly, she was the hottest fifty-seven year old in the medical community. The news of the disaster in Chernobyl inspired her to dig up her textbook on hematological disorders.

"My interns are tickled pink," Genie said to her niece. "They're a little freaked out, understandably. Who wouldn't be? It's not every day that nuclear reactors hiccup like that. But medical curiosity quickly triumphs over fear. What an exciting time to study oncology! We're about to see a drastic spike in tumors. The cancer centers will be overflowing in the coming months. My boys and girls will have no lack for study material. I remember my first biopsy. They brought me this giant red blob. It was still warm when I touched it."

Antonia tightened the belt of her bathrobe. "May I be excused? I'm feeling rather faint."

"Don't be such a sissy!" Eugenia puckered spitefully. "I swear, you're just like your mother, skittish and squeamish. I could never have an intelligent conversation with Lily. She'd rather sit and draw her stupid bridges and locomotives all day. The moment I'd bring up blood and body parts, she'd start cringing and barfing. It was our father's dream that all three of his kids would go into the medical profession, and Lily ruined that dream. She chickened out and became an engineer instead. So don't start feigning symptoms of radiation poisoning in my living room, dear girl."

"It's not that, Aunt Genie. My side really hurts. They just snipped one of my tubes, for crying out loud."

"So?" Eugenia shrugged and slammed the textbook shut. "It's been two days since the surgery. If there had been any complications, they would've surfaced by now. I've done enough surgeries to know that. If the internal stitches had come undone, you'd be on the floor, unconscious. You wouldn't be standing here, pouting and whining. Seriously, Toni, how long do you plan on playing that pity card? You're setting a bad example for your daughter. She'll grow up thinking that it's acceptable to moan and groan every time she has a cramp."

"All right, I get it," Antonia said, staring down at the tips of her slippers. "Tomorrow I'll be a brave Soviet soldier, but tonight I need to get some sleep. I washed the dishes in the kitchen and cleared the counter top. Tomorrow I'll make Maryana mop the floors and scrub the toilet. Can you let me be a useless sissy for one more night? That's all I'm asking for."

Eugenia folded her glasses and rubbed the bridge of her nose. "Fine," she said half-audibly. "Go and feel sorry for yourself. There's nothing I can do to make you behave like a mature able-bodied woman. You shouldn't take all the blame. It's your mother's upbringing. She convinced you that you're an invalid just because you had a tiny hole in your heart. The doctors told her you had a few minor birth defects, and she panicked, as usual. Go and be that invalid for one more night."

"Thank you," Antonia exhaled, clasping her hands. "Tomorrow your apartment will be spotless."

"One more thing," Eugenia said, raising her finger, "before I forget."

"Y...yes, Aunt Genie?"

"Next time you want to engage in philosophical discussions with your boss long-distance, do it on your own ruble. I'll let it slide this time, because you're still frazzled and can't think straight. Next time you can go to the post office and use a booth there. Last but not least, don't use that good Indian tea. I keep it for special occasions. You're welcome to help yourself to some Georgian tea while you wait for your advance and start buying your own groceries. Are we clear on the house rules?"

Chapter Six
OPEN WIDE, LITTLE COUSIN

Smolensk, Russia – May, 1986

The highlight of Maryana's stay in Smolensk was spending time with her cousin Demetrius. He was in fourth grade and shared his grandmother Eugenia's passion for anatomy. When left with Maryana alone for the first time, he undressed her and gave her a full physical. The next day he drew blood from her finger using a piece of broken glass and removed a suspicious looking mole from the back of her neck with a pair of scissors. Maryana endured the torments stoically, determined to overcome her fear of blood and pain, but when Demetrius recommended a tonsillectomy, she drew the line.

"Enough," she said firmly, pulling up her underwear and buttoning up her shirt. "I don't want to play hospital anymore."

Demetrius looked perplexed and vaguely insulted. "But why? You don't need your tonsils. They're useless."

"There's no such thing as a useless organ."

"Sure, there is! Some people are born with a vestigial tail."

"I don't have a tail. You've seen my butt a million times. There's no tail growing out of it."

"But you have tonsils." Demetrius folded his arms with the laidback confidence of a docent. "They're just sitting there in the back of your throat, accumulating germs, rotting away. That's what my dad says. He's the best ENT surgeon in the city. He extracts thousands of tonsils every year. He gave me his old kit to play with. It's almost complete. I have all the instruments I need. You can see and touch them if you want to. I know his method to minimize blood loss." Demetrius put his hands on his cousin's shoulders, restraining her. "It won't hurt at all, I promise. We'll go out for ice-cream later on."

Maryana shook her head. "I don't think so." Demetrius tightened his grip and pushed his face against hers. They spent a few seconds staring into each other's eyes. Maryana could see the budding pimples on the tip of his nose and smell the minty gum on his breath.

"Come on, little cousin," he cajoled in his hypnotic whisper. "You know there's no escape. You're getting your tonsils out today. It'll have to happen sooner or later. Everyone gets their tonsils out nowadays. You can trust me. We're family. Would you rather let some stranger back home cut you up?"

Maryana closed her eyes and leaned forward. She could hear his victorious chuckle. A second later she kicked him in the groin and ran out of the apartment. She flew down three flights of stairs, nearly knocking down the old cleaning lady who was mopping the hall. All the while she imagined

Demetrius chasing after her with a scalpel. That image would haunt her in her nightmares for years to come.

Antonia was sitting on a bench under a blossoming apple tree, fanning herself with the latest edition of *Burda Moden* magazine. Over the past few days she could not get cool, even though the temperature outside never exceeded twenty degrees. She kept panting and sweating. A local doctor explained to her that her body was working hard to regenerate the lost blood.

At the sight of her frantic daughter, Antonia jumped. "What now?"

"Mama Cat, take me away from here." Maryana grabbed her mother's hand and tried to pull her up. "Please, please, take me away, and never leave me alone with Demetrius. He wants to cut me into pieces. He's evil."

"Don't be silly. I'm sure he was only joking."

"Trust me, he's not joking!" Maryana turned around sharply and pulled up her tony tail to expose a bloodied bandage on the back of her neck. "See what he did to me? He cut out the melanoma and poured his father's aftershave to sterilize the wound."

Antonia gasped and dropped the magazine. "Good grief..."

"Now you believe me?""

"I do." Antonia choked up and pulled her daughter into her lap. "My poor baby, I'm so sorry that you had to go through this ordeal. I'd really hoped that Demetrius would turn out to be different."

"Different?" Maryana looked at her mother with suspicion. "From whom? In what way? What aren't you telling me, Mama Cat?"

"You see, darling," Antonia continued, stroking her daughter's hair, "Sergei, his father would do the same thing to me when we were children. He'd follow me around day and night, nag me, beg me, threaten me even, but I wouldn't give in. So one day Sergei slipped a bunch of sleeping pills in my juice and pulled two of my baby teeth with a pair of pliers. The teeth weren't even loose. I just blacked out, and when I woke up, there was a bleeding gap in the back of my mouth. I still have a gap there, believe it or not. The adult teeth never came in. There were no permanent buds there. It must run in the family, this fondness for cutting and pulling things."

Maryana fidgeted on her mother's knee. "Did you tell anyone, Mama Cat?"

"I tried. I went straight to our grandparents to present my case, but the odds were against me from the very beginning. Sergei had hidden the extracted teeth, so I had to open my mouth wide to show the damage. He didn't deny pulling my teeth out, but he told everyone it was my idea. He said I'd asked for it because I was too scared to go to a real dentist. Aunt Genie jumped in to stick up for her boy, naturally. Our grandparents took her side, as one should have expected. Eugenia always was their favorite, all rational and methodical. Lily was the hysterical one."

* * * *

Antonia and Maryana spent the next few days walking through the Central Park founded in 1830 in the heart of Smolensk. The main attractions included a fountain, a granite bust of the composer Glinka, a Napoleonic era cannon and a statue of a deer extracted as a trophy from the hunting lodge of Kaiser Wilhelm. Over the course of those few days Antonia made a shocking discovery—her eight-year old daughter was not a complete idiot after all. Far from it. She actually appreciated art and history. The realization Antonia full force when they visited a museum that contained one the largest collections of religious artifacts.

"The artists always get it wrong," Maryana said, pausing in front of the showcase containing 16th century icons.

"What did they get wrong?"

"The crucifixion. They always put the nail marks on the palms of Jesus' hands. In reality, he was nailed by wrists. And his ankles should be crossed, with one huge nail run through them. You see, Mama Cat, the artists don't care about historical accuracy. They do whatever they want, whatever will sell the most paintings."

"Who told you that?"

"Papa Josey."

"You...you actually talk to your father?"

"Sometimes." Maryana licked her lips and looked down. "He doesn't even need to open his mouth. He just looks at me, and I can read his thoughts. It's like...It's like we're joined at the brain or something."

Antonia squeezed her daughter's hand tighter. "Stop it, Cotton Paw." That telepathic babble was creeping her out big time. She remembered watching an American horror flick based on a book by some guy named Stefan Koenig. Or was it Stephen King? Anyway, that flick made a major splash at all the movie theaters in Gomel. The boys at the academy went to see it several times. It featured a weird kid who could read people's minds and his dad who went nuts from being cooped up at an empty hotel. Antonia had to sleep with the lights on for a week after watching it. She could totally see something like that happening in her family.

"It's not creepy," Maryana patted her mother's hand reassuringly. "It's kind of educational. They don't teach you that stuff in school. That's how I found out about Jesus. You can't believe painters. And you can't believe history books. Grandpa Lenin didn't die of pneumonia. He died of syphilis. He was not a father of a nation. He was just a philandering fanatic."

* * * *

When they came home at the end of the day, they found contents of Maryana's backpack scattered all over the sofa. Eugenia barred their entrance into the living room. Her pupils were dilated and her lower lip was quivering.

"Aunt Genie," Antonia said, "is there a reason why you are rummaging through my daughter's things?"

"My favorite amethyst earrings are missing."

"Oh, those..."

"Yes, those!"

The earrings had been in the family for almost a century. Antonia's quasi-aristocratic great-grandfather had bought them for his wife in St. Petersburg, and since then they had been passed on to the oldest daughter of the family.

"That's unfortunate," Antonia said. "Maybe they'll turn up."

"No, my dear girl, they won't turn up. For the past thirty years I've been leaving them in the porcelain dish on my dresser, and now they're gone. And I have a pretty good idea of who made them disappear."

"Sweet auntie, what in the world made you think you would find them in Maryana's backpack?"

"Because the child takes after her father."

"In what way?"

Eugenia tilted her head, soliciting candor from her niece. "Come on, Antonia, we all know what your husband is capable of."

"Could you please be more specific? I'm afraid I don't understand. Joseph is capable of many things."

"We all know who stole three hundred rubles from Uncle Ivan's box at the funeral. Joseph suffers from kleptomania, and it's hereditary. I know you don't read medical journals, but recent studies show that there's a criminal gene. Your husband is a thief, and so is your kid."

Antonia drew her daughter closer and covered her ears. Maryana wiggled, because she was dying to hear what would happen next. The conversation was just getting good.

"Aunt Genie, I understand you are upset," Antonia said, "but is it really necessary to traumatize the poor child? She's already been through enough."

Eugenia leaned back, her arms akimbo. "*The poor child,*" she mocked. "Seriously, Antonia, how much longer will you continue sheltering her from responsibility? I guess that's the problem with only children. They grow up selfish, maladjusted and entitled. Why should they learn that there are consequences to their actions? Mommy dearest will always come to their defense."

Saved By The Bang

Antonia uncovered her daughter's ears and pushed her forward. "Go on, I want you to look Aunt Genie in the eye and tell her the whole truth."

Maryana took a deep breath and blurted out, "I swear on the bleeding heart of Virgin Mary, the holy Mother of God, that I did not take your earrings."

Her declaration did not have the desired effect.

"Oh, that's rich," Eugenia said. "So you're a believer now? Is that a new trend among kids these days? You know, enlightened people, proponents of progress, had fought tooth and nail to purge the country of old-world superstition and give you a bright future. But I guess you don't want a bright future. You'd rather return to the dark ages. You steal, you lie, and then you confess to your imaginary God, and he makes you squeaky clean again. Such a clever way to work around your conscience, isn't it? I'm sure your father taught you all that. Oh, that man is good."

Antonia's eyes flashed. "Maybe your memory just isn't as sharp as it used to be, dear auntie. It could be an early onset of senility. All these chemicals you work with are making you paranoid."

"I open up my house to you and your thief child, and this is how your repay me? I've had enough. What happens to you next is of no concern to me. I want you out by tomorrow morning."

* * * *

First thing in the morning, while Maryana was still asleep, Antonia telephoned the music academy in hopes to get in touch with Vladimir Ivanych and negotiate the terms of her return. Galina Richtman, the twenty-six-year-old intern who allegedly could not tell Schubert from Schumann, answered the phone. At first the girl pretended that she did not recognize the caller and made Antonia identify herself several times. There were good reasons for this lack of cooperation.

Galina's biological father was from East Berlin where he practiced orthopedic surgery. He had not seen his daughter since she was an infant, though they kept in touch through postcards and magazine cutouts. Dr. Richtman would send her pages from *Burda Moden* featuring latest trends in European fashion. Galina was not a pretty girl—she was a well-dressed homely girl, single and on the wrong side of twenty-five, at risk of being shelved as expired goods. Her long-distance father had hinted that if she was not married by age thirty, he would take her in and try to set her up with one of the local bachelors. After all, German men are more practical and less fastidious when it comes to female beauty. Slavic men were spoiled and usually chose with their eyes.

Galina could not think of anything more humiliating than being patronized by her natural father and pimped out to his omnivorous friends, so she resolved to prove him wrong. She would not accept casual charity from the man who had walked out on her mother. She would be married by her twenty-seventh birthday, or twenty-eighth at the latest, and shut everyone up once and for all. She even had a perfect candidate in mind, a certain tenor from the music academy, but there was another woman in her way. That woman was Antonia Olenski. Bewitched by her, Nicholas was dead to the world. Galina could not compete with the sultry, cat-eyed semi-Jewess. Even if Galina starved herself, she could not get that dainty hourglass shape. She could not do anything about her bone structure. Every time she picked up another custom-made dress from the tailor, she could not help thinking of how much better the dress would look on Antonia.

"Ah, it's you, Olenski," Galina finally said in a sour tone. "You should've identified yourself at once. That girl at the front desk is a total dummy. Vladimir Ivanych is indisposed."

"Is he having crepes and tea with that guy from Moscow Conservatory?"

"Something like that. What do you need him for?"

"In a nutshell, here's the situation," Antonia sighed into the receiver. "My aunt kicked us out. She accused Maryana of stealing her stupid earrings. Naturally, I stuck up for my kid, so now we're broke and have no place to go."

"That's awful."

"Tell me about it. You just can't trust anyone. Would you be good enough to give Vladimir Ivanych a message? Basically, I'm coming back. But first I need to put Maryana up at a sanatorium. I need money, Gal. Ask Vladimir Ivanych to wire me an advance. I'll earn it all back, every ruble. Hell, I'll even take over the internship program if need be. Tell him I'll be back in time for the showcase. And tell Nicholas I'll be able to play with him after all."

Galina was mortified by the prospect of her rival's return. Things were going so well for her. The showcase programs have already been printed with her name on it. With Antonia out of the picture, she was the new prima donna of the Gomel Music Academy. Above all, she and Nicholas Nichenko were really getting chummy. The other night she swore she felt the tip of his shoe rubbing her ankle.

"Don't be foolish," Galina said. "This is no place for you and Maryana. People are passing out on the streets and glowing in the dark. It's worse than Hiroshima and Nagasaki. If I had kids, I'd want to keep them away from this steaming pit for as long as possible. And you're still so very weak. I can hear it in your voice. Your red blood cells must be way below the norm."

"So what do you propose, Gal?"

"I have a summer home in Gurzuf, in a great location, right by the market. My aunt Kitty lives there all year long, but we rent a portion of it out to tourists."

"Gal, you know I don't have that kind of money. I can barely pay for this call."

"Who said anything about money? You can stay there for free!"

"Please, Gal, don't joke like that. I don't have time for it. My humor button has been temporarily deactivated."

"No, I'm dead serious. It's really no problem. I mean, you'll have to buy your own train tickets, but you won't have to pay for the room, and the food there is dirt cheap. Tell you what, I'll send a telegram to my auntie right away. The Black Sea air would do wonders for you and Maryana."

Galina's enthusiasm only exacerbated Antonia's anxiety. Oh, there must have been a catch. No way would the Richtman girl be so nice without a good reason, especially when the rest of the world was turning its cold ass towards Antonia. "Gal, I'm speechless. You'd actually do that for me?"

"In a heartbeat! What are friends for?"

"And are we friends?"

"Totally!"

"Since when?"

"Since whenever."

"Gosh, it seems so sudden, and a little unnatural, dare I add."

"Why?"

"Gee, Gal, I don't know." Antonia scratched the tip of her nose. "Maybe it's because my father is a Jew, and yours is a German, and your people used to bake my people in the oven. Remember the six million?"

"Of course, I remember. Who could forget stuff like that?"

"So in theory, you and I should be genetically incompatible, right? Or am I overthinking it?"

"Oh, you're *totally* overthinking it. It's not like that at all. My dad was too young to serve in Hitler's army anyway. I think our dads would've wanted for us to be best pals in the world. They weren't the ones who'd started the war in the first place."

"You're probably right," Antonia agreed reluctantly. "I guess ..."

"Besides, you and your husband have been so nice to me," Galina continued. "It's not easy being an intern in this place, unless you're sleeping with your supervisor. Vladimir Ivanych has his pets, and I'm not one of them. Everyone makes sarcastic remarks about my technique, except for you and Joseph."

"Well, yeah, Josey and I don't stoop to that level."

"Exactly. You two barely acknowledged my existence, and that totally made me feel at home. When I walk down the hall, everyone whispers and giggles, but you guys just keep on walking, like I'm not even there. It's sort of comforting."

"Well, I'm glad you feel that way." Nobody ever accused Antonia of spreading comfort. "Oh, Gal? One more thing. Take good care of Nicholas for me. Will you?"

"You can count on that!"

"Just don't play too loudly when you're accompanying him. He hates it when you drown out his magnificent voice. Perform with him, not against him."

Chapter Seven
AS CLOSE TO HEAVEN AS IT GETS

Minsk, Belarus – June, 1986

Joseph's vow never to touch another woman went out the window next time he came to Minsk. The moment he walked through the glass doors of the recording studio, he was ambushed by a blonde in an embroidered peasant blouse and knee-high red boots. She dragged him into one of the conference rooms and pinned him to the table. Accustomed as Joseph was to random sexual assaults, he struggled to remember where he had met that woman before. The two of them must have brushed against each other somewhere. Joseph had always prided himself on his sharp memory. The copious amounts of hashish he had smoked in the conservatory had not decreased his ability to memorize faces and names. The key metrics of his past sex partners were catalogued in his brain.

Halfway through the messy intercourse it started coming back to him. He could vaguely recall having a somewhat bold conversation with a precocious eight-year old girl he had met on a train to Gomel, who told him about her mother's infatuation with him. So this panting siren on top of him must have been Ilona Poplawski, the professor of Belarusian literature who had written her thesis on Janka Kupala.

"We owe this meeting to my daughter," Ilona whispered in Belarusian with a distinct western accent. "She's such a clever girl to have recognized you. How often we underestimate our children."

"I hope you have a convincing explanation for the girl's father," Joseph replied, zipping up his trousers and straightening his tie. Having trysts with married women was not something he did frequently, preferring the company of widows, underage virgins and old maids. Married or even freshly divorced women fell into the no-touch territory. The idea of a maniacal husband or ex-husband lurking in the shadows gave him creeps. "What would he do if he knew how you spent your afternoon, huh? Should I start worrying about my balls?"

Ilona averted her eyes. "Your balls are perfectly safe. My husband is in prison, actually. They have another guy subbing for him at the university."

"What did he do—steal chalk from the liberal arts department?"

"It's a little more serious than that. He's suffering for his faith."

Joseph looked at Ilona with a hint of interest for the first time. "Catholic?"

"No, Baptist. They caught him in front of an abortion clinic, distributing evangelical pamphlets. He had a couple of his students with him. Catholics don't do enough of that. Their faith is confined to their churches. Baptists take their faith out on the streets. That's the way Christianity was meant to be, preaching in open air."

"No kidding!"

"Yeah. The police arrested him for sedition. Pretty crazy, huh? His students got away with a smack on a bottom and a written warning, but my poor Tycho is behind bars now."

"Well, for what it's worth, your husband sounds like a really neat guy, the kind I'd like to have for a friend." Joseph slapped himself on the forehead. "Gee, now I feel bad for having slept with his wife. See what you've done? All this talk about Christ and suffering is making me feel like a total pig. You come out of nowhere, jump on me, and then pour all that ecclesiastic talk over me."

Ilona strutted towards him and fixed his tie. "Don't feel bad. My husband would've understood. I won't see him for another six months. If I had to sleep with another man, he would've liked it to be with someone like you. He would totally approve of my choice. See, I have enough respect for Tycho to consider his wishes."

"Wow, you must really know your husband well, if you know the type of man he'd prefer to see you screw while he's doing time."

"Tycho has an exquisite taste in men."

"I bet he does! I don't know why you call me your soul mate. Looks like you already have a soul mate. At any rate, nice knowing you."

Joseph had exactly five minutes to get into the recording booth. He opened the door for Ilona, but she was not in a hurry to leave. She remained on the table, her legs crossed.

"I'm not sure Tycho will be able to get his old job back when he gets out," she said wistfully. "If he can't go back to teaching, he'll be devastated."

"I would be too."

"This is where I was hoping..." Ilona bit her lip and batted her eyelashes. "I was hoping, and praying, and assuming..."

"Go on."

"Maybe you could write a petition in his defense. You know, so he could get his job back?"

"What makes you think anyone will listen to me?"

"You're such a prominent figure. You have all these accolades."

"So do you, Ilona. You aren't exactly Dasha the Hairdresser yourself. You're the fucking poetry scholar, and you aren't even thirty."

"True, but I'm Tycho's wife, so it's not the same. I cannot advocate for him alone. I need a third party to help me. If you and I unite forces, we'll have a better chance of having my husband exonerated." She laid her hand on Joseph's elbow. "By the way, this is *not* the only reason why I made passionate love to you, if that's what you're thinking. I'm still totally crazy about you."

In truth, Ilona's feelings were irrelevant to Joseph. The sex itself was very mediocre. He was not a fourteen-year old to get excited by mechanical aggressive humping accompanied by monotonous groaning. Ilona's above average hotness did not compensate for her unimaginative up and down technique. Joseph was beginning to regret the whole thing. He never should have sparked that conversation with the precocious first-grader on the train. When he told the girl he would be delighted to see her mother at the studio, it was meant as a joke. He had no idea the girl would deliver the invitation and that Ilona would take it to heart. And now he was sucked into the mission of advocating for an imprisoned evangelical martyr. How could he say no? Tycho Poplawski's ordeal moved him deeply. While Joseph would have no problem getting over Ilona, he could not get over the horrendous injustice her husband was facing.

"I think I have a plan," he said with a sigh of determination. "I'm not sure if it will work or not. We have to seek help from fellow-Christians. Meet me in three hours at the Cornflower bookstore."

"Why three hours?"

"I'm here to do a choir recording. Remember?"

"Oh, yes," Ilona muttered with a faint nod. "Can I stay and watch?"

"Absolutely not. Visitors aren't allowed in the studio. Besides, I don't want the male singers to get distracted. If they see you standing behind the glass, looking all hot, they'll get boners underneath their costumes. Meet me at noon. Here are five rubles for a coffee and pastry I promised. Keep the change."

Ilona accepted the money and slipped it into her pocket swiftly. "How do I know you you'll show up? How can I be sure you aren't just trying to get rid of me?"

"I swear to you on my Catholic faith, on the lives of my daughters, both bastard and legitimate. I won't forsake Tycho. I won't let him rot in prison along with thieves and hooligans."

* * * *

Five rubles went a long way in 1986. Ilona skipped the coffee and the buttery goodies. Instead, she bought a pack of American menthol cigarettes, a tube of Polish lipstick and an imitation Lithuanian amber broach from a street vendor. Those western luxury items made her feel like a queen. She could not stop marveling at Joseph's generosity. In the eight years of marriage, her husband had not given her as much money on "stuff". Tycho was pragmatic and egalitarian. He insisted that serious scholarly women like his wife did not need all that cheap imported garbage to embellish themselves, and if they still craved it, they should pay for it with their own money. For the first time in her life Ilona got a taste of what it felt like to be a kept woman. A man just gave her five rubles to spend at her discretion. She could get used to it, though she knew this pleasant episode was not likely to repeat.

Joseph showed up at noon, as promised.

"I'll take you to see Father Athanasius," he said in a mysterious whisper.

"Who's that?"

"An Orthodox priest from Novgorod. He's sitting a few meters underneath us, in the basement. The store manager is his sister. She allows him to receive visitors. Right now he's collecting donations to open a new Orthodox Church. We could really use one here in Minsk. From what I hear, he's a total hoot. You'll love him."

Before going to meet the priest, Ilona washed her hands to remove the stench of cigarettes from her fingertips and blotted away the lipstick. It distressed her that even after this emergency clean-up she still had that slutty aura around her. She sensed that somehow Father Athanasius would know how she had spent her morning. A holy man can smell a fallen woman a mile away. She pictured a traditional patriarch in a black cassock, with a somber ageless face and a beard down to his waist. She was surprised to find a bald, clean-shaven, middle-aged man in a Turkish sweater and jeans, eating an open cheese-and-bologna sandwich and gulping Fanta. In contrast to his casual apparel, his gaze was scorching and critical.

"Sister Ilona," he began, having wiped his mouth with a sleeve, "your husband is a Baptist, I understand?"

"Correct."

"You are aware that the Orthodox Church regards this frivolous parody of Protestantism as a sect."

"It's the only sect that's doing anything to attract young people." Ilona was not afraid to stand up to that pudgy Fanta guzzler. Who did he think he was, sitting there with crumbs on his chin? "Modern kids need Christ more than ever. Have you been to a farmers' market lately, father? Have you seen the stacks of imported pornography between the crates with cabbage?"

"I wouldn't have a reason to, as I don't eat cabbage." The priest crossed his arms and leaned back in his chair. "But I'll take your word for it, sister. If you are telling me that there's cabbage on the market, I believe you."

"What has the Orthodox Church done lately to win more souls?"

"Our Church isn't obsessed with finding new converts, sister. Salvation is not like a Fanta commercial." He shook the empty bottle in the air. "You don't sell Jesus to kids the way they sell bubblegum in the West. We care about keeping the ones we have and preserving our traditions."

Ilona pushed her index finger into the tabletop. "Bullshit. The only thing you care about preserving is your own collective ass. You sold out to the communist party. Admit it! You assisted Stalin's henchmen."

Father Athanasius took another swig of Fanta. "We did what we had to do in order to survive. What would you do, sister, if nine out of ten churches were destroyed? The people in this part of the world are spiritual orphans. They've been separated from their Heavenly Father. But the age of darkness is coming to an end."

"Is it really? The way I see it, the clouds keep thickening."

"You haven't been following the news lately, sister. Tell me. What do you think of the new General Secretary?"

"Gorbachev?" The priest's question took Ilona aback. "To be honest, I haven't been listening to his speeches. It's hard to focus on his words. I cannot stop staring at that birthmark on his forehead. It looks like a continent, though I'm not sure which one. I flunked geography in school."

"It's a form of stigmata," Father Athanasius said. "That thing on Gorbachev's forehead. It looks like a stain from communion wine. The man is precisely what our nation needs. God will work through him. He'll conduct the Holy Spirit the way metal conducts electricity. Wait and see. He'll make friends with Reagan and let us reopen churches. The American president is a man of faith. He will exude positive influence on our General Secretary. Now is a great time to be a Christian—a real Christian, that is, not an amateur evangelist."

"So you won't help my husband?"

"Your husband doesn't need our help. He wouldn't accept it even if we offered it to him. It may be hard for you to believe, but right now he is very happy. It's as close to Heaven as it gets here on earth. There is no greater honor for a Christian than to suffer for his faith. If we give him his freedom and his job back, we'll rob him of his martyrdom. He'll resent us for it. Take my word. I'm somewhat familiar with Baptist mentality."

Chapter Eight
CRIMEAN FEVER

Gurzuf, Crimea - summer of 1986

After eating white peaches for two weeks straight, Maryana could not stand the sight of those pudgy fuzzy giants that looked too much like severed bald heads. It did not help that her mother kept forcing them down her throat every morning.

"Eat the goddamn peaches," Antonia would hiss, standing over her daughter with a fruit knife dripping with juice. "Or else you'll get radiation sickness and die. That's right, your blood will turn white, and your hair will fall out. They don't show you that stuff on TV, but it happens every day. So eat your peaches and be thankful, idiot child. We're in paradise. This is where the party officials come to soak their feet. Do you realize what a privilege it is?"

Maryana would groan and choke on the slippery peach flesh—you just don't argue with someone who's holding a knife. Somehow she did not feel particularly privileged. For whatever reason everyone back home kept raving about that subtropical resort on the northern coast of the Black Sea.

Saved By The Bang

Gurzuf was a former Tartar village located in a valley resembling an amphitheater, surrounded by a semicircle of mountains. Antonia insisted that Maryana should venerate that place, if only for its literary significance, for it was there that Alexander Grin, the genius of Russian Neo-Romanticism, had found the inspiration for his most lyrical novellas. Along with the peaches, Antonia kept force-feeding her daughter Grin's greatest works. Maryana obeyed begrudgingly. In one week she had read his two fantasy pieces, *Scarlet Sails* and *Wave Runner*. The adolescent optimism of the author, his love for humanity and his dogged faith in a favorable outcome sickened her. Did some girls actually believe in that bosh? It surprised her that her own mother, who always had a blasphemous comment under her sleeve, would swoon over these tales.

Above all, the climate was not agreeing with Maryana. She hated the fishy breeze, the blistering pebbles under her feet and the nauseating humidity. Every day she would come up with phony symptoms from heatstroke to phantom premenstrual cramps to avoid being taken to the shore. She would rather spend her afternoons on the glass-encased balcony of her hostess' apartment.

Galina Richtman's aunt lived on the third floor of a historical villa that had once served as a summer home for a czarist army officer. After the Revolution of 1917 the officer's family had fled westward, and the villa had been broken up into apartments for the communist party leaders. The balcony of the villa overlooked the bay with the legendary Bear Mountain protruding from the water.

Maryana's vehement distaste for the Crimean climate did not dismay Antonia in the least. All too relieved to leave her daughter behind, she took daily walks to the beach on her own. It gave her an opportunity to flaunt her summer wardrobe and temporarily forget that she was a thirty-three year old wife and mother. In a place where nobody knew her, she could play any role her whimsy dictated. The route from the villa to the shore lay through a military sanatorium surrounded by a park with exotic trees—giant sequoias, Lebanese cedars and sculptures. The famous Midnight Fountain crowned with a goddess standing on a globe was the signature monument in the park. The architecture combined the Turkish, Greek and Slavic styles.

The windows of the sanatorium were wide open all day long, with laughter, profanities, cigarette smoke, male hormones and guitar music pouring out of them. Antonia's presence generated considerable interest from the residents. Whenever they heard the clicking of her heels, they would flock to the windows like kennel dogs in anticipation of a meal. To play her part, she would turn out her shoulders and wiggle her hips just a little.

She had one particularly loyal fan on the second floor. He must have figured out her schedule and would camp out by the window each day from nine o'clock in the morning. Antonia knew as much about him as he knew about her. All she saw was a perfectly proportionate, meticulously chiseled torso towering above the windowsill. His face was of an ordinary Russian peasant, but the torso—Christ Almighty— was worthy of Michelangelo's David. Whenever Antonia passed underneath his window, he would whistle. She had to admit, his whistle was sonorous and melodic, with multiple pitches and undertones, like a nightingale's warble.

Saved By The Bang

One morning she paused under his window and looked up.

"Young man, with impressive lungs like yours, one should consider taking up a wind instrument. Others would turn blue by now from lack of oxygen."

"My other organs are just as impressive, as many a woman will testify," he retorted. A second later his smirk waned. "I can tell you're not from around here. You look a little pale."

"Well, that's because I had a major surgery, and my hemoglobin is a little low, thank you very much." For some reason she felt compelled to explain her pallor to the young man. "I'm on a sabbatical, recovering."

"Then you're in the right place, lady. With so many army studs in the two-kilometer radius, you're guaranteed one hell of a sabbatical. We get hundreds of women like you passing through the park, and at the end of the season they all leave sun-burned and saddle-sore."

Tickled by the delicious obscenity of the address, Antonia decided to stick around, if only to see how far that conversation would go. She put her bulky canvas bag on the bench and assumed a more flirtatious pose. With the sun rising behind her back, penetrating through her sheer dress, she knew he could see the V of her crotch and the outline of her bikini bottom.

"I assume you're here getting treatment for syphilis," she said.

"Nah, nothing exciting like that." He wagged his hand self-deprecatingly. "Just getting some light physical therapy. Got banged up a bit in Afghan. You know?"

"Oh...nothing major, I hope."

"Just a couple of scratches. Doctors say I'll be good as new by September. And what were you doing before the sabbatical?"

"Playing piano."

"No way!"

"Why does that surprise you?"

"You're too hot for a pianist. I always thought it was an ugly girl's instrument."

"You're very wrong."

"Am I? The guys here are wondering if you're an actress or something."

"Definitely not an actress. You can tell your friends that much. My mother never would've allowed it. No way."

"Tell your mother she's robbed the Soviet cinema of a great star."

"Hardly. I'm not super photogenic anyway. My face is not super symmetrical. I have a deviated septum, and it's really noticeable on photographs. Anyway, I graduated from the Minsk Conservatory, and now I'm working as the lead accompanist at the Gomel Music Academy."

The soldier tilted his head. "I'm still not convinced. I think you're lying."

"Why would I lie about something like that? I've been playing piano since the age of five."

"Then prove it. We have a piano in the lounge. Stop by tonight and play for me and the guys. They're serving clams and wine at the dining hall. What do you say?"

"I say we have a date!"

* * * *

Saved By The Bang

The radio reported the casualties from the earthquake in India, but not a single word registered with Antonia. She was in the process of inserting ruby studs into her earlobes, humming a waltz from Shostakovich's Jazz Suite II, a piece that her colleagues at the music academy unanimously condemned as flippant and superficial. Maryana was laid up again with malaria-like symptoms in the care of Galina's aunt, which made it all the more convenient for Antonia to sneak out. She could not remember the last time she went out on her own after dusk. She had a date, for heaven's sake, with a young stud fifteen years younger than her! The red halter dress custom-tailored in Kiev took half a decade off. The stomach muscles around the incision were beginning to atrophy and sag, but the drapes around the waist hid it. Damn it, she had every right to flaunt her muscled arms and back. For a thirty-something, who had nearly died a few months earlier she looked pretty good.

The botanical garden in moonlight looked a million times more beautiful than in daylight. Running down the balmy alleys, she felt like a heroine from one of Alexander Grin's novels, the Wave Runner.

The dormitory building, the ever bustling beacon of testosterone, appeared unusually sleepy and quiet that night. Even the concierge looked comatose. Antonia had to cough and click her heels a few times to attract his attention.

"I'm here to see..." It suddenly occurred to her that she did not know the soldier's name. "I'm here to see the piano."

The concierge yawned. "Ah, that piece of junk? Follow me."

Instead of a spacious concert hall with crystal chandeliers and frescos depicting cherubs, Antonia found a dusty hovel without windows, with cardboard boxes piled up against the wall. Standing in the corner was a cripple of a piano with the lid missing. Did the soldier boy play a prank on her?

"Is this where you hold performances?"

"No, this is where we dump rubbish before the truck comes for it—broken chairs, old mattresses, you name it. If you want the piano, it's yours. We're not paying for the delivery, though."

"Of course, not," Antonia whispered. "I'd like to try it out, if you don't mind."

"Knock yourself out, lady. I'll be at the front desk if you need me."

It had been over a month since Antonia touched a piano, the longest she had gone without playing. The piano came without a bench, so she sat on one of the boxes. The bare lamp bulb dangling from the ceiling provided enough light for her to see the keyboard. When her fingers pressed on the scratched keys, the nerves in her wisdom teeth howled. Such a horrid sound! Not unlike a deathbed groan of an old man abandoned by his children. She had never played on such an instrument that was so dreadfully out of tune, so cruelly neglected. All three pedals were dead. She felt a spasm inside her chest, suddenly becoming aware of her mission. Higher powers had led her all the way to the Crimea so she could rescue that piano and give it a second chance in life.

"You're safe with me," she whispered. "I won't let them discard you. I'll take you out of here, have you repaired and give you a good home. You'll make music again."

Halfway through the piece she heard faint creaking of floor boards and squeaking of wheels.

Saved By The Bang

"Bravo, pretty lady," a familiar voice spoke from the dark hallway.

Antonia's hands froze on the keyboard, and her breathing quickened.

A wheelchair rolled in from behind the corner. She recognized the ruddy peasant face and the sculpted torso, but there was not much below the torso, only short stumps wrapped in cloth.

"I honestly didn't think you'd come," the soldier said. "When they told me someone was here to see the piano, I had to come up and see if it really was you. The stupid elevator wouldn't cooperate."

"I'm a woman of my word," Antonia whispered, looking him in the eye. "I promised to come, so here I am. Now you see that I told you the truth about myself. I've been straight with you from the very start, though I don't even know your name."

"Sorry for the oversight," the soldier said. "I got so tickled by our acquaintance that I totally forgot to mention a few basic things about myself, like my name and my rank. Private Matrosov, at your service."

"Professor Olenski. But you can call me...You can call me just that. Professor Olenski will do."

The soldier glanced over his shoulder and whistled. "Hey guys! Come on in. The entertainment is here."

From her wooden pedestal, Antonia watched the tiny room fill with crippled soldiers. They poured in from the hallway, crowding around the piano, enclosing the petrified performer by a ring of wheelchairs, crutches, canes and artificial limbs.

"Comrades," said the ringleader, "I give you the star of the Moscow Conservatory."

"It's Minsk," Antonia corrected him coyly. "Minsk Conservatory."

"All the better!" He slapped the stump of his thigh. "This dainty thing, who looks tasty enough to spread on your toast, came here all the way from the radioactive Belarus to play a concert in recognition of our sacrifices for the motherland. I presume it's not too much to ask?"

"No, not too much at all." Antonia ran her hand over her teased crown. The humidity was causing her hair to curl at the root. "But this instrument needs some serious therapy."

"No, it's perfect for the occasion. A crippled piano for a crippled audience."Antonia cleared her throat and wiped her sweaty hands against her dress.

"What would you like me to play?"

"Whatever you feel like. Surprise us." He surveyed his comrades. "We're not picky, are we, guys?"

"You want a surprise? I'll give you one."

So she gave them Schubert's ballad, which sounded like a river carrying the sorrows of humanity. Schubert, a homely, sexually repressed outcast, knew a thing or two about loneliness and suffering.

Her performance was interrupted rather crudely.

"Enough of that depressing shit," Matrosov said. "How about a few combat ballads?"

The rest of the soldiers supported their ringleader with a deep howl.

"Whatever makes you happy," Antonia said indulgently. Really, she did not expect these boys to appreciate the breadth of the melancholic genius. "If you have the sheet music, I'll be happy to play the accompaniment."

"Nah, sheet music is for pussies and other uptight academic types. We soldiers don't record our music on paper. The song is supposed to sound a little different each time you perform it. Every one of us throws in something personal. The melody and the poetry have to keep evolving. They can't stand still. I bet they didn't teach you that at the Conservatory, did they?"

"Of course, not," Antonia replied coyly, rubbing her knees. "We spent five years marching in straight lines and saluting Khruschev's portrait. Well, chaps, maybe one of you can sing a few measures, so I get a sense for what that ever-evolving melody is and pick it up on the piano."

Matrosov snapped his fingers. Three, two, one...He belted the first line, and the one-armed Armenian sitting next to him sang the second one, and soon the song was going around the room like a musical relay.

> *Smoke came down the tip of Kandakhar,*
> *The vodka and the ammo have run out.*
> *I'll pick up a few chords on my guitar,*
> *The company will sing along, no doubt.*

They all joined on the refrain.

> *Who gives a damn that we are broken, scorched and weary?*
> *Who gives a damn that death had stared us in the eye?*
> *We have a chance to sing a song, so make it cheery.*
> *Another sing-along before we die.*

* * * *

"How much longer do you have to stay here?" Antonia asked Matrosov. They were sitting on the patio across from each other, drinking warm beer.

"Another month or so, unless the psychiatrist gives me an extension," he replied. "If I can convince the old goat that I'm suicidal, maybe he'll keep me here until the end of the year. You can always get an extension if you know how to fake symptoms."

"So you like it here?"

"The food is pretty good, actually. A definite improvement on what they fed us in the army. Too bad there's less of me to feed now." Matrosov glanced down at his stumps. "When I first got here I stuffed my face, even though I had no appetite. If you sit on your ass all day, you don't get as hungry. Imagine having a slab of smoked butterfish on the plate, staring at you, so you stuff it in your cheeks and just let it sit there. Can't say I'm looking forward to going home."

"Where is home?"

"Some shithole outside Saratov. Definitely not look forwarding to dealing with all those fucking people. My girlfriend had a baby last year."

Antonia gave his hand a playful squeeze. "You rake!"

"Don't get excited. It's not mine. My former buddy had fathered the bastard."

"Oh..." Antonia's fingers slipped off his knuckles. That was the stuff Hemingway's novels were made of. Friendship, war, betrayal. She wondered if Private Matrosov was telling her the truth or merely trying to cajole her into pity sex. She wanted to believe it was the former, as she had grown to like him. "Look, if talking about it distresses you, we don't need to continue this conversation."

"Not at all. I'm beyond being distressed. I'm just giving you the back story. This dude and I used to be thick as thieves. We'd do everything together, skip classes, smoke in the bathroom, jerked off into the same toilet and beat up the nerds. Good times! We graduated the same year, but he didn't get drafted, because his parents got a note from the doctor saying he had tuberculosis. You see, my parents weren't as smart. Honest, law-abiding morons! They didn't even try to get me out of the service. It didn't even occur to them to chop off my trigger finger. Anyway, while I was in Kabul, Alecia got lonely. That asshole buddy of mine sniffed her out and knocked her up. They both missed me so fucking much they jumped into bed to comfort each other. You know how it is. I heard that my mom begged Alecia not to tell me while I was laid up at the military hospital. She was afraid I wouldn't take the news well. But to tell you the truth, I didn't care one bit. Those people don't mean shit to me anymore. So that's my story, Professor."

"You can call me Antonia."

"I like professor better. Every girl has a name. Not every girl has a title. I feel so important now being in your presence."

"But you *are* important, title or no title."

"Bullshit. You don't believe that for a moment, lady. Titles are everything. If my old man had a title, I wouldn't be here. I mean, I'd still be in the Crimea, just not in the amputee ward. I'd be on the other side of town, in a place that's gated from the ordinary people, where the kids of officers and party leaders hang out. I'd still have my legs."

"You don't know that. Those boys serve in the army like everyone else."

"Yeah, but they don't get sent to the war zone. They get stationed along the Baltic coast and disembark to go to rock festivals in Jurmala and grope tourist chicks. Guys like me are the battle-cattle, the proverbial cannon fodder."

Antonia leaped to her feet. "I can't leave you here like this. I just can't!"

"What are you going to do, Professor—tuck me into your purse and take me to Belarus?"

"Yes! That's exactly what I'm going to do." She started pacing around Matrosov's wheelchair. "My husband is an influential composer and musicologist. He has access to a recording studio in Minsk. He's friends with the man in charge of radio programming. Your songs need to be heard by the people of this country. If you let me transcribe them and show them to the right people..."

Matrosov reached out and caught the hem of her skirt.

"For starters, stop running in circles, or I'll wring my neck trying to keep up with you. My wheelchair doesn't spin that fast. It's not one of those fancy ones they have in the West with buttons and levers and shit."

"I'm sorry. I always brainstorm on my feet."

"Calm down, Professor. Aren't you taking this freedom of speech fluff a little too literally? Wake up. It's Gorbachev's gimmick to trick people into thinking they have a say, all this illusion of democracy. Those songs weren't meant to go beyond these walls. My buddies and I wrote them for ourselves. If you think they have the power to stop the war, you've been smoking hashish. The war will end when both sides run out of troops. That's usually how it works out in the end."

Saved By The Bang

Antonia scribbled her phone number on a napkin. "Here's my number in Gomel if you change your mind. My offer still stands."

Chapter Nine
THE INQUISITOR'S DUNGEON

Yuri Gagarin Magnet School, Gomel – September 1, 1986

The academic year of 1986 started with the customary morning assembly. Four hundred students, their ages ranging from seven to fifteen, poured into the schoolyard for the opening ceremony in a sea of white gauze and chrysanthemum pollen. The teachers and the administration were going out of their way to pretend that this year was no different from any other. At quarter after eight, a boy from the tenth grade put a kindergarten girl on his shoulder in observance of the tradition and carried her around the perimeter of the school yard as she rang the tiny brass bell. Halfway through the promenade, the kindergartener's nose started to bleed. She pulled out a handkerchief from the pocket of her black apron. Clearly, this was not her first nosebleed. Within minutes the handkerchief was soaked. Her blonde head adorned with bows started bobbing from side to side. The teenage boy who was carrying her gripped her knees tighter and kept on walking.

Saved By The Bang

Antonia was watching the ceremony from the back row where nobody could see her. Maryana, sandwiched between two taller classmates, kept jumping on her tiptoes, trying to spot her mother's face in the crowd. Antonia could not bring herself to smile or even make eye contact with her daughter. That day she did not have the energy to fake excitement. Her heart was heavy as lead, but not because so many children were showing symptoms of mild radiation poisoning. After two weeks in Gomel she had gotten used to the sight of bloody noses and discarded handkerchiefs in the trash bins. She had bigger things on her mind, like the upcoming meeting with her boss, who wanted to speak to her regarding certain changes to the staffing roster that had taken place over the summer.

As soon as the assembly was adjourned, Antonia slipped out of the school yard and ran towards the bus stop. Thankfully, the waiting booth was not stuffed with people. There were just two old ladies with fishnet bags sitting on the bench, which gave Antonia plenty of elbow room. She pulled out a powder puff from her purse and blotted her cheeks and forehead. The reflection in the tiny round mirror was not encouraging. Her Crimean tan was fading unevenly. There were still some dark patches above her eyebrows and around her nostrils. She had not highlighted her hair in ages, and the new gray streaks were particularly apparent in the harsh mid-morning light. Her eyes were still red and crusty from the remnants of conjunctivitis she had contracted on the train back to Gomel. The wrinkles around her mouth had deepened in the past three months. All in all, she did not look like she had spent her summer eating peaches at a subtropical resort. The boys from the opera department would notice her decline, no doubt. Antonia could already hear them make venomous comments in the bathroom. On another hand, her haggard appearance could actually play in her favor. If she showed up in front of Vladimir Ivanych looking refreshed and glowing, he would be more inclined to give her a draconian treatment, but if she came in wheezing and blanching, perhaps it would stimulate his chivalrous side.

The idea of playing damsel in distress sickened Antonia. She despised women who resorted to such tricks as well as men who fell for them. Alas, the Amazon attitude, instilled in her by her mother, would have to go out the window. Antonia would have to repress her pride and distaste for falsity in order to keep her job, because becoming financially dependent on her husband would humiliate her even more than groveling in front of her boss. Knowing Joseph, he would milk his newly acquired sense of superiority to the fullest. Oh, he would punish her for all those times she had outshone him professionally. The thought of having to beg him for seven rubles to buy lipstick frightened her more than all nuclear disasters put together.

* * * *

In her absence, the interior of the academy had been changed beyond recognition. The place did not look or smell the same. The oil portraits of composers that used to line the walls of the auditorium had all been taken down. The old wooden floors had been torn out and replaced with shiny checkered tiles. Antonia slipped and nearly fell when she first stepped on them. The building itself was rejecting her like a foreign object. These freshly painted walls seem to recognize her. The hallways were swarming with pedagogy interns in their early twenties dressed in stiff stonewash denim. This Polish-made junk was all the rage, apparently, and Belarusians were willing to pay a fortune for it at the flea market. College students would save their meager stipend for months to buy a pair of fake Levis or ankle-high Keds with neon-green shoelaces, and perhaps, a black t-shirt with a Disney princess iron-on. Of course, no clown costume would be complete without a hot-pink plastic bracelet and some pearly lip gloss that made you appear cyanotic. Nothing spells "sexy" like that exsanguinated zombie look. Those gum-snapping airheads believed that they were one shot of hairspray away from Tiffany or any other American pop queen. Ridiculous getup aside, Antonia found it annoying that none of them bothered to greet her or even make eye contact. Whatever happened to respect for the veteran faculty members? Was her status not apparent to them? Would they not identify it by just looking at her silk dress that was custom-tailored in one of Minsk's finest ateliers? No, they kept on babbling about the best place to buy liquid eyeliner and tickets to the latest Euro disco concert. Those bands featuring queer-looking boys who wiggled their hips and wore mascara were popping up like metastases all over Eastern Europe. No place was safe from this cultural cancer, certainly not the academy.

The only familiar fixture in the entire building was Vladimir Ivanych. He was still wearing the same gray double-breasted Hungarian suit he wore every day, rain or shine. The man would probably be buried in it. When Antonia stepped inside his office, he was reclining in his roomy leather armchair, his fingers twirling a jade pen. She mentally compared him to a medieval executioner twirling a torture device.

"Welcome back, Olenski," he said. "You look exhausted."

Oh, good. The boss picked up on her fatigue. Just what she had hoped for!

"The train ride was bumpy," Antonia explained in a dying voice, running her hand over her face. "We got stopped at the Ukrainian border for no reason and sat there for three hours. There was some problem with the tracks. And then gypsies stole my wallet at the station, which was a perfect ending to a dreadful summer. Those people, if you can call them that, totally took advantage of my fatigue. This woman with a child in her arms approached me, and..."

"Let's cut to the chase." Vladimir Ivanych had heard that railroad saga before. "You must have a pretty good idea why I asked you to see me."

He did not even ask Antonia to sit down. It looked like she was going to receive her death sentence standing.

"It's about the restructuring, isn't it?"

"Undoubtedly, you've noticed an array of new faces when you came in."

"I just assumed it was a vocational technical school on a field trip, judging from the way these girls dress. On my way to work, I see them smoking outside the textile factory."

"You're mistaken, Olenski. These young women are the future of this academy and classical music education."

"I didn't realize that the future of classical music lay with *Sweet May* and *Modern Talking*."

Saved By The Bang

Antonia bit her tongue a second too late. Was it the best time to unleash her sarcasm when her head was on the chopping block?

"These young women may not subscribe to your dress code or your Khruschev era sensibilities," Vladimir Ivanych said calmly, "but they are in no way inferior to you intellectually. We have an influx of new talent, so we need to rearrange the old talent a bit. I'm making you the head of student teaching program." He stamped Antonia's contract and slid it over for her sign. "From now on you'll be in charge of the pedagogy interns."

Antonia swallowed a lump of acrid saliva and backed away from the desk. The severity of penance knocked the wind out of her. She had expected a slap on the wrist, a very painful slap that would leave lasting red marks, but this was a punch in the stomach, a jab through the heart.

"This must be a joke," she muttered.

"I don't have time for jokes, Olenski, especially at the beginning of the academic year, while I'm still trying to solidify my staff. Are you on board or not?"

"Do I have to give you my answer now? You cannot drop a bomb like that on my head and expect a straight answer."

"You need more time to do some soul-searching? Three months in the Crimea wasn't enough. Hey, maybe you'll get a job with the Moscow orchestra."

"You shouldn't say such cruel things, Vladimir Ivanych. You know I didn't leave on a whim. I had a summer from hell."

"So did everyone else, my dear. The autumn is not looking good either. Get used to it. On a positive note, the administration sank all that money into remodeling the place to brighten up the interior a little, so it wouldn't look so old-fashioned and depressing. Wait until you see your new office. It's on the third floor."

"Please tell me it's not the one with windows overlooking the highway. I cannot work with all that noise and car exhaust. I haven't recovered completely, and I still fatigue easily."

"You don't have to worry about the noise, Olenski," her boss reassured her. "Your office has no windows. It used to be a storage room for the janitor. I thought it would be perfect for you. It gets a little stuffy in there, but the sound insulation is superb. I assure you, nothing will distract you while you write those lesson plans and evaluations."

"But this position is not exactly in my specialty. Not to mention, it's beneath me."

Vladimir Ivanych shrugged. "It's the only one I had available."

"It's only available because nobody wants it. Honestly, I can't think of anything more mind-numbing. You know I hate working with children or people who work with children."

"Then you should've thought about that before you skipped town. Plum positions like the one you had don't remain vacant forever. Galina Richtman stepped up to the plate when I needed her, so it's only fair that she should be given the job permanently. God knows, that girl really wanted it." Vladimir Ivanych shook his fists. "I could feel her hunger, something I haven't felt from you in a long time. She'd come an hour early every time just to warm up. You merely deigned coming to the rehearsals."

"That's because I didn't need all those rehearsals. Nicholas and I got those pieces right the first time. Galina needs all that extra work, because her natural abilities leave much to be desired."

"She's getting there."

"It'll take her another five years to reach my level. Her hands are stiff as rakes, and they grow out of her ass."

"Her technique is improving steadily. Galina has come a long way in the past few months."

"Well, you don't need her anymore now that I'm back. Let her deal with the pedagogy interns. If she's such a quick learner, she'll do a marvelous job with those delinquents. I've been here longer than her, so I think I'm entitled to preferential treatment. Wouldn't you agree?"

Vladimir Ivanych felt his eyeglasses fog up. He was a little annoyed with himself for having allowed this conversation go to that far. He had hoped that Olenski would simply countersign the contract and quietly go up to her new office on the third floor. This intense discussion about entitlement was really not on his schedule. Of course, with that woman, nothing was simple. What in the world made him think she would take the news of her dethronement humbly?

"For God's sake, I can't remove Galina just like that?" He snapped his fingers. "It's not like popping a zit. It's a little more complicated than that. If I reinstated you to your former station, it would raise eyebrows. I already had to jump through hoops to get the approval to bring you back. The hiring committee was resistant to the idea. If I show any more nepotism than I already have, people will start thinking that you and I are lovers. And I don't need this sort of scandal hanging over my head at my age. I'm not a footloose tenor in his early thirties who'd find such rumors embellishing to his image. When you were flirting with Nicolas Nichenko, I didn't say anything. It was hellishly cute and romantic—while it lasted."

Nicholas! Antonia had completely forgotten about him. How could she? They had not had any contact all summer. She had tried writing to him, she had even bought a few postcards with images of the Bear Mountain, but every time something would derail her attention. Now she was wondering what that encounter would be like.

"Does Nicholas know yet?" she asked. "Has he mentioned me in my absence?"

"To be honest, he's had many things to occupy his time."

"Nothing bad, I hope."

"Only good stuff. As good as it gets. And I was there for him every step of the way, to provide some fatherly guidance."

Vladimir Ivanych took a framed picture from his desk and turned it around so Antonia could see a glowing couple, a slender handsome man in a tailcoat with his arms around a horse-faced young woman with a giant doily on her head. The two lovers were Nicholas and Galina.

"This is a distasteful joke," Antonia whispered, rubbing her eyes. "For the life of me, I don't understand."

"Nobody expects you to understand it," Vladimir Ivanych said. "Accepting it is enough."

It took Antonia about a minute to connect the dots. Suddenly it all made perfect sense.

Galina's suspicious generosity, her desperate desire to keep her rival away from the academy and Nicholas. Antonia wondered if Galina had resorted to black magic to get the guy of her dreams. She probably paid one of those gypsies who camped around at the train station to cast a spell on Nicholas.

"When did this abomination happen?"

"While you were running from the nuclear holocaust. I helped Nicholas pick a bow tie. He was going to wear the one he normally wears to performances, but I advised him to splurge on a new one for such a momentous occasion."

Antonia traced the picture frame with the tip of her finger. "And you keep this thing on your desk because..."

"What can I say?" Vladimir Ivanych let out a sentimental gasp. "I'm a sucker for romance, especially at my old age. This brings back the memories of my first marriage. Mendelssohn's march, the smell of smoked sprats in the air, my bride's dress made out of old lace curtains. It all happened before you were born. Comrade Stalin was still alive. Mmmm..."

He smacked his lips and bobbed his head, reliving the spring of 1949. "Two divorces later, I still remember that boyish ardor I felt when I first walked down the aisle. So when I see my former pupil waltz into the same bear trap called marriage, I feel compelled to stand by his side. My own kids did not want me at their weddings. This is the closest I've gotten to playing father of the groom. I show this photo to everyone who comes into the office. I want this academy to be known as a place where people find love."

"This isn't love," Antonia exclaimed. "He only married her to get back at me. Once the thrill of revenge wears off, he'll be sorry."

"Keep telling yourself that, Olenski. Whatever gives you comfort. Love or not, they are expecting their first child."

* * * *

The bathroom was not the safest place to cry. The wobbly cardboard partitions did not provide any shelter from the malevolent curiosity of other users. Antonia took her grief and her fury into her new office on the third floor. Vladimir Ivanych was right. The sound insulation was second to none. The former janitorial closet could be turned into a recording studio. Antonia sat at her desk, laid her head on top of a giant music encyclopedia and howled for about twenty minutes. Crying did not ease the tension in her chest, but apparently it helped clear out her conjunctivitis. Apparently it was just what her eyes had needed. She had not cried in ages, and her tear ducts must have started getting atrophied.

"Get a grip, Olenski," she said at last. "You're demoted but not defeated, not by a longshot. Show that ogre what you've got."

Having blown her nose, Antonia examined her new digs. The room could use some serious jazzing up. The chipping lettuce-green paint evoked the depressing images from the oncology ward. Antonia would transform this dent in the wall into a hip European lounge where everyone would want to hang out. She would use her own money to buy a stereo system, a lava lamp and a coffee machine. Everyone would be welcome—except for Nicholas and his horse-faced bride, of course.

* * * *

"How could you do this to me?" Antonia asked Nicholas when she cornered him in the coat room. "How could you marry her?"

Nicholas threw his arms up. "What was I supposed to do? I was alone, and she kept following me around in high heels. One night she brought in a bottle of wine, and...For God's sake, woman, I'm not made of stone! I'm not all high ideas and high notes. I have physical needs too, you know. It was springtime. Every man around here was getting laid, from Vladimir Ivanych down to the fourteen-year old section leader in the children's choir. I got tired of waiting for you to leave your husband."

"Do you even realize what you're asking me to do? I can't just pick up and leave Joseph. He loves me too much."

"Oh, and I don't?"

"You don't understand. Joseph is unstable. He's capable of anything. Back at the conservatory he slashed a pillow with a butcher knife in a fit of rage. If he gets sufficiently pissed off, he'll set the building on fire. He'll kill you. He'll strangle Maryana. I'm not about to start a Trojan war. I couldn't live with myself afterwards."

"How noble on your part," Nicholas muttered. "So I was expected to stay faithful to you, while you stay faithful to that Polish killer clown of yours? I'm thirty years old. Am I supposed to keep my cock tucked away in case twenty years from now you decide you want to toy with it?"

"Of course, not." Antonia placed her cat's paw on his elbow. "You are free to stick your cock anywhere you like. It's like any other man's, I'm sure. You're all the same below the waist."

"How do you know that?" As far as he knew, Antonia had only been with one man. "Since when are you such an expert?"

"My mother-in-law told me once after a few shots of vodka."

"You trust that woman?"

"Yes, I do. She was married at least four times. Why would she lie about something like that? So it doesn't really bother you that you share your bed with Galina or that she's pregnant with your kid. You're not doing anything mammals haven't been doing for millions of years. What irks me is that you share stage with her. It was supposed to be our domain, the holy of holies. So we didn't get together under the sheets. Big deal! At least we could always be together behind the velvet curtain. It was heavenly, ten times better than sex. I thought we could stay that way forever."

"And then what happens?"

"I take a sabbatical for a few months and come back to this. Forget the welcome-back party. Nobody even asked me how I was feeling after my recent brush with death. It boggles my mind how little it takes to lose everything! You sit down to catch a breath, and then you find yourself stripped of all your laurels. Vladimir Ivanych will be sorry for what he did. It was a really stupid move on his part."

"He doesn't look too sorry to me."

"Give it time, Cole. He'll be sorry, all right."

"Actually, he seems to be quite happy with his decision. Galina has been doing an adequate job."

Antonia jumped back, pointing her finger at Nicholas. "Ah, you said it! That word. Adequate. Not marvelous. Just adequate. Somewhere between C+ and B-."

Saved By The Bang

"What's wrong with B-? It's a passing grade."

"But it certainly won't get you noticed at international competitions. Let's be honest, Cole. This academy is no musical Olympus. It's a provincial pit, ignored by everybody who is anybody. If this place ever had any potential for greatness, it's because of you and me. Remember the reactions when we started performing together? Olenski and Nichenko! All of a sudden, people who were high up on the food chain started paying attention. What did they call us?" She scratched her chin. "Astonishing. Spectacular. You need me to pull out the newspaper clippings to refresh your memory? And now with Galina by your side, it's adequate. Seriously, Cole, is that where you want to be at thirty? You're entering your most influential decade."

"Yes. I'm quite content with adequate. If this is the script for the next fifty years of my life, I'll die a happy man."

"I don't believe it for a second. It's not you talking. It's the radiation. The air you're breathing is toxic."

"The only thing toxic here is...you, Antonia!"

"Huh?"

"That's right." Nicholas spoke very softly, as if repressing nausea. "While you were gone, it was so peaceful, so quiet here. At first I was restless and lost, but then once your poison worked its way out of my system, I felt strangely relieved, rejuvenated, liberated as if a veil had been lifted. I can finally see clearly, after eight years. Sick as it sounds, this thing in Chernobyl was sort of a blessing. It gave me that much-needed breather away from you. Saved by the bang, if you will!"

Antonia turned to the murky mirror and finger-combed her eyebrows.

"Don't fool yourself, Cole. You'll never break free from me."

"But I already have. Wake up, Olenski. I'm as free as..." Nicholas snapped his fingers, looking for an adequate comparison. "As free as a Yankee! Find yourself another victim for your boy harem."

"As matter of fact, I already have. He's barely twenty but has seen so much already, things your cotton-padded brain cannot process. He has no legs, yet he towers over you. He's courageous, witty and brilliant, and he'll go very far in that wheelchair of his. I'll see to it."

"I am very happy for you—and very sorry for him."

Chapter Ten

THE ART OF SHARING AN ICE-CREAM CONE

Belarusian State University, Minsk – October, 1986

Next time Joseph visited Minsk, he brought along a portfolio containing a collection of combat songs written by some crippled Afghan veteran Antonia had met in the Crimea. According to her, that kid was a genius, the voice of the wounded generation, the groan of the working class, and his ditties were masterpieces that deserved to be recorded and played on the national radio along with "White Linen" and "Veronica". Joseph did not know what to make of his wife's sudden plunge into philanthropy and advocacy. In the past Antonia had not been one to show much concern for the disadvantaged or the disabled. Under normal circumstances her response would've been along the lines of "Let them eat caviar." Social justice was not high on her list of noble causes. Joseph had always been the charitable one in the family. Perhaps, this sudden redirection of heart had something to do with her recent demotion at the academy, a wake-up call to humility or something like that. Or maybe it was the fallout from Chernobyl causing benign mutations in her personality. Whatever the reason, she would not leave Joseph alone. She kept nagging him to take Private Matrosov's songs and show them to the director of the recording studio. Joseph had no choice but to give in and take on her pet project. After a summer of piggish philandering, he felt he owed her that much. At least Antonia was not begging him to impregnate her with another baby. Hey, it does happen to high-achieving women whose career suddenly takes a plummet. They suddenly do a one-eighty turn and become obsessed with reproduction.

After having a pork chop lunch with the producer at the studio, Joseph swung by the Belarusian State University to say hello to a few of his Conservatory friends who were teaching there. When they found out Olenski was in town, they all cancelled their lectures and threw a party in the dean's lounge. Olenski's visit was a national holiday that called for champagne and chocolates that would normally be saved for New Year's. The faculty spent the next five hours trading sex jokes and badmouthing their enemies at the Moscow Conservatory. The festivities went on until it was time to close down the building.

Dragging his feet down the dark corridor, queasy from all the alcohol and sugar in his blood, Joseph heard someone call his name. He turned around with a shudder and saw a menacing-looking janitor with a dripping mop in his hands.

"Greetings, brother," Joseph said with a bow. "Do I know you?"

"You know my wife Ilona—in a Biblical sense, dare I mention."

"Ah, so you must be Tycho the Evangelist! What are you doing here?"

"Working. Can't you see? It's the only job I could get after getting out of jail. The department of history wouldn't take me back. The only way I could get back into the university was by accepting a janitorial position. Thankfully, I can still use the faculty bathroom and borrow books from the library. That was gracious of them. My former students still greet me in the hallway and turn to me for help with homework."

Joseph's bladder was screaming for relief, yet he was so drunk, he could not remember where the bathroom was.

"It's such an honor to finally meet you, Professor Poplawski," he said, "but I really need to be on my way. If I make a piddle right here, you'll have to mop it."

"You screwed my wife, didn't you?"

"Technically, she screwed me. I was on my way to the recording studio, and she appeared out of nowhere and jumped on me."

"Yeah, that sounds like her," Tycho muttered with a nostalgic smile. "She did that to me freshman year. I was sitting in my dorm room, writing a paper, and she just barged in and ... The rest is history. So, what did you think of her?"

Professor Poplawski's casual confession eased the tension. Joseph assumed a more relaxed pause. Suddenly, the two of them were teenage boys in the bathroom, comparing notes.

"Okay," said Joseph, rubbing his hands, "you want the whole truth, or the truth you can handle?"

"Brother, after what I've been through in the past few months, I can handle anything. Spill it."

"Sex with Ilona is like soft serve ice-cream. The first lick is sort of exciting, but by the third lick the novelty dulls. You know what the rest of it will taste like. By the time you reach the waffle cone, you've had enough and you don't want anymore. You just can't wait to throw out the wrapper, wash your sticky fingers and forget the whole thing."

"Sounds about right. That's my Ilona, boring watery vanilla from head to toe. Though I still love her, and I want her to be happy." Tycho put his arm around Joseph's neck. "Listen, Olenski, I need a huge favor."

"Anything for a Protestant martyr."

"I need you to continue screwing Ilona. I know I can count on your discretion. Something happened in prison. One day I got into a heated theological discussion with an inmate. Things got really intense. He kicked me in the groin. Since then I've been having problems meeting her needs... you know?"

"Oh...I'm sure it's temporary."

"But she needs to get laid right away. Ilona isn't good at delaying gratification. Abstinence interferes with her academic process. She needs someone to hump here and now, and I don't want this to be just anyone. It must be a very special individual, hand-selected and approved by me. And I already know I can trust you, Olenski. I just don't want her to go back to that Lithuanian prick Dominic Amantas. He works as a choreographer at the ballet theater."

"No kidding! I thought Dominic was queer."

"I thought so too. Apparently, he and Ilona have history of some sort. By now you should know that I'm pretty forgiving and open-minded, but I cannot stand that pompous cocksucker. His sexier-than-thou attitude just gets under my skin. I swear, he uses more creams and hair products than his leading ballerinas, and I just don't want the mother of my child coming home smelling of his cuticle moisturizer. Do you understand what I'm saying, Olenski?"

"Totally. So you'd rather have Ilona smell of naphthalene and bacon? No problem. That can be arranged."

* * * *

Minsk Ballet Academy

Dominic Amantas spent a good chunk of the rehearsal filing his nails. The company was gearing up for the opening of *The Nightingale*, a signature Belarusian ballet by Michael Kroshner. Thirty girls, their ages ranging from twelve to sixteen, and their individual weight not exceeding thirty kilos, were fluttering around the stuffy studio. They knew that the choreographer had radar vision. Even when he appeared to be looking down, he could still see every error, every improperly turned ankle. He had a long wooden ruler that he did not hesitate to use. Half of the girls had bruises on their thighs and buttocks seeping through the white leotards.

When Dominic saw Joseph's face pressed to the glass window in the door, he snapped his fingers, giving the accompanist a sign to stop.

"Take five!" he exclaimed. "Run, piggies, run. Oink, oink! Bathroom break. If I find any cookie crumbs on your leotards, I'll slaughter you for bacon."

He always referred to his dancers as "piggies." The girls giggled at this endearment. Dominic Amantas was actually one of the nicer choreographers. He may have whacked their asses with a ruler, but at least he did not strip them and circle their fat areas with toxic markers like some of his female colleagues.

As soon as the ballerinas vacated the studio, Dominic tiptoed towards Joseph and laid his manicured hand on the guest's shoulder.

"Looking good, Olenski. Radiation certain agrees with you. It gives you that sultry golden glow." A second later Dominic recoiled. "Do I smell cream puff on your breath?"

"Guilty as charged. I stopped by the coffee house on my way here, and the pastries looked divine."

"*Tsk, tsk*, Olenski. Keep this up, and you'll lose your boyish figure. I saw your last performance on television, and your tail suit was practically bursting at the seams. Of course, camera adds five kilos. You really have to watch these things. Metabolism slows down after thirty. By the way, how do you like my scarf? I have a beret to go with it."

Joseph pushed Dominic's hand away. "Stop clowning around, Amantas. I have a serious situation. *We* have a situation."

Dominic bit his nail. "Oh, dear. You make it sound so dire. What is it?"

"Poplawski's balls got damaged in a prison brawl."

"What balls? You mean Poplawski actually *had* balls at some point? That's news to me. He always struck me as a bit of a neutered pussy."

"Stop being a self-enamored asshole, Amantas. A colleague is in trouble, and you're cracking your insensitive egotistic jokes."

Dominic's long eyelashes fluttered. "I'm sorry, Olenski, it's hard to break old habits. Please, go on. I'll behave, I promise."

Saved By The Bang

"As you know, Professor Poplawski went to jail for promoting his faith," Joseph continued. "His male equipment got mangled in the process. Now he can't make love to Ilona, so he wants to dump that responsibility on me, just so she wouldn't be tempted to come to you. He has some sort of grudge against you. His self-esteem is kind of fragile, which is understandable, so he's looking for a stand-in dick for Ilona, as long as it's not you."

"I can't say I blame him," Dominic muttered. "I'm so damn handsome and witty that I get jealous of myself sometimes. Anyway, go on."

"I hate saying no to Poplawski, but my schedule is kind of full, and I can't add this sort of responsibility to my plate. It's logistically complicated, since I live in Gomel. I come to Minsk every few months, and Ilona needs to get laid a lot more often than that. So I figured, maybe you would take over the job for me. After all, you're local, and you two have history. I'll make Professor Poplawski believe that I'm the one screwing Ilona, but in reality it will be you. So everyone will be happy, and my own marriage will be safe. What do you think?"

Dominic scratched his goatee. "Gosh, Olenski, that sounds deliciously intriguing, and even five years ago I would've said yes, but I'm not the same person I was before. My tastes have changed radically. Truth be told, I don't think I can get it up around Ilona anymore."

"Sure you can! You've done it before."

"It's not that easy. I spend my days surrounded by sixteen year old girls. Ilona is pushing thirty. That's grandmother material in my book."

"You're such a pig," Joseph said with a hint of envy and admiration.

"Look who's talking," Dominic reciprocated coquettishly. "Besides, I think I'm done with women. The only reason why I can still function around teenage girls is because they look like boys from the back."

"God, don't tell me you're one of those..." Joseph snapped his fingers, struggling to remember the proper slang word. "Indigo boys?"

"To be honest, I don't know what I am anymore." Dominic removed his beret and ran his hand over his highlighted hair. "I just know that I don't want Ilona or any other woman who looks like her. The very thought of boobs and hips and plump thighs turns me off. I like to see bones and angles."

"But that's unnatural."

The smug smile vanished from Dominic's face. "The very foundation of my profession is unnatural, Olenski. It's not natural for a body to function on five hundred calories a day. You realize most of these girls don't get their periods because their body fat percentage is so low? Everything that happens in this room is in defiance of nature, brutal abuse of joints, bones, muscles, and above all, psyches." Dominic tapped himself on the temple. "These girls are going to end up mental and social invalids by the time I'm done with them. I get paid to break these girls, to ruin their chances of leading normal lives. Most of them won't go anywhere. They'll do a few more shows, realize they've hit their ceiling and get factory jobs. It's not like they are cultivating any other skills. Every one of them believes she's on her way of becoming the new Maya Plisetski. Every one of them works her bruised little fanny off. It's that false hope, that boundless determination that keeps them looking decent on stage. There's no sacrifice these poor little mites won't make for their art. For nine out of ten these sacrifices won't be justified. If I had kids, I wouldn't let them go into performing arts, not in a million years."

Joseph stooped in silence, still processing Dominic's candid unapologetic tirade.

"What are we going to do about Poplawski?" he asked, suddenly remembering the reason why he came to visit the ballet theater. "We still haven't found a solution. I don't want to take on his wife, and neither do you. Someone has to do the dirty work."

"I have a couple of boys in my troupe," the choreographer replied. "I'll talk to them. Maybe one of them will be willing to satisfy a lady professor. Poplawski will never find out. "

Chapter Eleven
MAY HE PERISH OF CHOLERA!

Western Belarus, Gervyaty village - June, 1987

Buried in the dense marshy woods of northeast Belarus not far the Lithuanian border, Trinity Cathedral had survived both communists and fascists. So strategically inconvenient was its location that the enemies of Catholicism had never gotten around to destroying it. They would have drowned in the swamps. Perhaps, they did not even know of its existence. Constructed at the turn of the twentieth century by a Vilnius builder, it became known as Belarus' most beautiful cathedral, Notre-Dame of the East. It was the only ecclesiastic edifice in Belarus designed with complete adherence to the Gothic tradition. The facade was carried out in a uniform style with signature wooden crosses covered in elaborate carvings and statues of saints decorating the front lawn. Hundreds of locals had participated in the construction, with more than seventy villagers toiling on any given day.

A separate factory had been built behind the village to produce high quality bricks from the clay gathered from the bottom of the nearby river. The tiles for the roof were imported from Germany. Having miraculously withstood two world wars, the territory of the village falling under the control of various governments, the cathedral towered as a beacon of Christian solidarity, drawing believers from the entire district of Grodno. The number of parishioners kept growing. By 1987 atheism was going out of fashion. With allegiance to Moscow waning and hostility towards the centralized government escalating, Belarus was clinging tighter to her Catholic neighbor to the west. Poland was regarded as an aloof though generally benevolent birthmother, while Russia was the ruthless stepmother that milked and bled all her stepchildren for her own profit. Poles may have had a history of exploiting the Belarusian people, keeping them as indentured servants, but Russians exploited the Belarusian land itself, usurping and dividing it into collective farms "for the benefit of the Union and advancement of communism".

Russian developers would chop down the primeval forests, dry out the marshes, reroute rivers, build dams and hydroelectric stations, dump pesticides into the soil and royally fuck up the ecosystem. Every year the population of wild lynxes, wolves and cows kept shrinking. Entire species of fish would disappear from the ponds. Once an enchanted woodsy paradise praised by poets like Jakob Kolas, Belarus was now a communist colony, and her inhabitants were "servants of the state". Only in the west could you find remnants of the old ways. Grodno and the suburbs was one of the few remaining pristine patches untouched by the callused Muscovite claw.

M.J.Neary

* * * *

On a Sunday afternoon in early June, there was a folk music festival in the village of Gervyaty. Immediately after the mass the parishioners of Trinity Cathedral began streaming towards the watermill house. According to the rumor, there were three barrels of beer donated by the local brewer in support of the arts.

By twelve-thirty the churchyard was empty with the exception of two peasant women in their mid-sixties sitting at the foot of St. Michael's statue. Their names were Teresa Wolski and Natalie Olenski. Both wore sporting loose linen dresses, flowery headscarves and slippers with cardboard soles. It was close to lunchtime, and their stomachs were beginning to growl. Having neither cigarettes nor bubblegum on hand to suppress hunger, Teresa and Natalie snacked on sunflower seeds, spitting out shells into the hems of their dresses.

The promise of free drinks did not entice them. They personally knew the brewer in Gervyaty and agreed that his beer tasted like salted piss. He was a well-intentioned chap, but he had no idea what he was doing. The brewer back home in Isobelino, on another hand, really knew his craft. He actually had proper equipment set up in his basement and was using an ancient German method to deliver the smoothest, richest brew. Having tasted his ale, Teresa and Natalie were spoiled for life. Gulping watery malt from a communal barrel was infinitely beneath them. Not in a million years would they grind elbows with those pimple-faced schoolboys. No, sir, these two fine ladies were a cut above the rest. On the surface they looked like ordinary farm workers, but on the inside they were gems of sophistication. Their morality, esthetic sensibilities and tastes in beer were formed at a time when Grodno was still under Poland's control. Born in the early 1920s, Teresa and Natalie had completed seven years of parochial schooling and spoke a colorful mixture of Polish and Russian, occasionally injecting a Lithuanian word here and there. Before the Nazi invasion Teresa had worked as a dental assistant in Grodno. On occasion her boss had allowed her to drill and pull teeth for high-profile patients, bankers, factory owners, even clergy. Natalie had managed a private theater company at a Polish aristocrat's estate. In the old days every noble family was expected to keep an acting troupe, and Natalie, who had played principal roles in all school productions, was perfectly qualified for the position. Her duties had included selecting repertoire for the season, casting the actors, taking care of the props and costumes and printing the invitations. Her employer, a well-traveled gentleman, had a fondness for Ibsen and Shaw. The enchanted world in which the two friends had flourished had been destroyed. The posh dental clinic had been burned to the ground. The magnificent rural estate had been flattened by the tanks. The privileged girls, who had always been two steps ahead of their peers, had been hurled into the same caldron of austerity. Only the Trinity Cathedral had remained as a reminder of their former life. The class distinctions were erased. First Germans, then Russians.

Neither one would drink beer just because it was free, or kiss a man just because he was available and eager. Incidentally, Teresa was on her third husband, and Natalie was on her fourth. The two friends had stuck together through the invasions and the bombings. Natalie, green-eyed and pragmatic, was the Eastern European version of Scarlett O'Hara. She faced life with a sort of cheerful fatalism. There was no Polish equivalent for "fiddle-dee-dee," but every time Natalie's youngest son Joseph would have an asthma attack, she would say, "You can't always cup your hands and catch 'em when they fall." Her oldest son Alexander was an alcoholic and drove a gasoline tank, which meant he could veer off the road, drive into someone's house and cause a massive explosion. Natalie refused to lose sleep over that.

Teresa, on another hand, had an entirely different psychological constitution. Whenever a disturbing image would enter her head, she would nurse and nurture it until it would blossom into a tapestry of disaster. Teresa's eighteen-year-old grandson had just been sent to Afghanistan, and she was, in her own words, totally freaking out. No amount of premium vodka could lift her anxiety. She could not shake the vision of her little Darius dying somewhere in the mountains with his legs blown off. She followed the reports from Afghanistan. Natalie was getting tired of her friend's gasping and moaning, so she suggested that after the mass they take a trip to the market and try to exchange some organic goose eggs for Polish lipstick.

The two ladies were engaged in elegant discourse.

"My entire summer just went down the shithole," Natalie lamented.

Teresa produced a sympathetic pout. "How come?"

"My Josey—may he perish of cholera—just dumped his brat on me."

"Stasia, the bastard, you mean?"

Saved By The Bang

"I wish!" Natalie shook her head regretfully. "Trust me, I'd jump for joy if he gave me Stasia for the summer. She's a big strong girl, and God knows, I could really use another pair of hands on the farm. But that stubborn son of a bitch won't bring Stasia here. Last I heard they moved her from the orphanage and sent her to work at some sewing factory. The conditions there are worse than in a gas chamber. I bet Sasia would love to spend a few months here, breathing fresh air, tossing hay and repairing bee houses. No such luck. It's Maryana he's bringing here."

"You mean the legitimate one?"

"Yeah, that one. The failed gymnast. All she does is stand on her head all day long, until her face turns beet-red. Not that she's getting any smarter for it. Her mother needs to get rid of her for the summer. Nobody else will take the kid."

True, in the past year Antonia had fallen out with most of her relatives. The light brush with death had made her cheeky and outspoken. Her human side waned, but her feline side blossomed. It seemed as if the surgeon had sliced away all of her inhibitions along with the damaged fallopian tube. Antonia emerged from under the knife a changed being. She experienced a sort of personal renaissance. Sarcasm started bursting out of her pores, often against her will. Her relatives were not used to that. They were not ready to accept the new Antonia. The price for this emotional catharsis was that she had no place to send Maryana for the summer.

At the same time, she did not want her daughter to spend three months in Gomel, splashing in the radioactive river. The only place where the girl was still tolerated was her paternal grandmother's hut in the village of Isobelino. Grandma Natalie had just recovered from her second heart attack and needed help on the farm, and Maryana, who was approaching her ninth birthday, needed some work ethic instilled in her. A few months of milking goats and plucking recently decapitated chickens would do wonders for her soul.

"Is Josey still married to that half-kike he met at the conservatory?" Teresa asked.

"Ah, he did what he had to. He needed an anchor in a big city, and she looked like a good catch at the time - top of her class, engineers' daughter, squeaky clean, with her hymen intact."

"Hymen intact?" Teresa gasped. "You don't see many of those nowadays, do you?"

"Not in the city, no. That one came with a hymen and her red diploma. A real find for a peasant lad like Josey! It's always been his dream to settle in a big city with a music academy. It all looked like a sweet deal in the beginning. Except now he's paying for it with his freedom. He can't eat, piss or fart without explicit permission from his mother-in-law. They all live in her apartment, and dance to the cracking of her whip. Poor Josey is suffocating."

"How do you know?"

"I just do." Natalie looked ahead solemnly. "The mother always knows. I see it in Josey's eyes every time he comes to visit. My boy wasn't meant for that life. I'm thinking now, he should've just kept sleeping with older women to get ahead. He's got a talent for pleasing middle-aged hags. And they paid for everything—his books, his records, his clothes. I tell you, Tess, after he turned seventeen, I didn't have to spend a ruble on his keep. Now he doesn't own anything, not even his cock. He needs visitation rights with his own balls. That's what happens when you consort with those damned Russians."

M.J.Neary

* * * *

Isobelino Village, Western Belarus

A horse-drawn cart rattled by. Matthew Wojtek, a jolly satyr of a man with a spongy gray beard and a lusty twinkle in his eye, tipped the brim of his cap.

"Mornin', lovelies."

Teresa and Natalie immediately assumed cocky poses. Their reciprocal greeting sounded more like "Bugger off".

Matthew pulled the reigns and stopped the cart. "My old woman has been laid up at the hospital for past two weeks," he said. "It's easy for a man to get lonely. Would you, ladies, care you stop by my house? I have a whole case of German beer that my son brought from Vilnius."

Natalia rolled her eyes. "As if...not in a million years."

Teresa tossed her greasy pony tail. "In your dreams, old goat."

Matthew, quite accustomed to this sort of reaction to his romantic propositions, tipped his cap again and continued trekking the dusty country road on his cart. At least he knew to keep his hands to himself. Local ladies would not hesitate to use a shovel, a pitchfork or even an ax to deflect unwelcome advances.

"He makes me sick to my stomach." Natalie huffed as she watched Mathew's cart disappear around the bend. "Would you believe it? He's been trying to get under my skirt since before the war. We went together briefly back in '37. He gave my parents a huge wall clock for Christmas. Later that night he cornered me in the cellar and groped me all over." Natalie

131

wiggled her juicy bust as if trying to shake off the disgusting memory. "For the past fifty years he's been on my tail. I swear, every time I bury a husband, he comes lurking around, smacking his lips and rubbing his hands. When Felix died, I thought I was going to die with him. He was the love of my life. Every day I'd go to the cemetery and weep on his grave for hours. And that snake Matthew would always slither nearby, hoping to catch me in a moment of weakness. He'd screw me right there on the grave if I'd let him. I hope he gets syphilis."

"Our men don't get syphilis," Teresa stated with a sense of pride. "It's a Western disease, like AIDS. It started with African monkeys, and now niggers and sodomites spread it to the rest of the human race. As long as Poles and Lithuanians don't mingle with primates, we're in safe."

Natalie shook her head reproachfully. "Tessa, Tessa! Have you been watching world news again?"

"What else am I supposed to do at night?" Teresa suddenly got weepy. "I cannot sleep. I keep freaking out thinking about my Darius in Kabul."

"Stop acting like you're the only woman whose grandkid is in the service."

"Easy for you to say."

"Yeah, especially after the Nazis shot my first husband."

"What do you think Darius is doing this very moment?"

"Fucking some Afghan prostitute probably."

"From your mouth to God's ears!"

* * * *

On Natalie's farm, every living creature had a wild streak. The barn cat was half-lynx, the guard dog was half-wolf, and the breeding bull was half-bison. Or so she claimed. The only creature that was fully domestic was her fourth husband, Franz Anthony.

"You senile jackass!" Natalie cried. "Why is the chicken coop open? I got my hens and roosters roaming the village."

Ten years ago Franz Anthony had walked out on his terminally ill wife to be with his much younger new flame. The incident was recorded as the sex scandal of the decade. The women of Isobelino could not stop whispering and hissing. The consensus was that Natalie was not to be judged too harshly, although she should have had the decency to wait for the first wife to die. After all, Franz Anthony was a desirable catch, and the two of them became something of a golden couple. At age eighty, Franz Anthony still had his hair and his teeth. He attributed his criminally youthful looks to his diet that consisted of baked potatoes with butter, smoked bacon, fried mushrooms, dill pickles and chicken cutlets. He was still reasonably dexterous with the scythe, although a few times he nixed his own foot. He spent his leisure on the porch, weaving baskets, even though eyesight was beginning to blur, and his hands were beginning to tremble. He was still on the list for herding duty. Cheese-making and butter-turning were huge, and most families in Isobelino had at least one milking cow. All able-bodied men in the village were required to participate in herding. They took turns getting up at four in the morning to drive the cattle across the field and back. Franz Anthony, because of his age, was excused from duty, but he opted to keep his name in rotation. He had some spiritual affinity for cows, but looking after chickens was way beneath him.

"It's not my fault the chickens are missing," Franz Anthony said to his wife. "If you're looking for someone to blame, you should blame Josey. While you were out, he dropped off his little rat. She went inside the coop because she wanted to play with the baby chicks and left the door open."

"So why didn't you close it up? She's a dumb kid who doesn't know squat about keeping poultry. Why didn't you do anything about it, you moron? I got my prized hybrid chickens on the loose in the neighbors' yards, and you just sit here, weaving your goddam baskets that nobody buys anyway."

"I wanted you to see the damage first." Franz Anthony extended a judging finger in the direction of the coop. "It's all your son's doing. He dumped that dimwit on us. Now we're stuck with her for the summer."

Natalie patted his withered cheek. "Be nice, old dog. I'll think of a way to make her useful."

"How? She can't lift her own piss pot."

"She's all we've got. You have money to hire farm hands? You have two hundred rubles lying around?"

"We have a barrel of moonshine," Franz Anthony suggested. "We could sell it to the youth club. Better yet, give it to the kids, and they'll work for free."

"Idiot!" Natalie whacked him on the chin. "That moonshine is untouchable. I'm saving it for guests of honor. Hear me? If the Pope ever passes through our village, I'll uncork that barrel, but no sooner than that."

* * * *

Natalie found her granddaughter inside the barn, covered in feathers and droppings. Maryana had been trying to round up the chickens and drive them back inside, but instead she got scratched and pecked to pieces.

"It's not my fault," she mumbled in self-defense. "I didn't mean to let them loose. Papa Josey said I could go in and look at them."

Natalie wagged her hand. "Forget the chickens. Listen, kid, I have a job for you. It's a very special job that all the children in the village are dying to do. They line up in front of my barn every day, begging to let them do it."

"What's that? Tell me!"

"Raking manure in the stable and sweeping the chimney. If you do a good job, I'll buy you some Polish lipstick and eye shadows. Blue, green, purple—pick your color!"

"But Grandma Lily doesn't allow me to wear makeup. She says only whores and circus performers—"

Natalie gave her granddaughter a wink. "Ah, but we all are whores in the circus of life, dearie. Grandma Lily doesn't live here."

"That's right, she doesn't." Maryana's eyes lit up with hope. Suddenly, the summer was looking up.

"Her Stalinist shit won't fly under this roof," Natalie continued. "For the next three months you'll be playing by my rules. Franz Anthony and I don't tyrannize people. We believe in rewarding hard work. Ask any of the local kids we've hired over the years. We pay them a pretty penny for cleaning up horse dung, and they spend that money on Polish jeans and underwear. Think of how fine you'll look when your cousins take you to the disco club. You'll be the cutest stinking tart on the dance floor."

M.J.Neary

* * * *

Isobelino Village – July, 1987

Moonshine was not the only market-bound commodity produced on Natalie's farm. She made just as much money from her signature cranberry marmalade. The recipe involved mixing the berries with honey and vodka, then packing the mixture into a jar and putting it into a clay oven on low heat for twelve hours. Two hundred grams of that delicacy went for ten rubles on the farmers market in Vilnius. Harvesting the key ingredient was a perilous task as it involved trekking through the marshes populated with vipers. Before taking her granddaughter on a cranberry-picking mission, Natalie made her wear thigh-high rubber boots and armed her with a wooden pike.

Her safety instructions were brief. "If that bloody vermin wraps around your ankle, just pierce it through the head. And see that you don't get any venom on your skin. One of Teresa's girls got sprayed in the face, and her eye rotted away. Your mother won't be too happy if I send you back one-eyed, will she?"

They did not get much cranberry-picking or snake-slaying that day. In fact, they did not even reach the marshy area. Halfway through the potato field, Natalie started panting and sweating. Her heart was rattling again, and she had forgotten her magical nitroglycerin patch at home. Having spread her floral headscarf on the ground, she collapsed with a grunt. Maryana remained standing. She feared that if she sat down, she would give her grandmother permission to have another heart attack. Dragging an eighty kilogram corpse across the field seemed like an unfathomable task. What would she tell Franz Anthony? He would strangle her for allowing his wife to die.

"See over there?" Natalie pointed her swollen finger at the cherry tree. "That's where they hanged him."

"Who hanged whom?"

"The Nazis hanged Victor, my first husband. They dragged him out of the house with a noose around his neck and hanged him, to set an example, perhaps. He looked like a Jew to them. He had a strong beaky nose. Then they pulled his pants off and realized that he wasn't a Jew after all, but it was too late. His neck had snapped by then. So for the next two weeks I had to play hostess to them. They turned our house into an inn, ate all the sausages and drank all the moonshine. The year's supply of jam was gone in one day. All the cheeses, two huge bags of raisin croutons, an entire barrel of honey."

"Did you think of poisoning them?" Maryana asked. "That's what I would've done. I would've mixed a whole bottle of arsenic into the vodka and served it with a smile. Then I'd stand and watch them drop dead one by one."

"I'd thought of that. There wasn't a drop of arsenic in the house. We never needed it. Our cat was doing a marvelous job at keeping the rats away. He'd catch them and lay them out in a row by the entrance. So we never kept rat poison. It surely would've come in handy with the German guests, wouldn't it? For two weeks I just did what they told me. Just gave them what they wanted. Couldn't get too cheeky with them. I didn't fear for my own life, but I had my younger sisters with me, one of them around your age. We got lucky.

The soldiers spared our village. They could've burned it to the ground like the others. Maybe they spared us so they would have a place to stop by again on their way back. Who knows? At any rate, my hospitality paid off. Nine months later I gave birth to your uncle Ally. He came out fair and blue-eyed like nobody else on either side of the family. I still think he was Victor's. My late husband planted that child in me right before he died. At least that's what I kept telling myself just so I wouldn't drown him in the well. God knows, the temptation was great. Ally—may he perish of cholera— was a miserable child, who tortured animals. I couldn't leave him alone in the barn. He kept poking pigs and cows with a pitchfork just for the fun of it. Then he grew up to be a miserable man, who bullies his wife and kids. It would've been better for him to perish in infancy. He would've spared himself and others a whole lot of grief."

The habit of verbalizing the regret over the birth of a child was not unique to Natalie. Every well-mannered Polish woman was expected to periodically say these words as an expression of modesty and humility.

"For a long time I couldn't look at cherries, let alone eat them, not even in a pie. I kept thinking of the tree on which Victor was hanged. Nor could I think of bedding another man, not until about five years after the war ended. I was working on a collective farm, in charge of the dairy unit, keeping to myself. By then my baby sisters had all gotten married to local drunkards. Those little bitches had no pride, no taste whatsoever. They took turns showing up at my doorstep when they needed a black eye iced or a loose tooth pulled, sniffling and asking for pity, sometimes for money. Eventually I fed up and shut the doors of my house to them, so it was just me and Ally. Then this delivery boy started coming around. Felix was his name. He didn't look a day over eighteen. And I was thirty at the time, practically an old hag. He skipped about like a young sparrow, always whistling. Just by looking at him, you'd never think he'd seen any sorrow in his life. You wouldn't know he'd lost his whole family in the war. I could tell he was hungry, though, always chewing on a straw, smacking his lips, eyes searching for the next morsel. One time I took pity on him and threw him a slice of ham over the fence. The next day he got bolder and came into the yard. Before long he was doing repairs around the house for me. It didn't feel right that I should feed him for free. He fixed the leaky roof in the barn. I remembered how good it felt to have a man in the house, a real man. One day I woke up and realized I was pregnant again. 'Felix,' I said to him, very calmly, 'we have to make an honest man out of you now. We cannot let the villagers point fingers and say that an older woman had taken advantage of you.' So we got married. Little Ally wasn't pleased one bit. He hated the rival growing inside me. When I was seven months pregnant, he kicked me in the belly, causing the baby to flip. When it was time for your father to be born, the local doctors didn't know what to do. They tried to turn him around, so he'd come out head first, but they couldn't. After three days of labor, I was growing weak. My heartbeat was dropping. So the doctors gave me a choice—to have my belly cut open to pull the baby out, or to cut the baby up inside me and extract him piece by piece, which would actually be safer for me. They said it wasn't worth it to save the child at that point. Even if he did survive, he'd be an idiot. He'd spent too much time stuck inside me, without oxygen. There was no way in hell I would let them butcher my baby. So I gave them permission to slice me up from the neck down. There was no time for last rites. I don't think there was a priest in a fifty kilometer radius. I recall blowing my nose, and saying my prayers and pissing in the pot one last time. Then the doctor held a handkerchief soaked in chloroform over my nose until I passed out, and sliced my belly to pull out my precious Josey. When I woke up, and they showed him to me, it pleased me that he was nice and white and plump, and his face wasn't flattened—a definite improvement on Ally."

Natalie coiled her gray hair in a bun and secured it with a comb, then glared at her granddaughter with sudden hostility.

"What are you looking at, kid?"

"I'm not looking at anything. Just thinking."

"What are you thinking?"

"Oh, nothing in particular." Maryana's thoughts seemed to be tangled in the branches of the haunted cherry tree.

"Come on, tell me."

"I'm thinking you had a pretty fun life, Grandma."

Chapter Twelve
BALTIC AMBER

When Natalie got up to milk the cows the next morning, she discovered that fence surrounding the vegetable garden was completely demolished. She could tell right away that it was not a result of burglary or lightening. Such extensive damage could only be caused by Alexander's truck. That son of a bitch had been drunk-driving again! And he never bothered to fix the headlights. He drove right into the carrot patch. His gasoline truck was standing about thirty meters away from the house, blocking the lane. Alexander himself was nowhere in sight, though there were strange groans coming out of the barn.

"Ally!" she cried. "Come out, wherever you are!"

Armed with a pitchfork, she marched into the barn.

On a pile of hay she saw an empty flask of Maryana's mosquito repellent. In his desperation, Alexander Olenski drank it for the alcohol content.

Natalie picked up the flask and whacked her son on the head with it.

"May you perish of cholera!"

"I'm sorry, Ma. I'll fix the damn fence, I swear."

"What's the use? You'll tear it down again."

Natalie's anger waned as quickly as it flared up. She had given up on Alexander. She knew that his promises to fix the fence were as empty as her threats to kill him.

The passenger door of the truck swung open, and Natalie saw her two older grandchildren, Nadia and Paul. They were fifteen and twelve respectively but looked alarmingly small for their age. Both were showing subtle signs of fetal alcohol syndrome—short noses, thin upper lips, weak jaws and bulging eyes. Maryana, who did not know the history behind their features, found them endearing elf-like. To her they were magical creatures from a fairy tale. What she likes most about them was that they never dwelled on the same subject. It was impossible to carry on a conversation with them for more than thirty seconds because they quickly lost the train of thought. Their flightiness appealed to Maryana, as it countered her own tendency to obsessively ponder the mysteries of the universe. Malice and compassion were equally foreign to these two.

"Listen up, my Mongoloid lovies." Natalie addressed Alexander's children. "Granny made a new tub of cranberry marmalade to sell in Vilnius. Why don't you take Maryana with you this time? I'm sure she'd love to take a break from raking horse shit in the barn."

Nadia, a timid rabbit of a girl, nodded her head in compliance, but her younger brother, whose abstract thinking was a little better developed, furrowed his low brow.

"I don't want her with us. She'll speak Russian on the tram, and we'll all get kicked off."

Saved By The Bang

"It won't happen," Natalie assured him. "Your cousin knows what's good for her. If she needs to say something in a public place, she'll say it in Polish. We've been practicing."

Maryana had never been to Vilnius before, but she had heard her father's rapturous accounts of the magnificent Olde Towne that contained almost two thousand medieval, renaissance and baroque buildings surrounding the neo-classical cathedral and the town hall. It was long string of chemical reaction amongst the ethnic groups within the city —Baltic, Scandinavian, Slavic and Jewish—that had shaped the unique face of Lithuania's capitol. Ascending the legendary Gediminas Mountain was an absolute must for any first-time visitor. The climb was steep enough to give one a heart attack, but God, it was worth it. The view of the cobblestone streets and rooftops the color of caramelized cream was breathtaking. And the music! Joseph described the choir performance at the Vilnius Cathedral as the single most moving experience of his life, far more momentous than his first fuck or his wedding day. As for Antonia, she always raved about the beauty of Lithuanian men. She said it was their long necks that made them so striking and graceful, unlike the squat Muscovites whose square red faces sat directly on top of their bulky shoulders.

Intoxicated with Baltic fantasies, Maryana burst out of the cottage wearing a poppy print sundress with a denim jacket over it and a pair of white sandals with square heels, with a Zenith-19 photo camera around her neck. Joseph had left the camera with a roll of black and white film so she could take pictures of the interior of the Gothic church in Gervyaty.

When Natalie saw her youngest granddaughter all decked out, she burst into laughter. "Where do you think you're going, dearie—the opera?"

"I...I was hoping..." Maryana swallowed. "I was hoping to get up the Gediminas Mountain and take some photos of the Olde Towne."

The old woman knuckled the girl on the head. "The only thing you'll be shooting, dearie, is a row of sheep carcasses."

* * * *

Ordinarily the trip from Isobelino to Vilnius would take less than an hour by car, but since Alexander Olenski was drunker than usual that day, he accidentally took the wrong turn and started heading west towards the Polish border. His blunder went unnoticed by the children. Nadia and Paul were picking their noses, staring out the window, and Maryana was tinkering with the camera lens. After doing about fifty kilometers in the wrong direction, Alexander came to his senses—the effect of the alcohol had started wearing off. It suddenly dawned on him that the signs were in Polish. There were friendly-looking soldiers on the side of the road, sipping Polish beer and creating an illusion of vigilance. The sight of those shiny silver cans made Alexander salivate. It had been at least two hours since his last drink, and he was due to refuel. He slammed on the breaks and rolled down the window.

"Lads," he began insinuatingly, "you wouldn't by any chance want to trade a beer for a pack of cigarettes. I've got Belomors in the back seat. I'd give anything to moisten my throat. It's so parched, I can barely talk."

Saved By The Bang

The soldiers, quiet accustomed to bargain propositions of the sort, blocked his path and surrounded the car. A pack of Belomors did not sound appealing enough to men who were used to being bribed with Marlboroughs.

"Your papers, comrade," the lieutenant said.

"What kind of papers are you looking for?"

"Papers allowing you to cross the border."

Alexander rummaged in the glove compartment and produced a 1982 bootleg edition of Playboy.

"Comrade, I think you should turn around and go where you came from."

"I will, in a minute. Look, I'm not trying to break through the border. I'm asking for a sip of your beer. If you don't want my Belomors, you can have the magazine. There's no law that says you can't trade things with your fellow countrymen, is there? Look, we were on our way to the market and took the wrong turn. Stupidest thing."

The lieutenant puckered his lips and peeked inside the truck cabin. "Let's see what else you've got in the back seat."

Alexander blanched and shook his head. "Oh, no, comrade. Don't even go there. These girls aren't for sale."

"Oh, no? Then why are they made up like hookers?" Tormenting the drunken simpleton was so much fun. "Especially the little one."

"Hey, that's my niece. She's a good girl. Her father is a national laureate. He has his own TV show."

"Yeah, I can see that. You look like a cream of the crop sort of family. It's written all over your faces. I bet you have a few scientists in the family too. Your boy looks like he escaped from a lab." Having gotten bored with teasing Alexander, the lieutenant assumed a more businesslike tone.

"Anyway, I'd like to check out your merchandise. You said you were heading to the market, didn't you?"

"I guess...what's the matter with that?"

"Well, maybe we'll want to buy something from you."

Before things could escalate, Maryana pulled out one of the smaller jars with Natalie's cranberry marmalade and pulled off the lid.

The smell of vodka made the lieutenant reel with pleasure. He stuck his thick fingers into the marmalade and licked them. "Mmm...I'll be damned. Good stuff. You people don't skimp on vodka, do you?"

"It's Grandma's secret recipe," Maryana bragged, "and I'm not sharing it with anyone."

The lieutenant snatched the jar from her hands and backed away from the truck, having lost all interest in the family of trespassers. The jar was being passed around among the soldiers.

"Hey, that will be fifteen rubles!" Nadia cried indignantly.

The lieutenant waved his hand, as if shooing a fly. "Get out of here. Just go wherever you were going."

Alexander turned to his fifteen-year old daughter. "Baby girl, would you mind taking over for your old man? My hands are a little shaky."

Nadia responded with her usual shrug and a hum. Her younger brother started growling.

"She's always the one to drive. Remember how last time she drove into a tree? How come I never get to drive, Pa?"

"Because your legs are too short and can't reach the pedals," Nadia explained. "You're a midget, because you smoke too much."

Saved By The Bang

* * * *

Vilnius, Lithuania

By the time they reached their destination, it was two o'clock. To Maryana's disappointment, there were no sheep carcasses at the market. A couple old ladies selling berries and dried mushrooms. A few wooden crates with motley chickens, cages with rabbits and nutrias, barrels with live fish. The general ambiance was that of irritable drowsiness. Business was not going well that day. It was not the rowdy and exotic bazaar Maryana had envisioned. There was nothing for her to photograph.

As soon as Alexander dropped the children off at the marketplace, he headed out to look for a bar where he could refuel. He had been without alcohol for ten hours. The last thing he had drunk was Maryana's mosquito repellent. He wondered how many bars would be open during the day.

The agreement among the children was that they would rotate and take turns watching the stand with the marmalade. One of them would be on active sales duty, while the other two would be free to roam the market and the nearby area. It was decided that Maryana, being the youngest, would go up first. Paul needed a new pack of cigarettes, and Nadia needed a pair of fishnet stockings with metallic accents that were all the rage in her high-school. Since such high-end items were not available on the market, she would need to head deeper into the city and hit the major department stores. Never argue with a woman on a mission.

At least she was nice enough to spread the tablecloth over the stand and set up the marmalade jars.

Before leaving her younger cousin in charge, Nadia whispered the instructions in her ear. "Remember what Grandma said. If any buyers come up to the stand and ask you about the marmalade, speak Polish to them. They won't buy any if you speak Russian. Or worse, they'll smash the jars."

Maryana responded with a mock salute, anxious to be rid of her cousin with her mother-hen demeanor. Getting lectures on linguistics and international business from a girl who got held back twice in elementary school made her blood boil.

The mellow Baltic sun did not leave deep burns but it took no pity on the eyes. Maryana had not thought of bringing along a pair of sunglasses, and within thirty minutes she had a pulsating headache.

A morose-looking elderly man paused by the stand and stared at her chest with the critical attentiveness of an expert.

"How much?" he asked in Lithuanian.

Having realized he was asking about the Zenith camera, Maryana pulled her jacket over it protectively and shook her head.

The man shrugged and moved on. That was her only interaction with a customer that day.

* * * *

Nadia returned four hours later, sporting new fishnet stockings and a denim jacket with the Lithuanian flag embroidered on the back. The giant clock at the entrance to the market showed quarter past six. The vendors were starting to pack away their merchandise.

"Did you make any sales?" she asked her cousin in a stern whisper.

Maryana sighed. "Nobody even asked about it."

"That's because you're a Russian kike. These people can sense those things. You don't even have to open your mouth. I knew it was a bad idea to bring you along."

"If you think you can do a better job, go right ahead." She had been on her feet for the past four hours with a full bladder. Alexander and Paul were still missing. "If you're such an expert, why don't you show me how it's done?"

"Very well. Stand back." Nadia took off her jacket, started waving it above her head and screaming in crudely accented Polish, "Vodka marmalade! Free samples! Low prices for the people of Vilnius!"

As much Maryana would love to stay and watch that freak show for another minute, she needed to piss like never before. There was a commercial bathroom that charged two rubles for admission, but the experience justified the fee. That establishment turned out to be so much more than just a place for relieving bladders and bowels. It was a museum! The granite tiles, the clear mirrors lining the walls, the sparkling bowls with cushy seats, the bunny-soft tissue, the doors that actually closed, the steady supply of hot water, the fragrant liquid soap pouring out of the dispensers in straight even streams made a profound impression on Maryana. She stepped out of the stall a transformed, enlightened, westernized woman. How could she ever go back to relieving herself in those filthy public bathrooms inside train stations?

Tempted as she was to snap a few photos of the magnificent interior, she decided to save the film for the glorious Gediminas Tower. With only a few hours of daylight left, she had to make her way to the Olde Towne.

Maryana could not have picked worse time to travel. At six-thirty the buses and the trolleys were bursting with commuters. The people were not loud or smelly, but there were just too many of them. Within minutes Maryana's white sandals turned gray from other passengers trampling over her feet. She bore the pain stoically, reminding herself that in ten minutes she would be at the Baltic Mecca, watching the sun set over the tower.

Her heart skipped a beat when she heard a sinister crunching sound. It was not her ribcage being crushed. Far worse! Her precious Zenith camera got jammed between the window and another passenger's briefcase. The lens cap cracked and fell to the floor.

Forgetting everything Natalie and Nadia had warned her about, Maryana cried out in Russian. "It's not a toy, for heaven's sake. What's wrong with you, people?"

Her exclamation instantly galvanized and mobilized the crowd. The passengers forgot their daily cares and focused their attention on the brat who dared to violate the code of Baltic honor. The crowd became fluid, like a river, carrying her towards the entrance. The trolley stopped in a bottleneck, and the doors opened. Maryana felt a shove in the back and tumbled down the steps onto the asphalt. The trolley started moving again down the congested road, leaving the young Russophile on her fours, with cars passing by on either side of her.

Saved By The Bang

The pain itself did not bother Maryana. She had taken enough tumbles off the balance beam to take those nerve jolts with a straight face. The sight of her shattered Zenith, however, made her eyes tear up. The body of the camera had cracked in half and the film had fallen out. So much for the photo session at the Baltic Mecca! Her knees and ankles would heal in no time. The destroyed camera, on another hand, would be harder to explain to her parents. They would never trust her again with another piece of technology.

Stifling sobs, she swept the remnants of the camera into the hem of her dress, pulled herself up and made her way to the sidewalk. She had no idea where she was. The pedestrians glared at the girl in a dirty dress with bleeding knees, but nobody stopped to offer help. It did not take a genius to figure out how she sustained those injuries.

Throwing a self-pity party in the middle of a city filled with Russophobes seemed like an extravagant luxury. Maryana's brain kicked into survival gear. Since taking photos of the Gediminas Tower was not in the cards for that day, she moved on to plan B, which was to return to her grandmother's house without sustaining additional bodily harm. Trying to find Alexander and his offspring would only be waste of daylight. She would need to make her way to the train station, catch an express to Ostrovets, and from there take a bus to Isobelino. With any luck, she would be home before midnight. Then it occurred to her that she only had four rubles in her pocket, not enough to pay for the tickets. Perhaps, they offered discounts for children? Or did they only apply to Lithuanian children?

* * * *

Vilnius, 9 pm

By dusk the commotion on the roads had died down. The smell of cinnamon and vanilla exuding from the cafés filled the night air. The lanterns cast a soft glow upon the pastel walls of the city hall. Art students came out and set up their easels on the sidewalks.

After more than two hours of wandering the streets, Maryana accepted the fact that it would not be possible for her to get home that day, so she allowed herself to savor the beauty of Vilnius after dark. In spite of everything that had happened earlier, she did not get a sense that the city hated her. On the contrary, the trees, the street lights and the buildings were begging her to stay, apologizing for the behavior of the citizens. If only she would close her eyes and listen to the sleepy murmuring of the Neris River, she could engage in amicable discourse with the city where the inanimate objects had more soul than the people.

The spasm in her stomach reminded her that she had not eaten since that morning. Four rubles could buy her a mediocre meal at a bistro or a really kick-ass dessert. Chocolate-coated cheesecake bars were a famous Lithuanian treat, so Maryana bought one from street vendor. She did not engage in conversation with the sullen woman behind the cart. She simply threw a whole ruble into the money bin, grabbed the cheesecake bar from the cooler and walked away without collecting the change.

Maryana claimed a vacant bench alongside the river and surrendered to the most indulgent gastronomic experience of her life. At first she licked the chocolate coating off first and then sunk her teeth into the thick strawberry-flavored mass. Antonia would be horrified to see her daughter eat a fatty dessert in such a piggish way. Thank God, Antonia was not there. That evening belonged to Maryana alone.

As her sugar levels spiked, so did her spirits. A few yards away Maryana spotted a burly policeman in his late twenties with a square pink face and a low brow of a C student. A mischievous thought passed through her head. There was her chance to test her acting skills. Having tossed the sticky wrapper in the trash bin, she came over and addressed him in English. "Hello. My name is Lucy Kennedy. My parents are American diplomats."

Andres Balciunas—that was the officer's name according to the tag pinned to his uniform—had failed in English in school, but he understood the last two words. *American diplomats.* To him those words spelled windfall. His official salary being so meager, Balciunas had grown to rely on occasional bribes. One time he was paid fifty rubles just to look the other way while the owner of a burgeoning denim co-op set his competitor's warehouse on fire. This time he was looking at being compensated in dollars. The girl's parents would have to thank him properly for delivering her to them in one piece. Perhaps, he would never have to work again! Of course, he could do the responsible thing and take her to the police station to file an official report, but that would mean forfeiting the reward or having to share it with others. No way! Fate would never smile upon him like that again.

Maryana had a pretty good idea what was happening inside the officer's head. To reinforce her point, she added, "Disneyland? Mickey Mouse?"

Balciunas punched the air playfully. "Chuck Norris? King Kong?"

So they had an understanding. Nothing bridges cultural gaps like American pop culture. The next step was for Balciunas to find out in which hotel the girl's parents were staying. It was probably Europa Royale or Shakespeare Boutique at the Cathedral Square. Those were two places worthy of American diplomats that came to mind. Both hotels were within fifteen minutes.

But then he started thinking. The longer he would make the girl's parents wait and worry about her whereabouts, the more jubilant would be their reunion, and the more generous would be there reward. Besides, he could not return her in such a wretched state. Something needed to be done about her knees. Without making any more Hollywood references, he scooped Maryana into his arms, threw her in the back seat of his van and drove off to the station. Using the back entrance to avoid unnecessary witnesses, he carried his little American heiress into the lounge where he and his partner hung out between shifts.

Maryana put up no resistance. It felt nice being carried around for a change, especially in such strong arms. She liked the smell of the officer's aftershave. In her mind, that was how a Baltic man was supposed to smell. In spite of being a tad overweight, he had a well-defined neck, just like her mother had described. Most importantly, the officer doted on Maryana in his own unrefined working-class way. He seated her on the couch and went to fetch some peroxide, iodine and bandages. His meaty hands trembled as he tried to clean the dirt around the forming scabs while causing her minimal discomfort. Maryana was all too familiar with those procedures and tolerated his clumsy manipulations with a straight face. One time her knee twitched involuntarily, and her foot ended up between the officer's eyes. Balciunas recoiled and rubbed his forehead. Maryana giggled.

Mickey Mouse. Donald Duck. Her eyes twinkled.

Donald Trump, thought Officer Balciunas.

He wanted to treat the little American guest to something special, something unique to Vilnius, so he gave her a bottle of Baltica beer. Having inhaled the pale lukewarm brew, Maryana started nodding off. Balciunas put her down on the couch and covered her with his jacket. He was not going to go back out on the streets again that night.

* * * *

2 am

In the middle of the night, Officer Megenis came into the station.

"Why are you still here, Balciunas?" he asked his partner. "Your shift was over five hours ago."

"Was it? I didn't notice."

Megenis nodded at the sleeping girl behind the glass wall. "Who's that?"

"Oh, that? That would be...my niece."

"Huh? I thought you were an only child."

"It's...complicated." Balciunis was grateful that the sunburn on his face concealed embarrassment. "Someday I'll tell you, just not today."

Megenis, who was paying support on two children, felt his heart imbue with sympathy for his partner. "Oh, I get it. No need to explain. This is your...destitute kinswoman?"

"Rrrr...right. She had a day from hell. You should see her knees. Her mother is going through another psychotic episode, so I took her in for the night."

"That sucks. Are you filing a report?"

"I haven't figured out what I'm going to do yet. If her mother goes to the loony bin, I'll have no choice but to take the kid in, and my wife won't be too thrilled."

Megenis blinked a few times. "Your wife? You're not even married."

"I am, sort of," Balciunas was improvising on his feet. He had underestimated how much his partner really knew about his personal life. "We were separated for a while, but now we're trying to get back together, and I bring this kid into the equation, it's going to ruin the whole thing. I love Inga with my whole heart, but this kid...she's my blood."

"I hear you."

"So you understand why I can't look the other way while her psycho mother smashes her knees with a crowbar. As you can see, it's awfully complicated, on all fronts. And I'd appreciate it if you didn't say anything to anyone."

* * * *

9 am

Officer Balciunas came in chewing a burned bagel and sipping Baltica. He imagined that his next breakfast would be at one of the posh bistros at the Cathedral Square.

Maryana turned to face him. "Shame on you, comrade," she said in Russian.

The movements of the cop's jaw slowed down, and a few breadcrumbs rolled down his chin.

"You've disgraced the entire law enforcement profession," Maryana continued chastising him. "You really have to pretend being an American in order to get some first aid around here?"

"Little girl," he said, having recovered from his embarrassment, "it's not a good idea to mess around with cops. Most of them aren't nice like me, especially the Russian ones. They'll sell you for body parts. That's why we're trying to kick those fuckers out of our country, those parasites who rape our land."

"That's funny." Maryana crossed her legs. "You sound just like my father. You know who he is? Joseph Olenski."

"From the *Belarusian Hour*?"

"Yeah, that's him. And I'm not lying this time." She crossed her heart. "He really is my father, not that Kennedy guy."

"Then you should've said so! I have tons of respect for that man. He's such an icon. I try to watch his show whenever I can."

Maryana frowned. "Now you're sucking up. Nice try, officer!"

"Look, kid, I feel lousy about what happened last night. For what it's worth, I'm sorry for what happened to you yesterday. Just tell me where your real parents are, and I'll take you to them. They must've sent a search party for you by now."

Maryana shook her head. "Nobody is looking for me."

"Then a few hours won't make any difference. I have an idea. How about a proper tour of Vilnius? We'll go up the Gediminas Mountain in my van. Honest to God. You can stick your head out the window and snap photos. Would you like that?"

Maryana sighed. "My camera's busted."

"Don't worry about it. I'll buy you a new one."

She looked at him like he was crazy. Those Zenith models were not cheap. It would be one hell of a consolation gift, especially on a cop's salary!

"I'm dead serious," Balciunas said, feeling giddy as a schoolboy, like Ebenezer Scrooge in the final chapter of *Christmas Carol.* "Now let's go, before I change my mind."

* * * *

A new Zenith camera was not the only gift Maryana walked away with that day. Balciunas also bought her an amber bracelet, a ragdoll in a traditional Lithuanian folk costume and a coffee table book with photos of Olde Towne. She returned to Isobelino with a bag full of Baltic treasures.

Chapter Thirteen
The Other Olenski Girl

Gomel – October, 1988

Joseph could really use a friend, even a fake one. His bastard daughter was dying of leukemia at the pediatric oncological center in Minsk. The classical regimen of chemo that had successfully sped up the deaths of so many Belarusian children and teenagers was liquefying Anastasia's vital organs without doing much damage to the malignant blasts in her bone marrow. After about a week of trying to hammer the cancer into remission, the doctors pulled the IV needle out of her arm. All in all, they felt petty handing her the death sentence along with one free long-distance phone call.

After getting the news, Joseph spent the night pacing around the apartment with his hands locked behind his head.

"Give me your cousin's number in Smolensk," he asked Antonia, who was in the process of applying makeup for an upcoming concert.

"It's no skin off my back, but I don't see how this can be of any use. Sergei is not an oncologist."

"But he's well connected."

"Connections are useless when you are dealing with cellular biology. It's always the same treatment protocol, and the same outcome. So she'll spend her final days in a fancier hospital with brand new tiles on the floor. Is it really worth the jostling?"

Joseph yanked the powder puff out of her hand. "Will you stop painting your muzzle for a second? A child is dying here."

"Children are dying all over the country, in case you haven't noticed. Still, there are worse things than being dead. Nicholas and Galina had a lobster. Did you know that?"

Joseph looked perplexed. "A lobster...you mean, for dinner?"

"No, you moron. Galina gave birth to a baby with deformed hands that look like lobster claws. There's a fancy name for it—ectrodactyly. Which is a crying shame, because supposedly the kid has a great musical ear. He'd make a great pianist. I don't know of any composers who write for lobster hands. What can you do? An entire generation is screwed."

"Screwed, huh? That's all you have to say?"

"What do you want me to say? Hey, at least I was able to save *my* child." Antonia raised her manicured finger like a referee on a soccer field. "Let's not forget the sacrifices I made. I put my career on hold to get Maryana to safety. Have you done anything for Anastasia? No. Then why does it surprise you that she's dying?"

Joseph released the powder puff in disgust. "You'll answer for your words before God!"

"Oh, please." Antonia resumed grooming her eyebrows. "You were the one who fathered the girl and stuffed her in an orphanage. I tolerated her existence, always turning the blind eye, always taking the high road, without as much as a venomous comment. And now you're threatening me with your God? That's Polish logic, I suppose. Now, if you don't mind, I'd like to get ready for my concert."

Maryana was sitting in the kitchen, just a few meters away. She could hear every single word. The sound of her parents arguing was music to her ears. They were so busy insulting each other, they would not yell at her for failing an algebra test. With any luck she would end up like the girl next door whose parents were divorced and never checked her homework.

As soon as Antonia was out the door, Joseph went into the kitchen to open the bottle of vodka he had gotten as a birthday present. He noticed that the table was covered with modeling paper, sequins, sparkling streamers left over from the New Year's celebration and magazine cutouts. There was no paper glue in the house, so Maryana was using the pungent industrial kind.

"I'm making a get-well card for Anastasia," she explained. "What should I write on it?"

That was when Joseph lost it. He grabbed the bottle with glue and squirted the content over his daughter's head, rubbing it into her hair.

"She's not going to get better, you troll! You're saying this fucked up shit to mock me. You and your mother are two heartless kikes!"

Maryana grabbed a pair of crafts scissors and pointed them against her father's navel.

"Stop it, Papa Josey, or I'll spill your guts."

Joseph dropped the empty glue bottle and crawled into a corner, covering his face and bawling. Maryana stood over him, with sparkles and shreds of color paper stuck to her hair.

"Take me to see Anastasia."

* * * *

City Oncological Clinic, Minsk

When Joseph and Maryana walked through the reception area, they were greeted by a monstrous Mickey Mouse smiling at them from the wall. Above their heads, Donald Duck was careening in a biplane. The funds allocated by the government to benefit the victims of Chernobyl would not be enough to buy state of the art equipment or even to repair what was already in place. Still, those rubles had to be spent somehow. Money that sits in limbo for too long is at risk of making its way into the wrong hands. The director of the hospital could not deal with an embezzlement scandal, so he opted for a light cosmetic renovation. The decrepit walls of the cancer ward were painted over with images from American cartoons. This way the young patients could take an imaginary trip to Disneyland before dying.

"This place looks more like a lunatic asylum," Joseph said.

As they entered the patient wing, Maryana pulled out a handkerchief to block the smell of chlorine and vomit.

Saved By The Bang

Walking down the corridor that seemed to be getting darker and narrower with each step, she battled the urge to grab her father's hand. That would be a really wussy thing to do, especially since she was the one who had insisted on coming to the hospital in the first place.

Around the corner, they bumped into a bald teenage boy in an oversized Turkish sweater. The wheels on the IV stand kept jamming, causing the chemo bag to dance.

"Nothing works in this fucking place," the boy complained to Joseph. "If I need to take a piss, I have to walk to the third floor to get to the only toilet that flushes. The elevator isn't working. The TV only shows one channel. If you see the director, tell him to suck my cock."

"I will," Joseph promised earnestly. "Do you have any idea where I can find Anastasia Melnik?"

A lascivious smirk cut across the boy's exsanguinated face. "Oh, that hottie with acute leukemia?" Clearly, chemotherapy did not affect his sex drive.

"Yeah, *that hottie*." A sudden rush of paternal pride came over Joseph and for a moment tuned out all other emotions. Damn straight, Anastasia was hot. Even on her death bed. She was his daughter, after all. It made total sense that she would be the most desirable chick in the cancer ward. "You know her well?"

"Of course. She's the only one with hair. You can't miss her. They stopped the treatments before she went bald."

"Where is she now?"

"At the nurses' lounge, watching Tom and Jerry."

* * * *

Joseph saw a stick figure wrapped in a plaid blanket. He recognized the blanket. It was the same one he had brought to the orphanage when Anastasia was still a baby. The colors had faded, but the sturdy woolen fibers were still intact.

Joseph threw a ping pong ball at the screen to grab his daughter's attention. She turned around and pulled the paper mask off her face.

"Papa Josey! I didn't think you'd come."

Anastasia's giddiness led Joseph to believe that the first round of chemo had destroyed the cells in her brain where the awareness of mortality was stored.

"Stasia, I want you to meet Maryana," he muttered apologetically, as if ripping off a bandage to uncover an ugly wart, as pushed his youngest daughter forward. "This introduction has been long overdue."

At the sight of her half-sister's bald head, Anastasia gasped. "Is she also sick?"

"Nah, this one will outlive us all." Joseph pondered the irony of the situation. His healthy daughter was bald, and his dying daughter still had her hair. "The nitwit poured some glue on her head, that's all."

"I see." Anastasia reclined against the back of chair. "You know what they do in America? People shave heads to show support for family members with cancer. It's some weird solidarity thing."

Joseph shook his head. "Well, Stasia, I assure you that this girl is not capable of doing anything out of solidarity. She only thinks about herself, just like her mother. Nevertheless, she wanted to see you. So here she is."

Saved By The Bang

Anastasia's interest in her half-sister lasted exactly two seconds. Having scanned Maryana from head downward, she turned her attention to her father.

"Did you bring me the family cross?"

Joseph patted his pocket nervously. "Damn it, I could've sworn I had it."

Maryana unbuttoned the collar of her shirt and pulled out the silver-plated Catholic crucifix from the Gate of Dawn cathedral. "Is this what you were looking for?"

Joseph closed his fist around it. "How the hell did it end up on your neck?"

"Because it's mine by right." Maryana did not blink. "Grandma Natalie gave it to me for cleaning the stables. I earned it."

Anastasia looked down. "She never gave *me* anything like that. And I'd spent many an hour inside the pigsty feeding the pregnant sow. Most I ever got for my work was a tube of lipstick."

Joseph thought it was kind of cute that his two girls, who had just met, were already bickering over jewelry, just like real sisters. He swiftly unclasped the chain and pulled the family heirloom off Maryana's neck. "It's yours, Stasia. It's yours for as long as you have on this earth."

After such an unceremonious transfer of property, there was not much more for Maryana to say or do. She buttoned her collar back up and stuffed her hands into her pockets, while Joseph and Anastasia continued talking over her shaved head. Maryana remarked that her half-sister was infuriatingly Slavic, like Basilisse the Fair with Golden Hair from the folk tales.

"So, what's the game plan?" Joseph asked in his back-to-business voice. "What are those mad scientists going to do to you next?"

"Nobody tells me anything." Anastasia shrugged. "They'll try transfusions first to boost my thrombocytes. Finding a donor is a real bitch. It doesn't help that I'm O-negative."

"I'll ask around at work. We'll find you a donor."

Suddenly, a sinister howling from inside the wall startled Maryana. "What was that?"

"It's the pipes." Anastasia explained. "They haven't been cleaned in thirty years. When it gets cold, the pipes start singing. The nurses are so funny. They say that those are the souls of the patients who died. Pretty soon it will be me howling in the pipes."

Chapter Fourteen
THE "L" WORD

Gomel Sports Academy - September, 1989

"There's a name for girls like you," the gymnastics coach said to Maryana. "Lesbian. Girls who hug and kiss other girls in the locker room are called lesbians."

Maryana exhaled, relieved and satisfied. At last, someone gave a scientific term for what she and the Romanian prodigy Deena Danilescu did in the shower after practice the day before. It had started with an innocent request for a massage. Deena begged Maryana to rub the sore area between her shoulder blades. At first Maryana found it baffling that someone of Deena's caliber was capable of feeling pain. The coaches could bend this girl backwards and twist her into a pretzel, and she would not as much as wince. Her dexterity and pliancy were superhuman. All her victories seemed so effortless. However, as a dutiful teammate, Maryana could not refuse. It would be a great honor to service a gold champion. So she entered Deena's shower stall and worked her over with a lathered sponge. Filled with gratitude, Deena returned the favor. Then one thing led to another. Their slippery hands went everywhere. All of a sudden, it did not matter than they were on the opposite ends of the totem pole. It did not matter that one was a venerated star and the other a comic relief. For a moment they became one lump of squirming prepubescent flesh. Their gleeful giggles echoed through the locker room, attracting the coach's attention. So they were lesbians! The word sounded so flirtatious, musical and exotic.

"You cannot stay on the team," the coach proceeded, poking her chipping fingernail into the folder with Maryana's medical forms. "Such aberrant activities won't be tolerated on school premises. It won't be good to the morale. What kind example would it set for the rest of your teammates? Out of respect for your father, I intend to keep the matter discrete. The last thing he needs is a scandal. I'm dismissing you on the ground of ill health and inaptitude. Olenski, you are officially off the team. I doubt that this will break your heart."

More good news for Maryana! No more practices at seven o'clock in the morning, no more crash tea-and-cabbage diets, and above all, no more torn ligaments. She and Deena would have all the time in the world to love each other. They would escape into a world without rivalry and pain. They would spend their afternoons rolling in the autumn leaves and go to matinee shows at the Jubilee movie theater, holding hands. They would give each other full body rubs and play with each other's hair. During winter they would build a snow fortress in the woods on the other side of the river.

Before exiting the building that had been her torture chamber for the past five years, Maryana took a moment to say goodbye to her locker. One last time she stuck her head inside the wooden box and inhaled the smell of musty towels and eucalyptus ointment. These smells were about to become a thing of the past, much like the uneven bars and the balance beam. She packed the rainbow legwarmers her grandmother had knit for her but left the photo of the team glued to the door. She never cared for those avaricious bitches anyway.

Stepping outside into the golden September morning, she remarked that the sun appeared brighter, and the air appeared cleaner. The tiny park in front of the sports complex was bustling with young athletes getting ready for practice. They were using the benches to stretch. How haggard they looked in their navy jogging suits! Maryana's eyes found her partner in crime. Nimble and swarthy, Deena looked like a short-haired version of Esmeralda. She was standing inside the gazebo, talking to the acrobatic trio famous for their routine on the trampoline. Oh, the things she was dying to do to this girl!

"They're kicking us out!" Maryana shouted. "Lesbians can't be on the team."

She opened her arms, ready to receive Deena in her embrace, but the little Romanian recoiled with an air of hostile disgust.

"Get away from me, you freak!"

Maryana remained standing in the middle of the gazebo, her arms still open.

"What...what did you say? What did you call me?"

"I called you a freak. That's what you are, Olenski. A sick, twisted freak. Now, get away from me."

"I don't get it ... Where did this come from?"

Daria, the tallest girl from the acrobatic trio spat on the ground. "I'll make it clear to you, Olenski. Never set your foot here again, and never ever, come close to Deena."

Maryana remarked that Daria, in spite of her Slavic complexion, had Negroid features—a flat wide nose, puffy turned out lips. Her frizzy wheat-colored hair would look great in cornbraids. Maryana was raking her brain to come up with a most potent insult.

"Deena," she said, throwing one last glance at her would-be lover, "do you really want to hang out with these girls? I mean, Daria looks like her mom had an affair with an African exchange student. You really want to be seen with her?"

The impish Romanian pushed her in the chest and jumped back. "Never speak to me again, you lesbian kike."

"Fine," Maryana muttered, nodding her head. "I may be a kike, but at least my parents are respectable people. Your parents are gypsy thieves. They live at the train station. I guess it makes sense that you should hang out with a Negroid bastard."

That day Maryana would be taking home one last injury, as a souvenir from her days on the balance beam. The three acrobats jumped at her at once. She made no attempt to defend herself. She just fell backwards and took the punches, as the sky and the golden trees span above her head. Girl fights were not that uncommon at the sports academy, but the usually took place in the locker room. For a brawl to break out in plain sight there must have been a pretty good reason. The young athletes, the future stars of the Belarusian Olympic team, dropped their equipment bags and ran over to watch Olenski getting the shit beat out of her.

Saved By The Bang

Before blacking out, Maryana heard Daria's low-pitched voice, "This lesbian kike insulted our families."

* * * *

Discovery of his daughter's aberrant inclinations stirred a mixture of emotions in Joseph. On one hand, he was tickled pink. In his wild travels he had never met a real, honest-to-God lesbian. And now he had the curious privilege of having one under his roof. There was something irresistibly piquant about the situation. On another hand, he was a little nervous about the fate of his biological lineage. It occurred to him that with Anastasia dead and Maryana officially off the breeding market, he would have no grandchildren. Of course, there was the slim chance of Maryana coming to her senses and reverting to heterosexuality, but the chance of her getting killed by a homophobic gang somewhere in a dark alley was much higher. The miserable girl would be lucky to last until graduation. The evolved, refined part of Joseph told him that his legacy lay in his art, not his gonads. Was he not a republican laureate after all? His folk songs would be playing on the Belarusian radio until the end of time. With the Soviet Union bursting at the seams, his work was more relevant than ever. Still, the savage, instinctive part wailed with sorrow.

He could not carry her on his shoulders anymore. She was not even pretty. If she could no longer play the role of his little princess, he would turn her into the son he never had. His mother-in-law would die of humiliation.

To his dismay, Lily remained unfazed.

"I think we should check Maryana's radiation levels," she suggested over dinner. "The doctor may prescribe iodine pills. They should resolve this temporary sexual confusion."

"You think pills can set our little lesbian straight?"

"Anything is possible with science. My sister Genie believes that radiation is affecting everyone's DNA. Maybe one of Maryana's X chromosomes got brittle. You know, some species are able to change sex under certain conditions."

* * * *

Later that night Antonia silently handed him an unmarked envelope.

"What's this?" Joseph asked, pretty confident it contained divorce papers.

Instead, he found some documents in English, signed and stamped.

"Remember my cousin Aaron?" Antonia said, her voice cool and enticing. "The one who lives in the States? He sends his daughter' hand-me-downs to Maryana."

"Oh, that pompous kike?"

"Yes, that one. Well, he invited the two of us to spend New Year's with him. He's paying for the whole thing. Come on, Josye, we've had a year from hell. It would be good for us to visit a civilized country."

Chapter Fifteen
YANKEE GOLD

North Stamford, CT - January, 1990

Joseph realized he looked like a total savage playing with the buttons inside the limousine that was taking him and Antonia from LaGuardia to their destination in southern Connecticut. The Sikh driver was probably rolling his eyes at the juvenile antics of the foreigner. Joseph just could not get over how cool the upholstery felt or how quietly the tinted windows rolled up and down in response to the pressing of the buttons. There were separate buttons to control the temperature and to play music. He was not paying any attention to what was happening outside the vehicle.

"Don't you want to see New York?" Antonia asked him, placing her hand over his to keep him from changing the radio station for the tenth time. "Look, isn't that the Trade Center?"

"Not now," Joseph replied, snapping and unsnapping the buckle. "Your cousin promised to take us on a tour. I don't want to spoil the surprise. I want to feel like Alice in Wonderland when Aaron takes us to the Statue of Liberty."

Saved By The Bang

His eyes blazed up when they fell about a tiny cupboard built into the wall. "Wow, this ride has a bar? Check it out! Is that scotch? Can you read what it says on the label? I left my glasses in the suitcase. If it's Jack Daniel's, I want it. It's always been my dream to try American whiskey. Before we left, I made a promise to the boys at the academy that I'd taste of the water of life."

"Please, don't get trashed now," Antonia pleaded. "There will be plenty of booze at my cousin's house. Nobody leaves his parties sober, I promise you. Don't fill up on this heavy stuff. What will people think if you step out of the limo shaking and barfing?"

Joseph growled and fell back against the cushions. Their journey had just started, and Antonia was already nagging and instructing him as she would a delinquent child. This would happen every time they went on vacation together. She would keep him from trying certain dishes offered at the hotel cafeteria, lest he should get indigestion. She insisted on buying her own produce and cooking her own bland unimaginative food, because she had heard too many horror stories of tourists getting food poisoning and dying.

She also insisted on bringing her own bed linens and towels, because she assumed every hotel had bed bugs. It was entirely in her nature to nip the spirit of fun and adventure in the bud. Antonia had not always been like that. In the first years of their marriage she was mischievous and spontaneous and appreciative of his boyish antics. This uptight, mildly paranoid behavior had started after her surgery. To his great dismay, Joseph noted that Antonia was beginning to resemble her austere humorless mother more and more. Even their sex life had gotten dull and awkward.

With her IUD removed for good, Antonia was constantly worrying about getting pregnant. She would make Joseph wear two condoms and then immediately after the intercourse turn on the light to inspect the rubbers for holes. This double-bagging was getting old. Antonia's overbearing dotage was also getting old. Perhaps she was projecting onto him the feelings meant for their unborn child. Even though Antonia had never mentioned the tiny embryo that had briefly lived inside her tube, Joseph suspected that his wife was still holding on to that phantom. One thing he knew for certain—their American trip was going to be a drag. Still, he had no choice but to comply, because they were going to see *her* cousin, who was paying for their flights and the limo ride.

Aaron Rosenberg, MD spent his days breaking, filing and reconstructing nasal bridges at his private clinic in Westport. Instead of picking up his international guests at the airport himself, he sent his personal chauffeur. This way his overeducated yet still grossly underprivileged cousin and her husband would taste of neo-Yankee luxury from the moment they stepped on the American soil. Aaron did not trust Antonia to find her way from the airport to Grand Central and catch the right train. The silly girl, who had spent the past twelve years of her life in a drab quasi-provincial Belarusian city where the biggest bus was the size of a Toyota minivan would surely get lost in New York.

* * * *

After thirty minutes of sulking, Joseph peeked outside the window and discovered to his astonishment that the scenery had changed. Instead of the Manhattan skyline, he saw a wall of pine trees covered in snow. Joseph reached out for his wife's hand.

"Where's he taking us?"

"To Baba Yaga's cottage, you nitwit," Antonia hissed and pulled her hand away. "Where do you think?"

"I don't know what to think. Maybe he's going to rob us and dump our bodies in the woods. Haven't you heard horror stories of tourists disappearing?"

"Don't be stupid. What is he going to steal?"

"What about those gorgeous wooden trays we are bringing for your cousin? You'd pay a fortune for those at a souvenir shop."

"You mean those tacky trinkets from a craft fair in Grodno that your mother imposed on us? Those goddamn things take up a lot of space and weigh as much as atomic bombs. I was secretly hoping the customs officer would confiscate those atrocities."

Joseph nudged her resentfully. "Hey, those are masterpieces of folk art. Your cousin will love them. They'll remind him of his motherland."

"I'm not so sure it's such a good thing. Aaron doesn't take well to pan-Slavic memorabilia. A mere sight of a *matryoshka* doll will give him a panic attack. As for the driver...Trust me. We don't have anything that would tempt this fellow. He probably makes more money in one week than we do over the course of a whole year. Welcome to America, my love."

An hour and a half later, the limousine stopped in front of a peculiar edifice that looked like a cross between a Swiss ski lodge and a Japanese pagoda. Out came a tall bearded man in a rough-knit sweater with a cigar in his teeth. He looked more like a Scandinavian captain from a Jack London novel than a Jewish surgeon. He used his right hand for holding alcoholic beverages, and his right hand for digging up words from thin air.

"Shalom, pretty cousin!" he greeted Antonia and threw one of his arms aside for a half-hug. "Welcome to my temple."

Aaron Rosenberg had immigrated in the early 1980s through Vienna and Italy. He attributed his success to his refusal to fraternize with his former compatriots. He could have settled on Brighton Beach among other Russian-speaking Jews and resolved to eat beets, pickled herring, gefilte and mayonnaise-smothered salads for the rest of his life. He could have married some nurse named Sonia or a math teacher named Larissa. To take the path of least resistance would have meant selling out. So he went straight for the Yankee gold and soldiered his way into the seemingly impenetrable Connecticut elite. It was no small victory for a boy who had once been denied entrance into the top medical school in Moscow because of the sound of his surname. He had found a niche performing ethnic nose jobs. Having implanted himself firmly into the reformed Jewish community in Fairfield County, he had no shortage of clients.

Having stuffed a one hundred dollar bill into the chauffeur's hand, Aaron took his awestruck guests on a tour of his mansion designed by his very own wife Esther, a graduate of the Yale architectural program. Her client list included a few local millionaires who had made their fortunes in private banking. Still, her dream of dreams was to design a thoroughly modern synagogue with walls of white clay and windows of thick tinted glass with swirls of blue and green. This way, whenever sunlight would penetrate the temple, the inside would look like the bottom of the ocean, and the members of the congregation would feel like fish.

Frankly speaking, Joseph was not particularly impressed by Aaron's digs. In his understanding, a rich man's house should resemble Louis XIV quarters with massive chandeliers, gold trimming along the ceiling, a canopy bed, a gurgling fountain with exotic fish and marble statues of naked goddesses. If Joseph has a fraction of Aaron's money, he would have splurged on a set of rococo chairs with images of bosomy shepherdesses and a nice reproduction of the *Birth of Venus*. Dr. Rosenberg lived like a goddamn samurai. He slept on what looked like a stack of wooden sticks covered with a wrinkled linen sheet and bleak paper lanterns hung on the walls. There was no soft cozy place in the whole house to rest one's weary ass. Joseph could not help feeling sorry for his host. He surmised that Aaron's sex life was just as drab and puritanical as his décor.

As for Antonia, she was hardly paying any attention to the interior, fully captivated by the dazzling white grand piano in the middle of the living room.

"What's a Steinway doing here?" she asked her cousin.

"Serving as a prop for my wife's trinkets," Aaron replied with a shrug. "Esther loves bringing stuff from her business trips. Last year Sarah said she wanted to take piano lessons, so naturally, I picked the most expensive thing from the catalogue."

"Just like that, huh? I'm speechless. Your daughter murmurs something about taking piano lessons, and—boom! —you run off and buy her a Steinway?"

"You got it! Nothing but the best for my Jewish princess. Of course, she lost interest two days later. You know how kids are. So this lacquered monstrosity just sits here unused."

Antonia choked on her wine. "Monstrosity? Do you realize how many of my colleagues in Gomel would kill to play on this...monstrosity?"

"Knock yourself out, pretty cousin." Aaron pulled out the bench for her. "The instrument is horribly out of tune, so please don't kill me for that."

"No, no, I won't kill you. Not tonight. After all, it's not your fault that you are a callous philistine."

Suddenly, a brilliant idea struck Aaron. He pulled out a book of music and flung it into Antonia's lap. "Why don't you play this for the guests? It would be such a treat."

Warily, she flipped through pages. The scale looked suspiciously jazzy.

"Gershwin?"

"Even worse. Rodgers and Hammerstein."

"Never heard of them," she fibbed, turning her nose.

In reality Antonia was familiar with the golden age of American musicals, but she could not admit to it without compromising her elitist image. "That sort of rubbish didn't get covered at the conservatory."

"That sort of...rubbish...is what my guests are used to. They'll start showing up around seven. Don't you want to run through the pieces at least once?"

"Then you better hurry and set up some chairs for the audience."

Aaron wagged his hand, as if chasing away a pesky fly. "They won't be sitting down, silly. They'll be drinking, bumping into each other and gossiping. That's what people do at parties."

Antonia winced. Her cousin's requests were getting more and more insulting. Was he asking her to provide a pleasant non-intrusive background noise?

"You came to the wrong person," she said, pushing away the book squeamishly. "You see, I'm a performer, not an entertainer. When I play, I expect utter silence and undivided attention, no matter how vulgar the program."

"Please, pretty cousin," Aaron implored. "Humor me, just this once. Nothing catastrophic will happen, I promise. You won't turn into a frog. As a token of appreciation, I'll take you to the Guggenheim Museum this weekend. Talking about high culture overdose! And I'll ask Sarah to go through her closet and pick out a few items for Maryana. I swear my daughter doesn't wear the same outfit more than once."

* * * *

Fluttering her way through the medley from *Carousel*, Antonia wondered what her colleagues in Gomel would think of her if they saw her. She could see them wrinkling their noses, shrugging and rolling their eyes. At the same time, engaging in a clearly demeaning activity tickled her dark, plebeian side. Playing show tunes was a sort of metaphysical experiment. Would she really turn into a toad? Is that what American culture does to European artists? Antonia's imagination suddenly took flight. She began wondering about the private lives of the self-proclaimed purists, the shameful secrets behind the squeaky facades. What were those haughty, intolerant people doing behind closed doors? She pictured Maryana's gymnastics coach, who would begin every practice by putting the girls on the scale, stuffing her face with bread generously buttered and topped with thick slices of Dutch cheese and washing down that cholesterol bomb with pear-flavored soda. Then she pictured her Russian literature professor reading poorly translated American potboilers that respectable bookstores did not carry. What guilty pleasures did these people indulge in to stay sane? Before long, she was humming along to *June is Bustin' Out All Over*. Indeed, Broadway was a form of narcotic. Antonia had to pry her fingers away from the keys before the sticky tune sucked her in beyond the point of no return. She yearned to wash her hands, to scrub those infectious Americanisms from under her fingernails.

Aaron sat down on the piano bench next to her and surveyed the shuffling crowd. "You realize, there's not a single natural nose in this room," he said. "It's all my hard work. For how much they like to scream about taking pride in their long-suffering heritage, Jewish women never bypass a chance to get that Anglo-Saxon profile. Operating on a Jewish nose is a breeze. I can do it with my eyes closed. You just break the bones, file down the bump, reposition the bones and secure the new structure with a light cast. Done! The trick is to not scoop out too much. Now, Hispanic, African and Middle Eastern noses are much more challenging. They tend to have less cartilage and thicker skin, with a lot of spongy soft tissue in between, which makes it hard for the surgeon to predict what the final result will look like. There have been some rather daring attempts to thin out the soft tissue with cortical injections, but the complications can be devastating."

Antonia cleared her throat. "Are you trying to tell me something?"

Aaron blinked innocently. "What do you mean, pretty cousin?"

"This lecture on tissue density wasn't delivered in vain, was it? There must've been a good reason for you to share such intimate technicalities from your practice with me. Perhaps, it's your way of telling me that I need work. For the past five minutes you've been staring at me, and not with kindred tenderness. Just admit that your hands are itching to stick a scalpel in me."

"Fine, you've exposed me," Aaron exclaimed with a gesture of abdication. "I'm as addicted to my craft as you are to yours. To me people are never just people. They are potential patients, regardless of their ability to pay. I just happen to be fortunate enough to live in a place where people are able and willing to pay." He squeezed Antonia's hands. "Please, let me do it to you."

"Do what?"

"Everything! Just give yourself to me. I'll transform you." His voice dropped as he lowered his eyes. "As a boy, I adored you. That last vacation we spent in our summer house near Kiev was the most blissful time of my life. I'd lie in bed fantasizing about straightening your nose, thinning out your nostrils, redefining your lips, enlarging your breasts. You were my inspiration for pursing plastic surgery as a profession. I wanted you to come to America, to see the artist

I've become and to meet my patients. Pretty cousin, I could turn you into a goddess, if only you'd let me."

His ardent speech strengthened Antonia sense of privilege. How lucky was she to have relatives in the medical profession who were eager to test their skills on her! First Sergei pulled her teeth when they were children, and now Aaron was after her entire soft tissue.

"You're very sweet," she said. "And I am terribly proud of you. I'm just a little too old for such bold experiments. Last time, anesthesia did a number on my brain. Brahms' entire rhapsody in G minor had been erased from my memory. Can you believe it? I used to know that piece by heart. God knows what else I might forget if I go under the knife again. How about a compromise? I will give you Maryana after she turns eighteen."

"Your Maryana?"

"Yes. That girl needs work like nobody else. You can cut her into pieces if you want."

* * * *

Rachel Horowitz, Esq. a languid giraffe of a woman with a bandage across her septum floated towards Antonia. "So... tell me. How is it—living in Russia?" She asked, pausing after every word. "Do they really have five feet of snow all year long?"

"You can talk to me at your regular pace," Antonia retorted in a lightly accented but perfectly fluent English. "I'm not retarded."

Saved By The Bang

Rachel's Judean eyes were ready to pop out beyond the charcoal liner. Her sinewy hand trembled, creating a storm in on the bottom of her wine glass.

Aaron pinched Antonia's cheek. "I believe the proper term is 'mentally challenged' or 'developmentally delayed'. In case you didn't know, Rachel advocates for special needs children. She's written numerous articles on the subject of civil rights and successful integration."

"Well, I'm not one of her patients," Antonia said, staring back at her offender. "I watch PBS tapes without subtitles and read Hemingway in the original, thank you very much. For starters, Belarus is a distinct, soon-to-be autonomous republic. Gomel is about as culturally similar to Moscow as Cancun is to Montreal. Attorney Horowitz, I beg you, don't make such mistakes in front of my husband. He will—how do you Americans say it? Totally freak out."

Aaron sprayed red wine over his wool sweater. "She's a real spitfire, my cousin. As you can see, Rachel, she's been reading the Bible of American Slang."

"Undoubtedly, Attorney Horowitz has heard tales of bears riding Romanov carriages on the streets of Moscow, drinking vodka, playing balalaikas, reciting Dostoyevsky and juggling Faberge eggs," Antonia resumed. "That's not all. We use World War II tanks to fire homemade nuclear missiles on America, but for some reason they keep landing in Afghanistan. That's the beauty of Soviet engineering for you. The civilized world should be afraid of us, very afraid."

* * * *

"Bravo, pretty cousin," Aaron said when Rachel was gone. "Now Attorney Horowitz is traumatized for life."

"She's lucky I didn't crack a bottle of Stolichnaya on her head," Antonia replied.

Aaron backed away in jocose surrender. "Hey, now, she also happens to be one of my most loyal patients. I just got done operating on her nose. Her boobs were next on the list. Now I'm worried that she'll go somewhere else to get them pumped with silicone."

"Seriously, how can you surround yourself with such ignorance?"

"What do you expect from these people? God created dumb Americans for the amusement of sophisticated Europeans. Don't be cruel, cousin. Don't destroy their quaint little Cold War fantasy. Telling an American that there are no vodka-drinking bears in Moscow is like telling a child that there's no Santa Claus. Their whole world would turn upside down. Indulge them instead. Tell them what they want to hear."

Antonia's lip curled. "You mean, about the food rations and Stalin's purges?"

"Exactly!" Aaron winked. "They love stuff like that. These people grew up on Dr. Strangelove and James Bond. I used to tell all sorts of horror stories to my professors in medical school, just to see their reaction. They'd look at me in terror, shake their heads and tell me what a strong young man I was, and how lucky I was to have found my way to America. Then they would give me an A and write stellar letters of recommendation."

Saved By The Bang

Antonia gasped and moved away as far as the parameters of the couch allowed. "I don't believe it! You actually played the pity card?"

"Sure did, cous. And guess what? It worked. Look at this place!" He made a swaying gesture with his free hand and glanced at the ceiling. "Hey, a Jew's gotta do what a Jew's gotta do. I'm pretty sure God approves."

A second later the lights went out. Darkness engulfed the posh glass house. God clearly was giving Aaron a sign that He did not appreciate taking His name in vain.

"This isn't good," the host muttered. "The damn generator again. It always hiccups at the worst possible time. I better call Ethan."

"Who's Ethan?" Antonia inquired. The ominous way in which Aaron pronounced that name suggested that the individual behind it had some divine powers.

"My Man Friday, the only one I trust to repair my generator. He's also the only one who'll drive up here on a night like this. I'll pay him double for the trouble. Otherwise in a few hours the temperature will drop below freezing, and Esther's bonsai trees will die. We cannot let that happen. I couldn't care less about the people in this house. But those trees are Esther's babies. She talks to them. They have names."

* * * *

The Man Friday arrived within half-hour. Aged thirty-eight, Ethan Schwarzwald was a compelling mixture of sinister and swashbuckling, a cross between Cardinal

Richelieu and Indiana Jones, with religious-themed tattoos peeking through the thick golden fur on his forearms.

As soon as the last guest pulled out of his driveway, Aaron poured the remains of his wine in the sink and grabbed a few beers from the refrigerator. He looked relieved and revived. Now the party could start in earnest. In his heart he was grateful that the generator broke again and gave him an excuse to kick out the prissy guests. Ethan was the much-needed burst of oxygen. Aaron would not be caught dead fraternizing with a blue-collar man in daylight, but in the privacy of his glass mansion he could let his guard down. He found Ethan's company far more enjoyable than that of other plastic surgeons and lawyers.

Having spent ten years on a nuclear submarine, Ethan was an expert on international brothels and had the best whore stories ever! The particularly memorable one was about a certain Thai girl who had her private parts pierced and decorated with a tiny silver bell that rang with each thrust. It pained Aaron to admit that he did not have such exciting stories. He was just a sheltered Jew who had built his muscles at a gym with a personal trainer. The Man Friday had built his muscles repairing equipment on a nuclear submarine. Clearly, Ethan was far more experienced and worldly. To his credit, Ethan never rubbed his superiority in his employer's face. He shared the stories of his carnal escapades with eagerness and eloquence but without arrogance.

"Only in America can you have a German working for a Jew," Aaron said, as the Man Friday was tinkering in the breaker room. "His Aryan ancestors must be flipping in their graves."

Saved By The Bang

"You spend a great deal of time pondering the eternal Semitic question," Antonia noted. "I thought the whole point of living in America was divorcing your ethnic grudges. I thought Americans were like water lilies, floating freely, ignorant of their roots."

"Bah, that's what *I* thought too when I first got here. Nothing could be farther from the truth. America is where nations settle their ancient grudges. Chronic resentment can be so delicious. You sip it like aged wine."

"Or you gulp it like Pepsi—by the gallon." This pseudo-Semitic angst was beginning to wear on Antonia's nerves. She longed to get away from the Judeo-Aryan conflict. The magnificent Steinway grand piano was summoning her. "Now that your friends are gone, can I play some real music?"

Aaron dismissed her with a weary flick of the wrist. Frankly, he was anxious to get off the subject.

Antonia sank her fingers into the keyboard the way a hungry man sinks his teeth into a loaf of bread and began playing Chopin's polonaise opus 53 in A flat minor from memory. The piece held a sacred place in her heart as she had played it at her conservatory entrance exam. All the artistic victories of her youth were summarized in this polonaise. Pressing her foot against the pedal, she remembered the scorching tightness of her strappy white sandals. She and her mother were so poor after her father's death, and Antonia only had one decent pair of dress shoes. Lily had bought them at a no-return consignment shop, and Antonia was stuck with those torture devices. She kept those sandals exclusively for performances, as she could not walk very far in them.

M.J.Neary

On that day in the spring of 1972 she was Cinderella, and the admissions committee was the royal court. The polonaise lasted seven minutes. Those seven minutes would determine the course of her career. Three-quarters through the piece Antonia already sensed that she had won the judges. She hammered the last measures of the piece with an air of boastful triumph. But her trials were far from over. As she was descending the stage after the performance, the ankle strap on her left sandal burst. Beet-red, she hobbled out of the auditorium, leaving the damaged shoe on the steps of the stage. A young baritone who was sitting in the front row waiting for his turn to audition, picked up the shoe and tried to run after Antonia, but by then she was out of sight. She later learned that the young vocalist was Joseph Olenski, the notorious boy-whore of the conservatory with at least one bastard to his name. It would be four years until they would speak again.

One day, when they were in their senior year, Joseph showed up at the doorstep of her dormitory room with a bouquet of anemic looking pink carnations and the missing shoe with the strap fixed. When Antonia finally accepted his request for a moonlit rendezvous, he confessed that it was her rendition of Chopin's polonaise that had captivated his heart. In a voice both coy and ardent, he begged her not to judge him for his sexual past. After all, he did not sleep with all those women because he enjoyed the game of seduction. He only did it to advance his career. Surely, his cock had been to some very dark places, but his heart was still virginal and pure, and it belonged to Antonia.

Now that he had earned all the accolades available in the vocal and the sexual departments, he no longer needed to

191

warm the beds of the dried up matronly administrators. He would abandon his philandering and become an adoring husband to the girl who played polonaises and mazurkas so divinely. And Antonia believed him, or at least pretended to believe him. At the time her romantic prospects were as meager as her artistic prospects were abundant. So the prissy virgin said yes to the boy-whore, on a bench in a moonlit park. And it had all started with a polonaise and a pair of sandals.

* * * *

"This is some serious kick-ass rendition of Chopin," Antonia heard above her head when she stopped playing.

Man Friday was standing by her side, cracking his knuckles, a towel over his shoulder. He had just finished fixing the generator.

"You think so?"

"Totally! I have the same polonaise on vinyl, recorded live at Carnegie Hall. Got it at a garage sale. There was an old lady living next to your cousin, a hardcore music lover. She wouldn't think twice about flying out to La Scala to hear Pavarotti sing. If she heard of some major concert in Europe, she'd be there in a heartbeat. Vienna, Budapest, Prague—you name it. I used to fix her swimming pool. Nice lady. A little lonely too. When she died, her kids let me raid her vinyl collection, so I pulled out a few Chopin albums. I must tell you, it's just not the same. Too smooth, polished, sterile. The recording lacks that mysterious Slavic touch that you add to the piece. Your rendition is edgy and tumultuous, much like

Poland's history. Elegance through bitterness. Flirtation with doom."

Antonia giggled coquettishly. "I bet you say that to all pianists."

"Oh yeah, I'm just surrounded by classical musicians." Ethan threw the towel into his tool box. "Bump into them every day. Sure! At the ball bearing factory where I work, that's the most popular conversation topic. Chopin, Dvorak, Liszt...That's what our guys discuss on their lunch break between cans of beer and packs of cigarettes. Secret life of the blue-collar workers!" The droll self-deprecating smirk disappeared from his face. "Anyway, it was worth coming out in this ungodly weather, just to hear you play."

Antonia could not believe how much mileage she was getting out of one polonaise.

"Are you in the mood for some Ravel?" she challenged him.

"Yes, the *Bolero* theme. Bring it on."

* * * *

At quarter past midnight the phone rang. Antonia was still busy entertaining Man Friday, while Joseph and Esther were working his way through the collection of California wines. Aaron was the one to take the call. The conversation lasted about twenty seconds. When he came into the living room, his face bore that foreboding "yikes" expression that cut Antonia's performance short.

"What's wrong?" she asked.

"Bad news for Josey, I'm afraid," Aaron replied. "I just spoke with his niece Nadia."

Joseph looked up with an air of dread. He knew that the mousy girl would not make a transatlantic call just to remind him that she wanted a pair of genuine Levis. So he played dumb for a few more seconds before immersing himself into reality.

"Your mother died of a heart attack, Josey. The funeral is in two days. There's no way you can make it back in time."

* * * *

His head hung, Joseph continued sipping his wine, while his wife was running her fingers up and down his spine. They were sitting quietly in the dark living room.

Then the hunky electrician broke the silence.

"My old man kicked the bucket on the way to chemo. Pancreatic cancer, at age sixty-one. I remember that day well."

Aaron rebuked him. "Not now, Ethan."

"It's all right," Antonia said. "We want to hear the story. Let your Man Friday speak. If Joseph has a hard time following, I'll translate it for him."

"So I was driving my old man to the hospital for another round of treatment," Ethan continued. "When I glanced in the rear view mirror, I realized he wasn't breathing. In other words, I spent close to an hour being stuck in traffic with a corpse on the back seat and Beach Boys playing on the radio. My mother's passing was entirely different. She had the same disease, but in a different part of the body. She'd spent the last weeks of her life hooked up to an oxygen tank. My brothers and I would camp out at the foot of her bed. She waited for us to go outside for a smoke and turned off her oxygen flow. When we came back in, she was gone. She purposely timed her death so we wouldn't be there to witness it. Why am I telling you all this, Mr. Olenski? So you don't beat yourself. We shouldn't assume that our parents always want us by their bedside as they draw their last breath."

Another moment of silence followed. Antonia and Esther were blotting their eyes from Ethan's stoic and heartfelt narrative.

"I think we should stick to the original plan and go to the Guggenheim on Sunday," Joseph said at last. He put the empty glass on the table and stretched his back. "Then we can swing by St. Patrick's Cathedral and light a candle for Mama. She'd like that."

Chapter Sixteen
WEIRD SCIENCE

Yuri Gagarin Magnet School, Gomel – December, 1990

Maryana experienced her first orgasm during a chemistry exam. She had spent all night cramming and in the morning she gulped three cups of black coffee. Coming to class with a full bladder was definitely not the best idea, but she did not get a chance to use the bathroom before the bell rang. The stalls were occupied by three eighth-grade girls. Maryana recognized them by their large lacquered shoes with square heels and peeling tips. Last time she found herself in their company, it did not end well. The burly blonde girls pressed her against the wall, frisked her down, emptied her pockets and took the plastic ring she had won at an amusement park. Disappointed and infuriated by the meagerness of the booty, they yanked at her ponytail a few times and promised to break her neck if she reported them to the principal. Maryana knew too well that turning to authorities was useless. The bullies would get to her sooner than the principal would get to them. Having famous parents granted her no immunity from the three burly girls. Thankfully her neck was intact, but her bladder was bursting. It was impossible to think of anything else except for the throbbing pressure below the belt. She froze over the basic equation. The formulas she had spent all night studying suddenly evaporated from her memory. Above her head, the clock was ticking. With every shift of the arrow, she came closer to failing the exam. The teacher, Edward Moiseich, was a gorgeous austere Jew in his late thirties, with Biblical features and a baritone as deep and sweet as kosher wine. He was strolling up and down the aisle, watching his delinquent flock like a good shepherd, holding his wooden pointer like a staff. Maryana always found him terrifying, in a mysterious, romantic way.

Suddenly, she felt the tip of the teacher's pointer on the nape of her neck and heard his voice.

"Olenski, are you feeling all right?"

That was when it happened, the explosion inside of her, the silent roar. All the dread, self-loathing and humiliation poured forth in one sweet avalanche. She had heard other eleven-year old girls talking about orgasms in the bathroom between classes. They would huddle in the corner over a poorly translated copy of some German ladies' magazine and whisper. As result of those peak-and-giggle sessions Maryana had been under the impression that the pinnacle of bliss could only be achieved with copious amounts of wine and strawberry-scented lubricant. And there she was, twitching with pleasure in front of the man who terrified her.

"See me after class," Edward Moiseich said.

Saved By The Bang

* * * *

Edward Moiseich held his audiences with students in the chemistry lab adjacent to the main classroom. That scientific oasis was off limits to the school janitor. Only the top chemistry students hand-selected by the teacher himself were allowed to come in and service the fragile equipment. Dusting the microscopes and arranging the glass tubes was considered a huge honor, one that could be easily rescinded for a minor offense like a bad grade or a nick on a slab. Edward Moiseich was not particularly liberal with second chances. Maryana had been one of his prized Playboy bunnies since sixth grade. When he asked her to see him after class, she assumed it was because he had decided to take her off lab duty and ask that she return her white smock. When the bell rang she froze in the doorway to the sanctuary.

"Come in, Olenski," he said with an elegant and gracious welcome gesture. "This isn't Spanish Inquisition."

Her eyes still downcast, Maryana tiptoed into the lab. "You wished to see me?"

"Elementary. You're one of my favorite people."

"And you're one of my favorite teachers. And chemistry is my favorite subject. And this lab is my favorite place on earth. I'd rather be here than anywhere else."

Maryana bit her tongue. She may have gone just a little overboard. A man like Edward Moiseich, who valued dignity above all things, would not take kindly to groveling. If he had already resolved to dethrone her, no amount of sucking up on her part would make him change his mind.

"I've been watching you, Olenski."

"Have you?"

"I like to observe people and try to understand them on the molecular level. You seem awfully chummy with Morozov and Veretenik nowadays. Those two flank you everywhere you go, carrying your book up the stairs. In my ten years here I haven't seen such chivalry."

"It's not what it looks like, I assure you."

Edward Moiseich brushed the tip of the pointer across her knuckles. "Nothing is what it looks like, not when the brightest girl in the seventh grade is involved. You put certain tenth-graders to shame, Olenski. There's a reason why they appointed you class president."

"Titles mean nothing," Maryana said bitterly. "Everyone knows that the president is the scapegoat of the student body."

"But you changed that tradition, didn't you, Olenski? You rule with an iron fist. Amazing how the bullying and the hooliganism have stopped since you've taken over. Morozov and Veretenik, the two strapping delinquents, have transformed under your regime. Your Russian literature teacher is telling me that the quality of their writing has improved considerably, as if someone had pulled out the cork and unleashed all that soaring prose. In fact, their progress was so dramatic, that they were recommended for regional literary competition. Surprisingly, or not, they failed miserably. Might you have any theories on why this happened?"

"How would I know?"

"Oh, I think you do know, Olenski. Those eloquent compositions, so strikingly similar in style, weren't really written by Morozov and Veretenik. Were they? The diction has a distinct feminine slant."

Maryana shrugged. "Fine, I'm the one who's been writing their compositions. I did what I had to do. Morozov and Veretenik were torturing Finkelstein, so I made a bargain with them. I promised to help them with their written assignments on the condition that they'd leave the poor kid alone. Now I'm their hostage. If I refuse to write their assignments for them, they'll turn me in. You know that the enabler gets punished twice as harshly as the cheater. I'll lose my office, and Finkelstein will lose his protection."

Edward Moiseich nodded. "I see."

His lack of judgment was disconcerting. At the same time, he made no indication that Maryana was off the hook. "Well," she said, "are you going to turn me in?"

"No, I leave it up to you. If you get tired of your hostage situation, you'll turn yourself in. "He breathed on a glass tube and polished it with his handkerchief. "By the way, Olenski, don't lose sleep over today's test."

"I'm pretty sure I flunked it."

"So what? Chemistry a useless subject."

Maryana could not believe her ears. "What did you say?"

"It's a waste of academic hours, unless you plan on reinventing the atomic bomb. You should focus on perfecting your English instead." He rummaged in his drawer and handed Maryana a dictionary of American slang. "One day you may decide to move to a more civilized country, where people of our stock are allowed to prosper."

"Our stock? I'm not even a full-blooded Jew."

"I'm neither. Looking the part is enough. One dark curly gene goes a long way. I knew your maternal grandfather."

"You knew Eli Rosenberg?"

"I learned watercolor techniques from him. He used to teach art classes at the youth center back in the late 60s." Edward Moiseich nodded at an inconspicuous still life on the wall right next to the table of elements. "It was refreshing to have an instructor whose last name ended with a –berg."

* * * *

Before returning to class, Maryana stopped by the coat room to get a piece of hard candy from her jacket. She desperately needed a sugar boost before the algebra test. The elderly custodian lady was applying lipstick in the bathroom, so Maryana could sneak inside without being noticed. Ordinarily the coat room was off limits during the school hours, because ninth-graders had used it as a place for hookups. Whoever wanted to retrieve pocket money between classes would need to plead with the custodian to be let in. The old lady applied endearments like "whore" and "slut" quite generously, to fifth-graders and nine-graders alike.

The smell of fur, wet wool and cheap hairspray permeated the air. As she was rummaging through her pockets, a gloved hand reached out and grabbed her wrist. Maryana gasped and dropped the bag with candies. Standing before her was a tall yellow-skinned woman in a raspberry coat with a matching hat. Maryana recognized Leah Finkelstein, the mother of her tormented classmate.

"Just the girl I've been looking for," the woman said, burrowing Maryana with her lobster eyes. "I'd greatly appreciate it if you stopped meddling in my son's affairs."

"What do you mean?"

"You got the entire administration and the student council worked up over some bullying incidents."

"I had to. Some kids were stealing his lunch money and kicking him in the locker room."

"Look, my Ephraim is neither big nor athletic, but he is proud. Do you know how humiliating it is for a boy to be defended by a girl?"

"I'm not just any girl." Maryana lifted her chin. "I'm class president. It's my job to ensure safety for my classmates."

"I can see you're full of good intentions. Why don't you pick another cause, like aiding the victims of the earthquake in Armenia? Leave Ephraim out of your noble endeavors. This flamboyant advocacy will destroy him sooner than all the bullying in the world."

"So you want me to look the other way, while your son is being beaten to a pulp?"

Maryana stepped back and smoothed her black apron. "Very well. From now on, Ephraim is on his own. Just don't forget to invite me to his funeral."

Chapter Seventeen
NOBLE FURY

When Maryana left school that day, a blizzard was in full rage. The wind lifted the skirt of her dress, like a bawdy hooligan. She felt an urge to slap the sky. Such weather stimulated her belligerent side. A perfect day to start a war!

Through the curtain of swirling flakes, she saw her father. Joseph was sitting on the railing, wearing tight stonewashed jeans with Rambo iron-on decals. After his mother's death Joseph experienced a sort of regression and plunged into adolescence. Dressing and acting like a twelve-year old nurtured the illusion that Natalie was still alive. His students at the music academy found the transformation delightful. In a world that was growing increasingly tense and grim, Professor Olenski's class provided a safe haven where the future musicians could rediscover their juvenile side. The only person who did not find his transformation endearing was Maryana.

"Hey, troll, you're getting kind of fat," Joseph said to his daughter.

"I'm growing," was her sullen reply.

"In the wrong direction, at the wrong rate. Your mother and I can't keep buying you new clothes every three months."

Sadly, there was truth to Joseph's words. Ever since she got kicked off the gymnastics team, Maryana has been adding padding to her small frame. Hey, that's what happens to athletes who go from burning three thousand calories a day to only nine hundred. An ugly girl cannot afford the luxury of being fat too. There's just more of her to despise. A fat girl makes for a larger target. There is more surface for bruising.

"What are you doing here, Papa Josey? You didn't get fired, did you?"

"I don't have any students for the next three hours," he said, jumping off the railing. "So I swung by to see you in your natural environment. Don't change the subject though. Pretty soon your tits will reach your knees if you don't get your appetite under control."

"Save your compliments for your choir girls, Papa Josey. I bet you've had a chance to grope all of them between rehearsals."

"Oh yeah? Who's been groping you lately?"

"None of your business."

"I bet it's that chemistry teacher. Don't get too excited, troll. You don't stand a chance with him. Jews don't fall in love with other Jews. They want natural blondes, the forbidden fruit."

Trading ethnic and sexual jokes was a new custom between the two. Joseph had officially abdicated the remnants of paternal authority and settled into the role of a delinquent older brother. It seemed hypocritical to demand modesty and chastity from his daughter when he practiced neither. Their private conversations were so deliciously and liberatingly inappropriate. Maryana was reluctant to admit it, but she enjoyed the new development. In some respect she had risen above her peers. She seriously doubted that many other seventh-graders had such discussions with their parents. It's so much more gratifying than talking smack with other girls in the bathroom.

Joseph reached into his pocket and pulled out a pack of German gum. Maryana was more interested in the miniature comic inserts than the gum itself.

"Mama Cat would have a fit if she heard us talk," she said, having finally settled on the piece with Maja Bee.

"At least I'm not one of those sanctimonious assholes who grope anything that moves and then insist that their daughters stay virgins until the age of forty." He squinted quizzically. "You are still a virgin, aren't you?"

"What do you think? It's not like I have the entire soccer team lining up under my window."

"Don't lose heart, troll. You'll get laid one day. I'm sure there's a strapping Lithuanian shepherd boy waiting for you. Hey, if you ever need an alibi or condoms..."

"Nice to know I can count on you, Papa Josey."

"By the way, guess who died."

"Franz Anthony?"

Maryana shrugged and adjusted the straps of her backpack. "About time. I didn't like that grouchy old coot."

"I didn't either," Joseph admitted. "Come to think of it, I don't think I ever approved of any of my mother's boyfriends or husbands. None of them was good enough for her. You think it's a form of Oedipal complex?"

"I don't know. Talk to a psychologist. How did old Franz die, anyway?"

"You wouldn't believe it. Teresa Wolnik told me he pretty much lost it after the funeral. At first he couldn't believe that she was gone. Every morning he'd set the table for two, load up her plate with pancakes and sausage. He'd play polonaises on the accordion, the ones they used to dance to. Late at night the neighbors could hear him arguing with himself. Then it finally hit him. He couldn't lure her back with the smell of bacon or her favorite tunes. He'd go to the cemetery every day and spend hours kneeling by her grave, rain or shine. He even tied one of her scarves to the cross so she wouldn't get cold. Pretty creepy, huh?"

"Like something Edgar Poe would write."

"One day he went and never came back. There was a major blizzard, worse than the one today. He just walked into the storm. A week later they found him on her grave, frozen, hugging the cross. He'd taken his coat off and thrown it over the grave. She'd always hated cold, so he'd given her his coat to keep her warm, just like he'd done in the early days of their courtship. Heavy stuff, eh? Kind of puts Romeo and Juliet to shame, doesn't it?"

Personally, Maryana preferred *Titus Andronicus* to all other Shakespearean plays. She glanced at her father. "If something happened to Mama Cat, would you visit her grave every day?"

"No, I wouldn't," Joseph replied after a second of deliberation. "I would've asked to be buried alive with her."

Maryana elbowed him. "You're full of shit."

She paid for that innocent shove dearly. Her father sent her flying across the pavement into a gutter. Her backpack burst open, and collection of wrinkled notebooks spilled over the wet pavement. Joseph walked a few meters ahead, then stopped and glanced behind. "Come on, troll, pull yourself together."

They walked through the Pioneer Park, past the circus. The smell of animals and fried dough seeped through the walls of the illuminated round building, spilling onto the street and mixing with the smell of melting snow and car exhaust. The visiting troupe from Moscow was on tour, and all shows were sold out. Confetti and candy wrappers were frozen into the sheet of ice covering the sidewalk. When Muscovites come, they bring chaos and litter.

Having reached the corner of the Victory Square, father and daughter saw a crowd gathering around the World War II tank monument, with posters wavering above the people's heads.

"What's all that?" Joseph squinted to read the signs. "Free bagels and tea?"

A pimply youngster in his late teens elbowed his way through the crowd.

"Professor Olenski!" He grabbed Joseph by the sleeve and pulled him towards the tank. "Thank God you're here. We need you like never before."

Maryana noticed that the youngster was wearing an embroidered Belarusian peasant shirt and a Catholic cross underneath his leather jacket.

"Mankowski, what's going on?" Joseph asked. "Are we starting a revolution on a Tuesday afternoon?"

"They're trying to squish our initiative," the student said. "Everything we've worked for. We can't let those Moscow whores win, can we, Professor?"

Saved By The Bang

The initiative. Maryana knew exactly what Mankowski was referring to. For the past year there had been talks in the nationalist circles about instilling certain linguistic reforms in schools for the purpose of purging the up-and-coming generation of the pernicious Russian influences. All subjects would be taught in Belarusian, and Russian would assume the position of a foreign language, like English. The brilliant proposal, championed by Joseph and his colleagues, had caused a great deal of outrage among the citizens of Gomel, given that most of them spoke Russian at home. The fact that the union was crumbling away did not surprise anyone. Gorbachev, the sentimental softie, had made it possible for the small nations to get cheeky with the Moscow government. The Soviet state was on its way out, just like an outdated car model. Still, most people of Gomel were not quite ready to embrace the quaint melodic language of the bards.

Maryana got a little nervous. In her father's gooseberry-green eyes she saw the familiar fanatical fire. She knew he would not let the revolution happen without him. The three of them were standing on the platform of the tank monument, above the sea of flags and posters. His one arm around his student and the other around his daughter, Joseph addressed the crowd.

"These are the final days of the Union," he spoke in Belarusian. "People of Gomel, we've suffered enough under the tyranny of Moscow. Russian education has turned your children into pea-brained Philistines who disdain the language of their ancestors. I've come here to give you a taste of freedom!"

"We don't want your stupid freedom, Olenski," one of the pro-Russian activists shouted. "Go back to banging your interns, you village clown."

Rocks and vodka bottles started flying. Maryana felt a sharp blow to her right temple. Blood streamed around her eyebrow, blurring her vision. The rumbling of the protestors below instantly muffled, as if someone muted the volume on a TV set. The last thing she saw was Mankowski's face as she tumbled down from the tank into the raging crowd.

* * * *

Central Hospital

"Fucking savages," Joseph murmured as they were waiting in the trauma center, waiting to patch up the gash above Maryana's eyebrow. "I can see why they'd want to aim at me. Not everyone wants to hear the truth. But never thought they'd actually try to harm a kid."

"I'm not a kid anymore." Maryana sighed. "Not a cute one, anyway. I'm an ugly fat teenager with Jewish features. You can't use me as a shield. If anything, I'm a magnet for stones and bottles."

"So what are we going to tell your mother?"

"We don't have to tell her anything. Maybe she won't notice. I'll just wear my hair down for a few days."

"Of course, she'll notice. She probably heard about the riot. My name will be all over the local news."

"Well, maybe I can come up with a plausible story. I'll tell her I fell off the bus or walked into a wall. I'll do the talking"

"Maybe on the way home, we can stop by the consignment shop. I'll get you those earrings you've been eyeing."

"Papa Josey, my ears aren't even pierced."

"Then I'll buy you a bracelet, garnet, amber, anything you want."

"I don't want anything...from you. I just want to get home." The truth was, she did not want to go home either.

"Come on, troll, we have a pact. Remember?"

"I don't want any more pacts."

* * * *

Telman Street

"What happened to your head, Cotton Paw?" Antonia asked her daughter over dinner. "It looks horrid."

Joseph continued stirring condensed milk into his coffee. Like Maryana, he had grown tired of lies. A part of him wanted to be exposed and turned in. He was curious to see if his daughter would actually go through with her promise to tell the truth.

"We were attacked by some hooligans outside the circus," Maryana said between bites of fried potatoes, "and Papa Josey protected me. He was very brave. Then he walked me to the trauma center and held my hand while they were sewing me up."

Antonia continued to spread butter on her bread. "Kids these days..."

Joseph tossed the sticky spoon into the sink. "Actually, this isn't what it happened at all. Maryana is lying to you."

Antonia batted her eyelashes in mock astonishment. "Our daughter, lying? No!"

"We were passing by the Victory Square," Joseph said through his teeth, "and got pulled into a nationalist rally by Mankowski. He made us climb the tank monument. The rest is in the accident report. Happy now?"

Antonia reclined in her chair with the majesty of a trial attorney. "Well, Josey, don't you deserve a medal for honesty. Father of the Year! You realize you can lose your teaching license if the administration catches a whiff of this? Disturbing the peace, using a twelve-year old as a human shield. Tsk-tsk..."

"What can I say?" Joseph threw his arms up. "I've outdone myself this time."

"Well, now that we are on a soul-purging spree, maybe you'll be a man and tell me how Maryana got the rest of her injuries. That broken rib that kept her out of the regionals back in '87. Did she really get it at practice?"

"If you despise me so much, why not file for divorce?"

Antonia had to give it some thought. Despise Josey? Absolutely. But divorce him? Not yet. She was hoping to torture him for another decade or two. Above all, she did not want Nicholas Nichenko to think that anything was wrong with her marriage. No, she would not give that ungrateful pup such satisfaction.

"My dear Josey," she said in a softer voice, "we don't need to divorce just because our political views are diametrically opposite. This plurality of opinions is what makes our marriage so exciting and sparkling. By the way, I'm enamored of Moscow government. I detest tyranny as much as you do. But Belarusian people need an iron fist. They cannot handle their freedom. What happened today at the Victory Square is only an example of what is yet to come. You unshackle slaves, and they trample over their liberators. Don't expect gratitude for setting your people free. When you must choose between freedom and order, the choice is obvious."

Feeling that the painkiller shot was beginning to wear off, Maryana excused herself and went into the living room to lie down. Rummaging through her mother's closet in search of a blanket, she came across a box containing a vinyl collection of Chopin's waltzes and barcarolles, recorded in New York. Enclosed was a hand-written note in English.

*Please accept this souvenir from a humble
American electrician, in memory of the night we
met.*

*Yours,
Ethan Schwarzwald*

Chapter Eighteen
ARYAN BLUNTNESS AND SLAVIC CHIVALRY

Gomel – September, 1991

Ectro-dac-ty-ly. After almost four years of fatherhood, Nicholas Nichenko was still struggling to pronounce his son's diagnosis. In all this time he had not even managed to bring himself to take a proper look at the boy's hands. He could not tell off the top of his head which fingers on Timmy's hands were fused, and which were missing. He did not feel comfortable with the whole idea of Timmy posing for the preschool photo. He had asked the teacher to move Timmy to the back, or at least have him hide his hands in his pockets, but Galina had preempted her husband and arranged for the boy to stand in the front row, holding the school banner, with his deformed hands in plain sight. In her opinion, it was only fair that Timmy should hold the banner, since he was the one who had painted it. The news of the lobster-handed art prodigy had spread through the city. Timmy's surrealistic masterpieces featuring elephants with two trunks and three-headed monkeys were gracing not only the hallways of the preschool but also the music academy where his parents were working. Galina was organizing a charity banquet for ectrodactyly awareness. The event had already received copious coverage in the local newspapers. The news crew was gearing up for filming. Rumor had it, the chief hand surgeon from Minsk going to make a guest appearance.

Nicholas found the whole affair distasteful. He realized it was not in his power to stop the spinning wheel and cancel the event. Timmy was already in the public eye, the genius lobster boy. He had already attracted a sizable circle of fans. They were writing letters to him and asking for autographs. The only thing Nicholas could do was ruin his wife's mood. If he could get her sufficiently flustered, maybe she would get a zit or two and look abysmal.

"You don't care about special needs children," he said the night before the benefit as she was ironing her velvet gown with a slit. "You're only doing this to get attention. You know damn well that nobody considers Timmy's works brilliant. It's nonsensical doodling."

"It's juvenile surrealism," Galina corrected him sternly. "I believe that's the correct term—thank you very much. Salvador Dali went through that phase."

"You don't believe a word of that rubbish, do you? Nobody would've noticed Timmy's projects if he was normal. When a kid with ten fingers splatters some paint on a piece of paper, it's called doodling. But when a deformed kid does the same thing, it suddenly becomes high art. Jesus Christ, woman, how cynical you must be to make a spectacle out of a family tragedy!"

Galina whipped him with her bra across the arm. "My only tragedy is being married to you, Cole."

"Huh?"

"You heard me. You're the weak link in this family, not Timmy. It's people like you who should be institutionalized. I happen to be proud of my brilliant exceptional son, and I'll make sure that his talents are recognized. I won't let you ruin my happiness. You know, when I first met you, I thought you were an operatic god! But over the years you've proven to be nothing but a humorless coward."

Nicholas took a step back. He did not want to stand too close to a woman with a hot iron in her hands. "Whom are you calling a coward?"

"I like calling things by their proper names. It's my Aryan bluntness." Galina leaned into the ironing board. "Truth be told, you are only concerned for your golden boy image. You expected me to produce a perfect baby Apollo for you, and when that didn't happen, our marriage became irrelevant."

"Now you're being totally unfair, Gal. Didn't I stick by you for all these years? Didn't I accompany you and Timmy to doctor appointments whenever I could?"

"And now you think you deserve a medal for it? Sure, you stuck around out of sheer politeness, just so you wouldn't look like a total bastard. But in your heart you've already checked out."

"We should open the windows, Gal," Nicholas said half-audibly. "These fumes from the laundry detergent are making you talk nonsense."

He pulled the curtains aside and wiggled the handle on the window, but Galina's menacing growl stopped him in his tracks.

"Don't even think about it! You'll cause a draft, and Timmy will catch a cold. Is that what you want?"

"Fine." Nicholas backed away from the window, his hands raised in surrender. "If you want to get high on the fumes, be my guest. By the way, you don't need to press the shirt so hard. It's polyester blend. You'll damage the fabric."

Galina would not let her husband change the subject so easily.

"Remember the day Timmy was born?" she said, resting the iron on the board and brushing her loose hair strands away from her red face. "Remember how the neonatal pathologist urged us to put him in an orphanage and tell the rest of the world our baby had died? I saw that twinkle in your eye, a glimmer of hope. I know exactly what was going through your mind." She made it a point to remind Nicholas of the incident in the neonatal unit at least once a day. "I should've just taken the baby and dumped you right there. The way you behaved that day showed me who you are."

"What kind of reaction did you expect from me?" Seriously, how many times did he have to apologize for that brief moment of confusion? "The doctors said it would be better that way, that Timmy would get proper medical care around the clock, something we couldn't give him at home. He'd be around other kids with missing fingers, who'd understand him."

"Proper medical care?" Galina let out a guttural laugh. "You seriously buy into that bullshit? Have you been inside one of those institutions? Garbage bins for rotting vegetables. That's what they are."

"Geez, forgive me for not having done my homework. I had no idea what it would be like to raise a handicapped baby in this country."

"This country is handicapped—not my son. That's why I'm taking him away."

Nicholas sneered at this outrageous declaration. "Where in the world would you take him?"

"To my father's house."

"In GDR?"

"There's no more GDR, you moron! Hasn't been in two years. In case you haven't heard, the Berlin wall was torn down. Germany is one country once again. Not that I'd expect you to follow world news. Anyway, I've been thinking about taking my father up on his offer and move to Berlin."

"You think that post-Nazi orthopedist can perform a miracle and reconstruct Timmy's hands?"

"On the contrary, my father thinks that a surgery won't be necessary. Timmy doesn't need ten fingers. He's perfectly adjusted the way he is. If anything, a surgery will disrupt his painting career."

"Wow..." Nicholas scratched his balding crown. "This is by far the most absurd thing I've ever heard in my life."

"Why don't you admit it, Cole? You're jealous of your son. You're not the center of attention anymore. The spotlight is on Timmy, and that just doesn't sit well with you. You're not ready to give up your crown. That's why you want Timmy to feel like a freak. God forbid he should be proud of himself."

Nicholas opened his mouth, gasped a few times, as if on a verge of an asthma attack. "So, you're just going to pack up and take our kid out of country? I don't get a say in all that?"

"Sorry, Cole. You've given up your parental rights the day you wanted to sign Timmy away. Now, I realize our breakup is a little untraditional. Usually, it's the man who walks out on his wife and special needs child. That's what the doctor said. Men don't like being burdened or embarrassed. Very soon you'll have all the freedom in the world. I'll find myself a real man, in a civilized country, and you can always go back to being Antonia's eunuch."

* * * *

The last parental duty Nicholas performed was packing his son's unwanted clothes, toys, puzzles and board games and taking them to the orphanage across the Sozh River, the same orphanage where Timmy would have been placed. The potbellied nurse hastily snatched the bag from Nicholas' hands and slammed the gate on him with a snarl. Ordinarily the staff would invite the donor to come in, inspect the grounds and meet the internees, if only to ensure that the donations would keep coming. On paper visits were allowed, even encouraged, but only the better-looking and better-behaved children would be shown to outsiders. The truly hopeless cases without any chance at adoption were kept in a separate room with insulated walls that would contain their incoherent groans. After the fire in Chernobyl the rate of congenital mutations skyrocketed. Certain sights were too disturbing even for those who had worked in the system for decades and thought they had seen it all. Who would have thought that nature was even capable of such violent hiccups? Oh, the endless possibilities that arise from a scrambled genetic code! The expanded spectrum of birth defects stretched beyond trivial microcephaly and skeletal malformations. The medical community studied them with horrified curiosity, but general public was not ready to see those images. There was enough panic in the air already.

Earlier in the year a particularly daring journalist posing as a donor had made his way into the closed-off-ward and snapped a few photos of the internees. Even though the photos had never made their way into any of the newspapers, they had been released to the public. Within the week the waiting halls of women's clinics filled with frazzled patients at various stages of pregnancy demanding abortions. At that rate the nation would die out. Someone had to put a lid on mass hysteria.

Nicholas would love to talk to the director about organizing a holiday concert at the orphanage or giving some pro-bono voice lessons. He certainly had the free time now. But that fat lady let him know in no uncertain terms that he was not welcome in the establishment, as if she knew what he had contemplated doing four years earlier. Or, perhaps he looked too much like a journalist yearning to write an exposé.

So Nicholas stood on the other side of the rusted fence and watched the children play in the yard in front of the dormitory. The padded autumn jackets concealed their deformities. That particular orphanage specialized in orthopedic handicaps. Most of the internees had clubbed feet and stunted limbs. Some had defects of the spine. The children bustled, crawled and giggled, oblivious to the melancholic onlooker.

The high-tech playground totally knocked his socks off. The equipment must have been a charitable gift from one of the bourgeoning co-ops. Local businessmen would make amends with the police by supporting orphanages and juvenile detention facilities. Even the most exclusive residential neighborhoods in Gomel did not have such snazzy turnstiles, carousels, sliding tubes and monkey bars. Buried in the heart of a maple park, the orphanage looked more like an oasis rather than prison. No. The real prison was outside the iron gate.

M.J.Neary

* * * *

Crossing the bridge on his way home, Nicholas spotted a teenage girl in school uniform. She had climbed over the railing and was standing on the narrow ledge, holding on to the bars with one hand. A thin train of blood was streaming down her bare leg, getting absorbed by the white knee-high sock. Nicholas caught a glimpse of the side of her face. Boy, she must have really pissed someone off. She was sporting a black eye and a swollen lip. Underneath the dirt and the bruises, Nicholas recognized the troll-like features of Maryana Olenski. He knew that girl had a talent for getting beat up. This last brush with society must have been particularly violent. God, what did she say this time? She was staring into the chirping gray rapids three hundred feet below.

Nicholas positioned himself behind her back, close enough to be able to grab her by the frizzy pony tail, should she take the leap.

"Does your mother know where you are?"

Maryana shook her head. "Don't say anything to her. She's getting ready for the concert tomorrow night. It's this huge benefit event. She needs to focus on her performance."

"If they fish your corpse from the river, I have a feeling it will put a damper on her plans."

He wrapped his arm around Maryana's waist and pulled her over the railing. She felt like a really heavy rag doll, neither cooperating nor resisting. One of her shoes came off and fell into the ripples of the Sozh.

"Fuck," she whispered. "It was my good pair. It was supposed to last me until next year. Grandma Lily will kill me."

Nicholas took a few seconds to scan her injuries. They were numerous but superficial. Her reflexes seemed in order, which led him to conclude that she had not suffered a brain concussion.

"Now, kid," he said, "let's get down to business. Who did this to you?"

"A bunch of ninth-graders. They called me a kike and a lesbian, so they wanted to show me what it felt to have a Russian man inside me."

The laconic immediacy of her reply took Nicholas aback. He had expected to spend at least some time pulling the truth out of her. To his surprise, he did not detect any trace of humiliation in her voice. The girl seemed more distressed by the loss of her shoe than her virginity. Still, possessing this information obliged him to taking some sort of action.

"Do you know their names?"

"Of course, I do. We go to the same school."

"Are you going to share them with me?"

"What for, Uncle Cole?"

"So I could cut their balls off or at least smash their knee caps."

Maryana tugged at the fringe of his scarf. "You're sweet, but I can't let you do this. You'll go to jail. And your family needs you."

"I don't have a family anymore." Nicholas stooped. "Galina is moving to Germany and taking our son with her. Her birth father talked her into it."

"Oh, that sucks."

"Not really." He forced a smile. "Maybe it's for the best. In a way, it frees me up to do things I wouldn't do otherwise, like castrating those bastards who hurt Antonia's daughter. I don't care if it's the last noble deed."

Nicholas looked so wretched that Maryana forgot about her own mishap for a minute. The notion that a thirty-five year old man of such caliber was baring his soul before her made her feel exalted.

"Noble deeds aren't appreciated anymore," she said, putting her arms around his neck. "The country is going down the toilet. Grandma Lily says so. Her father had fought in the war for this country, and the younger generation is fucking it up."

"Those were Lily's exact words?"

"Yep."

"I've always liked that lady. Though, I imagine it would be a bear to have her for a mother-in-law."

Maryana began to shiver. Nicholas removed his coat and wrapped it around her. He would have offered her a cigarette, but he had smoked the last one on his way to the orphanage.

"Just for the record," she added, "I'm not a lesbian. What happened with Deana earlier...It was totally not what it looked like. The reason why I fell for her was because she was one girl on the entire team who looked like a boy. I like broad shoulders, short hair and a deep voice, and Deana had all those things. In fact, I'm in love with someone else right now, desperately, miserably."

"Why miserably?"

"It's complicated," she said the worldly gravity of a woman who had been through at least three marriages. "We can't be together, not until I graduate. You see, he's my chemistry teacher, the smartest, sexiest Jew in the world."

Nicholas scooped her up in his arms and carried her off the bridge.

"It's getting late," he said. "I'll fix you a cup of tea with a shot of cognac."

"Make it two shots."

* * * *

Gomel Music Academy

Nicholas waited until Antonia's rehearsal was over to deliver the news. Barging into the concert hall with foam around his mouth would be excessive. He still possessed enough delicacy and concern for Antonia's public image. So he let her finish the piece. Incidentally, it was Aram Khachaturian's *Symphonic Poem*, the piece that had earned the composer the wrath of the Party back in the 1940s but had been later restored. To Nicholas this piece represented resurrection and second chances, all the things that eluded him. He did not have the heart to interrupt Antonia's performance.

When he ambushed her in the coatroom, the place of so many mid-afternoon hookups, the first thought that occurred to her was that he had come to her in search of sexual healing.

"Look, Cole," she said, "I understand you're feeling a little lonely with Galina gone, but I'm really not interested in reviving the wild passion of our youth."

He cut it straight to the point, "Your daughter got raped by a bunch of ninth-graders. She's at my house now."

Antonia's dainty crocodile skin clutch slipped out of her hands. Coins and makeup spilled all over the floor.

"I cannot believe it," she muttered. "My little Cotton Paw is all grown."

For the first time in his life, Nicholas came close to slapping a woman. "Are you out of your mind? She's not 'all grown'. She's a child who was violated."

"No, no, no." Antonia shook her head. "I won't allow my daughter to fall into victimhood. Self-pity is so addictive and crippling. I don't want her to be more crippled than she already is. She'll blow her nose, fix her skirt and march on. It's the only way."

Nicholas grabbed her by the shoulders and gave her a heartfelt shaking. "For God's sake, woman, can you drop your Spartan ethos for once? Your daughter needs a head doctor."

"So do you, Cole. Get your hands off me!"

"She was dangling off a bridge when I found her. Who knows what would've happened had I not passed by. I could very well be delivering much worse news this very minute. Preposterous as it sounds, Maryana got off easy this time."

Antonia slipped out of his grip and bent over the collect the contents of her clutch. "Don't get me wrong, Cole," she said. "I'm grateful to you for giving Maryana a place to lick her wounds. But please, don't lecture me after you've driven away your own wife and kid. You're no paragon of parental love yourself."

Saved By The Bang

* * * *

Prospect Street

It suddenly occurred to her that in the thirteen years of their acquaintance she had never been inside his house. All traces of Nicholas' marriage had been removed.

In the hallway Antonia wrinkled her nose.

"Do I smell cognac? Have you been drinking without me? I could really use a shot right about now."

"There's plenty in the cabinet," Nicholas groused under his breath. "And no, I'm not turning into an alcoholic, if that's what you're wondering."

Maryana was lying on the couch under a pile of plaid blankets, flipping through a German comic book. Galina's father had been sending Rolf Kauka's publications so his grandson would stay in touch with his German heritage. After moving to Berlin, Timmy would have access to all the comics in the world, so he left the old collection behind.

"Uncle Cole has *Fix und Foxi*," Maryana said without making eye contact with her mother. "This stuff is seriously collectible. Do you know how much these go for on the black market, Mama Cat?"

Antonia elbowed Nicholas and hissed in his ear, "It's a defense mechanism. Totally normal after a trauma like that, from what I heard. She's regressing into her childhood."

"One she never had."

"Oh, for heaven's sake, Cole! Not again. We've been through this already."

She knelt in front of the couch and pried the comic book out of Maryana's hands.

"Cotton Paw? Look at me. About what happened today... It's too bad your paternal grandma isn't around anymore. She would've told you how she was cornered by a contingent of German soldiers during the war."

Maryana exhaled and raised her eyes to the water-damaged ceiling. "Mama Cat, I heard that story a million times."

"Great. Then you know it has a happy ending. Grandma Natalie went on to have many boyfriends and husband afterwards. That run-in with the Nazis didn't turn her off men. It certainly didn't dampen her sense of humor or her libido. Same thing will happen to you, my dear. You'll shake it like a nasty head cold in no time."

"I don't know what you're talking about, Mama Cat. I don't have a cold."

"You don't have to pretend with me. What happened today doesn't make you dirty or anything."

"I don't feel dirty. I don't know where you get these ideas."

"Then why were you trying to take a bath in the river?"

"I don't know. It got a little hot all of a sudden."

Maryana had seen enough American movies to know what normal girls were supposed to act like after being raped —curl up in a ball, rock back and forth, scratch their arms, cry in the shower and shudder at every touch. No, she did not feel compelled to do any of the above. Either the directors of those movies were lying, or American girls were hysterical weaklings. In all truth, she did not feel dirty or defiled, certainly no more than she did on any other day. Another hematoma in a new place. She had reached a point where pain no longer hurt, and insults no longer offended. Perhaps that's what Buddhists call Nirvana, when you no longer twitch when poked with a rod.

* * * *

Telman Street

Around eleven o'clock at night the phone rang. Antonia crawled out of bed over Joseph's flaccid body. They had just finished having sex, and the freshly washed sheets were already wrinkled and damp. She was expecting a call from Prague regarding an upcoming tour, and the director of the philharmonic orchestra was notorious for ignoring the difference in the time zones. Through the copious static she heard a volley of smoker's cough. A little neon light went on inside her as she realized that the call was coming from across the Atlantic. *Ethan.*

"Your cousin is hosting this fancy-ass wine-tasting party," she heard him say. "His Jew friends blew the generator again. Anyway, he stepped away to take a piss and left his address book on the counter, so I found your number. I couldn't help it. The opportunity was staring me right in the face. I just wanted to hear your voice."

"You have serious balls calling me at home," she hissed into the receiver, "especially at this hour."

"Did you get my present?"

"Yes. And it really made me angry as hell."

"Gosh, I'm sorry. I just wanted to do something nice for you."

"What you did was juvenile and reckless. My God, Ethan, what were you thinking?"

"I wasn't thinking at all."

"How could you send those precious vintage records across the Atlantic without proper packaging? Do you realize how delicate vinyl is? It's a miracle they didn't crack. Callous men like you shouldn't be allowed to handle such relics."

"Just forget the whole thing. Calling you was a bad idea. I don't know why I do certain things, honest to God. And I've done some pretty random stuff. But don't worry. You'll never hear from me again."

"Now you're acting like a sulky child." Antonia adjusted the strap of her nightgown. A few meters away, her husband was growling and turning in bed. "You should call me on my work number instead. Aaron has it written down somewhere. Every day I take lunch between two and three. And remember, we're seven hours ahead of you. Anyway, there's a small upright piano in my office. Call me, and I'll play Chopin for you. Tomorrow I have a dentist appointment, but Wednesday is wide open. Do we have a date?"

The reply did not come right away. Antonia heard some indecisive humming on the other side.

"Hello, Ethan? Are you still there? Does Wednesday work for you?"

"I don't know if it's such a good idea. It might be too much for me."

"The long-distance bill? Just ask Aaron for a bump in salary."

"I wasn't talking about money. It's the last thing on my mind. I just don't know if I can handle listening to you play and knowing that I'll never see you again."

"Nonsense. Of course, you'll see me again. I'm not in another galaxy, for God's sake, just across the pond. I haven't made any public announcements yet, but I'm coming to America for good. I've found a way to pull that off."

* * * *

"What was that all about?" Joseph asked her when she returned to bed.

"Just some punks playing a prank." She yawned and turned her back to him.

"Oh yeah? Since when do punks speak English?"

"Since your daughter joined the Mark Twain appreciation society." Antonia was pleased with how smoothly and unaffectedly the fib rolled off her tongue. To make the story more believable, she elaborated. "These kids found out we have relatives in America, so they've been calling day and night. They need some blue jeans for a production of *Huckleberry Finn*."

Chapter Nineteen
BEYOND THE SHADOW OF DOUBT

Moscow, US Consulate - October, 1991

The waiting room at the American embassy in Moscow was bustling with Jews and Jew lookalikes who had come from various parts of the soon-to-be former Union, pursuing the same goal—to claim political asylum and get the hell out of the old country. The *coup d'etat* attempt in August was the long-awaited wink from God for those who had merely flirted with the idea of emigrating. Time has come for another exodus. The old machine was cracking, with bolts and screws flying all over the place. Gorbachev's naïve experiment in democracy had produced a growling mutant that was stomping its big ugly feet. Nobody knew what the new regime would look like, but one thing was certain. Things were not going to be pretty for those whose surnames ended with -stein, -berg and -man. Preemptive holocaust was not out of the question. Now was a perfect time to take advantage of the commotion and slip out. Only a fool would not recognize that opportunity.

Saved By The Bang

So the people came prepared. Each one of them had a weepy story to tell, but all stories sounded distressingly similar. The narrative usually involved a math genius named Boris who was denied entrance into the top informational technology program or an art prodigy named Ella who was barred from St. Petersburg Academy of Fine Arts, all on the account of ethnicity. The claimants had already jumped through the rings to get as far as the embassy. They had to fill out lengthy questionnaires, send them to Washington, then wait for several months to get the official invitation to interview with an officer. The oval room at the end of the hall was the final point where their fates were decided.

Maryana liked the idea of missing three days of school. The academic year had only started, and her hands were already itching to shoot half of her classmates, starting with Morozov and Veretenik. Earlier in the week during art she drew their dismembered bodies. Great! The first quarter had only started, and she was already having such vivid homicidal daydreams. The valerian root extract that Lily swore by did not seem to be working for Maryana. She still was the class president. The principal would not allow her to step down from her position as class president. What masochistic idiot would take her place? Those pubescent delinquents needed her diplomatic leadership more than ever. With any luck, it would be her last year in that school, that city, that country.

To kill time, she had brought along Pushkin's novella *The Captain's Daughter*. She just grabbed a random book from her father's shelf. Now she was wondering if she should have brought something by Sholem Aleichem instead. Or would it make it look like she was trying too hard?

Her dry curls were pulled into a high ponytail, leaving her shiny forehead exposed. The new hairstyle accentuated the bump on her nose. The strategically smudged eyeliner gave her eyes that woeful Semitic slant. For the past few years she had years she had worked so hard to neutralize her Jewish features, lightening and straightening her hair, contouring her nose with makeup to make it shorter and straighter. Today was one day when she needed to look like she had just stepped off the set of a holocaust movie.

* * * *

Ten minutes before their interview, Antonia pulled Maryana aside and laid her lotioned hands on her daughter's shoulders.

"Cotton Paw, remember how I always told you not to play a victim?"

"Uh-huh..."

"Well, today is not one of those days. Forget everything I taught you about pride and self-reliance." Antonia glanced behind. "There's a very influential American bitch behind those closed doors. I hear she's brutal. You must convince her that you truly are a victim of ethnic persecution, beyond the shadow of doubt. Dozens of people come here every day claiming that their civil rights are being violated, and most of them go home without the coveted refugee visa. We cannot be one of those losers. Understand? What you say today behind those doors will determine the course of our fate. We either start a prosperous new life across the pond or rot away in this radioactive anti-Semitic hole. You want to live in America, don't you?"

"More than anything, Mama Cat."

"I thought so." Antonia patted her cheek. "I know you don't subscribe to that patriotic bosh that your kindergarten teacher hammered into your heads. Screw Motherland! Just think of all the clothes and makeup you'll have when you're in America. You won't have to wait for Uncle Aaron to send you Sarah's hand-me-downs. You'll have all the pretty things in the world. You deserve it, Cotton Paw."

"I deserve it," Maryana echoed, envisioning a stack of Levi jeans. "Hell, yeah, I deserve it!"

"Remember, you're doing this for the benefit of the entire family. Never forget the sacrifices I've made for you, Cotton Paw. This is your chance to repay the debt."

"I'll do whatever you tell me to do, Mama Cat." At that point she would gladly throw herself under a tank.

"Just be candid with the lady, Cotton Paw. Spare no detail. Tell her how those nasty boys battered and molested you for being Jewish. Look sad, very sad, but don't cry. You don't want her to doubt your sincerity. Plus, your mascara will run."

"Okay, okay," Maryana jumping up and down like she did before gymnastics competitions. "Jesus Christ, help me..."

"Shush, idiot child." Antonia pinched her daughter's arm. "You can say 'damn' or 'fuck' or any other one-syllable word, but don't let them hear you say 'Jesus Christ'. Today you're Jewish. Jesus is not your friend. If you slip, our American dream will go belly up. Is that what you want?"

Maryana blinked and retreated into a silent prayer, "Mother of God, Blessed Virgin Mary, please help me be the best Jew I can be."

* * * *

The interviewer's name was Judith Beck. Or maybe it was Jane Doe. She looked like a cross between Candice Bergen and Linda Hamilton, the two American actresses most familiar to Eastern European audiences. By 1991 everyone had seen the shows "Murphy Brown" and "Beauty and the Beast". Platinum highlights, a strong leathery neck and a square chin placed the woman in that category that was affectionately referred to as "Yankee horse", the epitome of reformed Occidental womanhood. Her office was as bare as a KGB interrogation chamber. One would have expected to see some blown-up panoramas of New York on the walls. Nothing. Not a trace, not a hint of American promise. Maryana did notice a demure silver cross flashing under the lapel of her red blazer.

The interviewer greeted the Olenski family in excellent Russian and incidentally wished them a very, very happy Yom Kippur.

"Mrs. Rosenberg," she began by addressing the oldest member of the family, "I understand your late husband was Jewish."

Crisp and self-righteous, Lily threw her head back. "That's right." She was pretty gung-ho on the idea of going to America. Perhaps, she could revive her engineering career across the ocean. The George Washington Bridge could certainly use a facelift. "Eli was as Jewish as a bowl of matzo soup."

"And that must've affected you and your family."

Saved By The Bang

"Tell me about it! But I'll let my daughter do the talking. She'll tell you how she was rejected from Moscow Conservatory. She had to go to the one in Minsk instead. Everybody knows, it's a second rate institution. It mostly attracts provincial riffraff. Such an insult! With her natural abilities...As a result of this horrid act of discrimination, her musical career didn't go as far as it could have." Lily pulled out a starched handkerchief from her purse and blotted her forehead. "My daughter has the floor."

Antonia wiggled in her seat, assuming a more official attitude, and cleared her throat, ready to deliver her speech, but the interviewer was not looking in her direction. Her next target was Joseph.

"And how are you doing today, Mr. Olenski?"

He gave her a wry, self-deprecating, I'm-just-a-dumb-Pole, smile. "Me? I'm awesome."

The interviewer leaned in, locking her hands under her chin. "You are a public figure, Mr. Olenski. I heard your song on the radio this morning. You have an established professional life in Gomel. How do you feel about leaving it all behind?"

"I'm eager to follow my beautiful wife to freedom."

Joseph cast a buttery glance in Antonia's direction and reached out to take her hand. He knew all about her international phone trysts and with the American electrician. Gal Richtman had clued him in. The entire music academy knew how Antonia was spending her lunch breaks, including Nicholas and Vladimir Ivanych. Interns would congregate by the door, eager to partake in those Chopin-themed orgasms. Joseph was not ready to reveal his cards. He had not yet decided how he would punish his wife for this act of emotional infidelity, so continued to feign innocence. The punishment would have to be elaborate and sadistic. Jealous outbursts were beneath him.

"Incidentally," he continued, stroking Antonia's fingers, "I owe my happiness to that very horrid act of discrimination that my mother-in-law pointed out a moment ago. Had Antonia been accepted to Moscow Conservatory, we never would've met. Those anti-Semites who barred Antonia from the school of her choice actually did me a huge favor. But, just because I benefitted from this act of injustice, it doesn't make it right. I want her to go to a country where her talent can truly blossom."

Antonia pulled her hand out of his and went on to tuck a loose frosted strand behind her ear.

"Now, I don't want you to think that we're seeking a mid-life career boost. We aren't cynical opportunists milking the Jewish gene to get ahead in life. No doubt, you see people like that all the time, and I assure you, we are nothing like them. The main reason why we are contemplating emigration is for the sake of our daughter Maryana. Of all the family members, she has suffered the most."

"Maryana has her father's surname?" the officer asked.

"But she has her grandfather's features! Look at the poor girl! That nose, that hair. Just wait until you hear what happened to her last year." Antonia glared at her daughter. "Cotton Paw, won't you tell the nice lady what happened?"

Yankee Horse slammed the folder shut. "It won't be necessary. I've heard enough."

Maryana jumped up. "Wait! You must hear me out." No way were they going to send her home without giving her a chance to narrate the rape saga that she had spent so many hours rehearsing. "Please. I won't take too much of your time. Two minutes tops, I promise. Jesus Christ..."

There, she said it. The forbidden name that instantly blew her feeble Jewishness right out the window. Maryana knew she was dead. Now her long-suffering family would never see America because of her slip. Panting, she stared into the threadbare rug on the floor, waiting for the executioner's ax to drop.

"Are you all right, little girl?" she heard the interviewer say. When Maryana looked up, she saw the leathery face beaming with solidarity and understanding. "There's no need to shout and frighten the people waiting in the hall. Everything is well. Your visas will be ready tonight."

* * * *

Gagarin Magnet School – October, 1991

The students knew something was up when the class president showed up wearing a denim button-down mini dress instead of the uniform.

She poured out her treasures—tubes with pearly lipstick, half-empty miniature flasks with perfume, packs with bubble gum, hard candy, flashcards, scented markers, erasers shaped like baby animals, plastic neon bracelets, glow in the dark shoelaces and bright polyester headbands. Suddenly her desk looked like a tray of a Polish street vendor. The only thing Maryana did not surrender was the amber bracelet given to her by Officer Balciunas. That Baltic souvenir from her magical night in Vilnius would follow her to America.

"Help yourselves, bitches," she said, backing away from the pile as if it was toxic waste. "First come, first serve."

At first the girls did not know what to make of her bizarre behavior. This gesture of generosity was totally out of character. Maryana Olenski never shared her stuff. She never was one to let a friend borrow her chap-stick or take a bite out of her apple. Not that one would expect any better from an only child, whose parents were local celebrities. Why was she suddenly giving her stuff away? Had she been diagnosed with some terminal disease?

Dana Dubrowski, the vice president, reached out and felt Maryana's forehead.

"Are you delirious, Olenski?"

"Yes," Maryana replied hoarsely, "with joy. Finally, I'm getting out of this shithole. You can split my junk among yourselves. I don't care who gets what. Won't need it in America."

"America?" Dana pulled her hand away, as if scorched. "What? You're leaving us, Olenski?"

"Don't pretend like you're sorry to see me go, Dubrowski. That makes you the class president. I know it's always been your dream to preside over these delinquents. Now dig in, bitches, before I change my mind."

Thick-skulled as the girls were, they sensed they should be feeling insulted by Olenski's words. Their indignation was short-lived. The magical fruity smell emanating from the pile of Polish souvenirs neutralized their pride. Pushing each other aside, they dug into the booty. Watching her classmates pinch and shove each other over her trinkets filled Maryana with grim satisfaction. Arms folded, she leaned against the bookcase and savored every squeal coming from the crowd. "Mine! Mine!" Ah, that was her revenge for the years of torment. The skirmish continued even after the bell rang and the physics teacher came into the classroom.

"Olenski is leaving us," Dana announced with affected sorrow. "In the middle of the academic year, too! Edward Moiseich, she's going to America."

The handsome Jew graced Maryana with one of his smiles, balmy as the breeze from the Dead Sea, which for a second made her stoop in shame. She had allowed herself to go too far. True winners do not gloat. She had no right to despise those kids.

Chapter Twenty

FRANKLY, SCARLETT...

Sheremetyev Airport, Moscow – February, 1992 – 11:00 pm

Strolling along the row of duty-free gift shops at the airport, Maryana felt her sympathy for her former classmates deepen. Those wretched girls who were ready to kill each other over her meager hand-me-downs would never have access to such a vast selection of magazines and designer purses. She knew that such high-end items would never make their way into the department stores in Gomel, not for another decade or two. And there she was, preparing to plunge into the bottomless ocean of glamour. While at the Chanel outlet, she sampled at least twenty fragrances. The cuffs of her denim jacket became sticky from the moisturizer. The skinny salesgirl with her hair in a sleek bun must have been used to such barbaric behavior from bedazzled provincial teenagers, because she volunteered to teach Maryana the smoky eye technique that involved a charcoal pencil and three different types of brushes. Paired with burgundy lipstick, it was the hottest New York look. And it only took forty minutes to achieve. The salesgirl knew she was not dealing with a paying customer here. At least the young savage would sit still in the makeup chair and not break any tester bottles. Maryana emerged from the outlet a changed woman, thoroughly westernized, reeking of bergamot and sandalwood.

Joseph had been unusually quiet and contemplative all night. He had not made a single sex joke. Like a true gentleman, he volunteered to hold Antonia's carry-on, while she was sampling perfume and lip gloss at the Estee Lauder stand. He looked endearingly pathetic with the tiny opera purse in his hands and mist over his eyes.

When the boarding was announced, he suddenly trembled, as if jolted with a shot of caffeine, and handed the purse over to Antonia.

"Go easy on the lipstick," he said. "That shade makes you look whorish. You can always tell a Russian immigrant woman by the amount of makeup she wears."

"Very funny. Now get in line. I don't want us to be the last ones to get seated. My feet are killing me."

"Then you should definitely hurry. You want the aisle seat, don't you?"

Antonia cocked her hip. "Don't tell me...you have to piss, don't you? This very moment? Ugh...I told you not to drink those beers. What are you going to do now? The bathroom is on the end of the building. Can you at least wait until we're on the plane?"

"But you see, darling, I'm not getting on that plane. I'll surely miss you, though."

"Did my Polish village idiot get cold feet? It's all nerves. You've been up for twenty hours. Now take a pill, like a good boy." She pulled out a bottle of valerian tablets. "Take one. Better yet, take two."

Joseph took the bottle and tossed it over his shoulder. The pills scattered all over the freshly mopped floor.

"I don't have cold feet. In fact, my feet have never been warmer. They just won't dance to your fiddle anymore."

"Whatever your problem is, can we discuss it tomorrow in America?"

"That's the thing. I'm not going to America. They offered me a job in Warsaw, a dream job, with room and board thrown in, and I accepted it. I only came here to help you get your things on the plane. I'll send the divorce papers to your cousin's address."

For the next thirty seconds Antonia stood gasping and smacking her scarlet lips.

"Don't get so agitated, not on my account," Joseph continued. "I'm not the bad guy here. I'm only trying to make it easier for you to be with your American electrician boyfriend. Who am I to stand in the way of true love? I'm sure that blue-collar knight will be thrilled when you show up at his doorstep penniless with a kid. He'll sweep you up in his arms and carry you over the threshold of his trailer."

Antonia smacked her lips a few more times, and then the words finally came out.

"Impregnator of grannies! Look who's talking about fidelity. You've smeared your sperm all over Eastern Europe. I could've slept with the entire music academy, you know. I had countless opportunities to fuck some of the hottest studs in the vocal department, not just Nichenko. Still, I kept my legs closed, even when I knew you were banging that Poplawski bimbo, because unlike you, I still have traces of morality and self-control. More than that, while your bastard daughter was alive, I looked the other way when you slipped her ice-cream money, the money you could've spent on your real daughter instead. That's right. I pardoned you your rancid past!"

"That's the thing, my love." Joseph shook his index finger. "I don't want to be pardoned anymore. I'm tired of being put on trial and then pardoned. I'm tired of holding my farts around you. As long as I'm married to you, I won't be a free man, not even in America." Joseph had not intended to make this parting speech long and wordy. The boarding was about to begin. "Have a fabulous trip, my darling."

Mesmerized, Maryana watched the scene between her parents, dragging the tip of her boot across the slippery tiles. She had never heard her mother use so many profanities on one breath. In less than twenty seconds Antonia had managed to resurrect her husband's entire sexual history. Pretty impressive! Something told Maryana that was the fight to end all fights. Still, she found the scene was disappointingly anticlimactic, similar to the one between Clark Gable and Vivien Leigh in "Gone with the Wind".

Having broken eye contact with his wife, Joseph looked at his daughter and slapped his thigh with a whistle. "Come here, troll. Papa Josey would like to have a final word with you."

Maryana stepped forward like an altar girl ready to receive her communion. Joseph reached out to tousle his daughter's hair and frowned when she growled and bared her crooked front teeth.

"No need to get skittish," he chided her. "I'm not gonna hit you. We're in a public place, for Christ's sake. Don't worry. Pretty soon you'll have a new father. That ought to make you happy. Come on, give us a smile."

Instead of a smile, Maryana blew a giant gum bubble and popped it.

"By the way," Joseph added in a lower voice, "I've been meaning to tell you how impressed I was with your acting skills. That performance at the consulate? Priceless! The whole segment about being molested by a pack of Neo-Nazis brought me to tears. With a talent like that you'll go far in life."

Maryana punched him in the face, knocking the glasses off his nose. Stepping back, she rubbed her knuckles and grinned. It felt good.

* * * *

11:30 pm

Maryana bulldozed her way down the aisle of the Boeing and claimed the window seat. The cushion was still warm and dented from the previous passenger. The armrests were sticky from the pineapple juice. Maryana sniffed her fingertips and smiled. Ah, the smell of America, of freedom and prosperity! And her idiot father would not be sharing those blessings with them!

Right before the takeoff, Antonia burst out sobbing.

"Tears of joy, I hope," Lily said. The prospect of flying on a Boeing exhilarated her. As an engineer, she had tons of professional admiration for the brilliant people who designed such a magnificent aircraft. "I've waited my whole life to fly a Boeing. I don't know how anyone can cry on a day like this."

"Joseph's got the money," Antonia sniffled. "All of it. I locked it in my clutch and asked him to hold it for me while I was window-shopping at the airport. He never gave it back to me."

Lily clicked her tongue. Three thousand dollars in cash. That was the sum they ended up with after selling all their furniture, jewelry, furs, electronics and the coin collection. That money was supposed to cover their rent for the first few months in America before they found jobs.

"What did I tell you, Antonia? A man who grew up in a boarding school is bound to be a thief. You didn't believe me. On another hand, you know what they say. If you give a man three thousand dollars and never see him again, it was worth it. Good riddance! If there is a God, that money will go towards Joseph's funeral expenses. Now, girls, wipe your noses and buckle your seatbelts.

M.J.Neary

Epilogue
NORMAN ROCKWELL DOESN'T LIVE HERE

Gomel - November, 2002

Vladimir Ivanych's funeral was the most splendid farewell of the decade. The late department chair looked magnificent in his open casket, dressed in a double-breasted suit and covered in loose sheet music. That last esthetic touch was his students' idea. Since he died suddenly of a stroke, his corpse did not show the usual wear-and-tear of prolonged illness. Anybody who was anybody in the world of classical music or nationalist revival attended the funeral, including Ilona and Tycho Poplawski from Minsk. Galina Richtman could not come from Germany because she had another charity concert to raise ectrodactyly awareness, but she did send one of her son's finger paintings depicting the fall of the Berlin Wall.

With Vladimir Ivanych gone, his job was given to Nicholas Nichenko. Now it was his turn to throw angry fits, chide young lovers and groom the new generation of national laureates. The promotion came at a perfect time, as Nicholas had a new wife and a baby on the way. Moved by that morose sense of duty echoing back to the Soviet era, Nicholas took it upon himself the task of writing the obituary for the newspaper and delivering the eulogy at the cemetery. It began with the words, "We are standing at the dawn of a new century." In reality, he was just standing at the edge of his late boss' grave. His thirty-year old wife was fidgeting by his side, dying to go to the bathroom. The sound of the rain beating against the granite monument was exacerbating her desire to urinate.

Having returned home that day, Nicholas found an international letter with American eagle on the stamps. Skimming over the loopy whimsical calligraphy of the woman he had once worshipped, Nicholas felt a warm tingle of nostalgia, as if a cat licked his neck with her rough tongue. Suddenly it all came back to him, the cheerful austerity of the 1980s, the enormous flowerbeds with pansies in the riverside park, the squeak of floorboards at the concert hall, the smell of Baltic perfume and freeze-dried coffee.

My dear Cole,
Time flies when you ignore old friends, doesn't it?
Can you believe it's been ten years already?
Belated congrats on your latest marriage. I
find it strange that you never acknowledged
mine or Maryana's. Was that intentional? I
won't comment on your wife's age or her vocal
range. It's so predictable that the chair of the
vocal department should marry a soprano. I
would've expected more originality from you.
But Cole, what in the world possessed you to
create another child at an age when most

sensible people already have grandchildren? Speaking of which, Maryana popped out a nuclear five-kilo giant back in April. I warned her not to eat so many pancakes with butter. The stubborn girl never listens. All those extra calories went into the baby. He split her open when he came out! The adorable little designer outfits I'd splurged on don't fit him, so I'll be sending them to you. You should expect a package in the next few months. I'm sure you could use a few donations, especially in light of the recent budget cuts. I still think it was rather cheeky of you to give reproduction another shot. Don't you know that chances of birth defects increase as you age? You already have one handicapped child. Aren't you in the least bit worried that genes will play a nasty trick on you again? Please don't misinterpret my bluntness as malevolence. I wish nothing but pure bliss for you, my dear Cole. You deserve it, after all the disappointments and failures in your life.
All my love,
Antonia Schwarzwald, Ph.D.

PS – I am enclosing a few photos of my new studio. Ethan repainted it from top to bottom, put in hardwood floors and recess lights. The acoustics are divine! Vladimir Ivanych would approve.

Saved By The Bang

* * * *

Southern Connecticut, 2002

Morning sickness was a real ass-kicker, and no amount of pickled ginger could alleviate it. Antonia strolled around her newly remodeled studio with a handkerchief pressed to her mouth. After a decade of sporadic flirtations with fertility drugs, Antonia had suddenly found herself pregnant at forty-nine, exactly twice the age she was when she gave birth to Maryana. Had she known the treatments would actually work, Antonia would have stopped them. She did not want another kid, not really, but she continued on the Clomid regimen, because it gave her and Ethan something to do, a common goal to strive for, like a chronic remodeling project. Now she was on par with Madonna and the rest of Hollywood grannies.

Above her head she could hear her six-month old grandson wailing and beer glasses clanging. Ethan was entertaining Maryana and her husband. The homely troll had blossomed into a moderately attractive ogress one nose job away from beauty queen, determined to make the world pay for the slights of her childhood. Her victim was a willowy Irish-American graphic designer by the name Bailey Griff, ten years her senior. During her last year in college she had bullied him into marriage, and now he was the one carrying the fussy infant while Maryana was cackling to her stepfather's racial jokes between sips of Guinness. A typical Friday night at the Schwartzwald house.

250

"Cotton Paw, keep it down!" Antonia implored from her studio.

The cackling stopped, but only for a few seconds. "What's the matter, Mama Cat? The baby is wide awake."

"I wasn't talking about your baby. My head hurts."

"Then have a drink, Mama Cat. A shot of whiskey should take care of that."

"I cannot drink. In case you haven't noticed, I'm a little pregnant. Hello?"

Maryana leaned over the railing, her milk-filled breasts spilling out of her size four Ann Taylor jacket.

"Well, Mama Cat, in case you haven't noticed, I'm suffering from a major case of postpartum depression. You're not the only one in the throes of a hormonal storm."

"Why do I have a feeling that you'll be milking that for the next eighteen years?"

Maryana huffed and recoiled. "You just can't stand the idea of someone else being the center of attention, can you? Admit it, Mama Cat. I had a baby, so now you are having one too. God forbid I should be one step ahead of you for once."

"Oh, Cotton Paw, you're in no danger of being one step ahead of me. At your age I was working on my dissertation, and you don't even have your Master's."

"Well, that's because you didn't pay for it. A real mother would've paid for her daughter's grad school. I mean, look at my cousin Sarah. Her parents took out a home equity loan to put her through Harvard."

"Oh yeah, and now she's chairing a non-profit, making whooping forty thousand a year," Antonia remarked with a touch of venomous pleasure. "A PhD in urban anthropology

—that's how people make millions. Her parents must be over the moon."

"That's not the point." Maryana raised her finger. "The point is Uncle Aaron made the effort to give his daughter the best education possible. He made sacrifices. When was the last time you made a sacrifice for me, Mama Cat?"

"Do I really have to answer that question?"

"Well, since you are rubbing my obvious lack of education into my face! Nice to know where your priorities are. You had to take that trip to Hawaii and renovate your studio. Gotta keep up with the oligarchs of Fairfield County! Oh, and let's not forget your fertility drugs. Those alone cost sixty grand. That's an MBA right there. Now thanks to you, I'm making half of what I'm worth. On top of everything, that Russian nanny we hired last week is already giving me grief. I think she's been sampling Bailey's scotch. Every time we come home, the place smells like booze, and there are wet spots all over the counter."

"Maybe you should put a lock on your liquor cabinet," Antonia suggested.

Maryana let out a jerky laugh. "A lock, seriously? Your faith in humanity is endearing, Mama Cat. When did a lock stop a Russian alcoholic? If she wants to get plastered at our expense, she'll find a way."

"You don't know that for sure. Don't be so hasty to accuse people. You could start by installing a camera. Hollywood stars do it all the time to spy on their nannies. Take a ride to Radio Shack before they close."

Maryana raised her empty beer can. "You want me to drive drunk in pouring rain? You really don't care if I get into an accident and die, do you?" Her padded shoulders collapsed. "Of course, you don't. I was never good enough, so now you're trying to have another kid, to get things right the second time around. You don't have a single picture of me at your house. It's like I don't even exist. In your eyes I'm just one huge birth defect, *spina bifida* in the human form."

"That's a slight exaggeration," Antonia said. "But there's no denying that you do take after your biological father in many ways."

"Sometimes I wonder if I should've gone to Poland with him instead of coming here with you."

"Don't be silly." Antonia exhaled in exhaustion. Those retrospective musings were hurled at her at least once a week.

"Joseph never loved you, and we all know that. Ethan is your father now. He loves you, in spite of your rotten genes."

"Not for much longer," Maryana objected morosely as she crumbled the beer can. "I know exactly what's going to happen. When the new baby arrives, Ethan will lose interest in me. I won't be his princess anymore. It's like when a family gets a new puppy, the old dog gets sidelined. How can I compete with a puking, drooling screamer? Funny how I had one genuinely good thing in my life, one benevolent father figure, and you had to take that away from me too."

Maryana flung her mercilessly straightened hair and strutted back to the kitchen to pour herself another drink. Bailey mumbled something in his mother-in-law's defense. The infant's wailing went up a few notches. Through the symphony of background noises Antonia could hear her daughter's tirade directed at her Irish-Pennsylvanian husband.

"Shush, Bailey! I'm sick and tired of hearing about your sore back. You just started your Daddy shift forty minutes ago. I spent the whole night walking up and down the hall carrying your kid, so you could get some sleep. Now it's your time to bond with him, man to man, so don't shove him in my lap. If I make less money than you, it's not because I'm any less intelligent, ambitious or hard-working. It's because my mother denied me proper education. You knew that when you married me. It's supposed to be an equal partnership. It's not some sort of patriarchy that you grew up with. Norman Rockwell doesn't live here."

Antonia crawled underneath her Steinway and heaved into her plaid handkerchief, like a cat coughing up a hairball, feeling the walls of her freshly painted studio close in on her.

The End

About the Author

Marina Julia Neary

A self-centered, only child of classical musicians, Marina Julia Neary spent her early years in Eastern Europe and came to the US at the age of thirteen. Her literary career revolves around depicting military and social disasters, from the Charge of the Light Brigade, to the Irish Famine, to the Easter Rising in Dublin, to the nuclear explosion in Chernobyl some thirty miles away from her home town. Notorious for her abrasive personality and politically incorrect views that make her a persona non grata in most polite circles, Neary explores human suffering through the prism of dark humor, believing that tragedy and comedy go hand in hand.

Her debut thriller *Wynfield's Kingdom* was featured on the cover of the First Edition Magazine in the UK and earned the praise of the Neo-Victorian Studies Journal.   After writing a series of novels dealing with the Anglo-Irish conflict, she takes a break from the slums of London and the gunpowder-filled streets of Dublin to delve into the picturesque radioactive swamps of her native Belarus. *Saved by the Bang: a Nuclear Comedy* is a deliciously offensive autobiographical satire featuring sex scandals of Eastern Europe's artistic elite in the face of political upheavals.

If You Enjoyed This Book

Please write a review.

THIS IS IMPORTANT TO THE AUTHOR AND HELPS TO
GET THE WORD OUT TO OTHERS
VISIT

PENMORE PRESS

www.penmorepress.com

All Penmore Press books are available directly through our website, amazon.com, Barnes and Noble and Nook, Sony Reader, Apple iTunes, Kobo books and via leading bookshops across the United States, Canada, the UK, Australia and Europe.

A Gathering of

Vultures

Donald Michael Platt

Murder, mutilation, and carrion... in paradise? "

"There shall the vultures also be gathered, every one with her mate." -ISAIAH 34:15

Professional ballroom dancers Terri and Rick Hamilton aspire to be world champions. Unfortunately, Terri's recurring back and health problems place that goal well out of reach. They travel to Terri's birthplace, Florianópolis, on the scenic island of Santa Catarina off the coast of Brazil to vacation and visit their best friends and mentors.

Along the picturesque beaches, dead penguins and eviscerated bodies wash up on the shores of paradise, and Antarctic blasts play counterpoint to the tropical storms that rock the island. The scenic wonder is home not only to urubús, a unique sub-species of the black vulture, but also to a clique of mysterious women who offer Terri perfect health and the promise of fame—at a terrible price.

Praise for "A Gathering of Vultures

PENMORE PRESS
www.penmorepress.com

WILDFIRE IN THE DESERT

BY

BRUNO JAMBOR

Action Adventure, Crime, Mystery,
Southwest History

Highly entertaining, well researched and original:

A Navy veteran returns home to his ancestral land to escape the pace of modern life. His nephew begs him to hide the drugs he is transporting to escape his pursuers.

An astronomer trying to find a replacement for his estranged wife finds solace in his work with the stars.

Police and the drug cartel try to recover the missing shipment, regardless of consequences, ready to sacrifice any opponent.

The antagonists crisscross the desert of Southern Arizona in a chess game where the loser will be eliminated.

Unexpected help comes from a famous missionary who blazed new paths through the same desert three centuries ago.

The climactic resolution will captivate readers of this thriller with deep spiritual undertones.

PENMORE PRESS
www.penmorepress.com

THE BOTTOM DWELLERS

BY

LEAH DEVLIN

Bioengineer and Party Girl...

Lindsey Nolan has it all: inventions paying large dividends, a dream job in the scientific village of Woods Hole, Massachusetts, and a stable of eager playmates. But when Lindsey wakes up in rehab with no memory of how she got there, her world is turned upside down. Her roommate, an HIV-positive teenage prostitute named Maggie, is the most volatile patient on the ward. The facility is plagued by disturbing thefts. And another theft unfolds when her competitor, an engineer named Karen Battersby, discovers and steals Lindsey's astonishing new invention from her Woods Hole lab. Lindsey and Maggie must face the consequences of past transgressions if they hope to deal with present perils and ascend from the desolate world of the Bottom Dwellers.

PENMORE PRESS
www.penmorepress.com

Force 12 in
German Bight
by
James Boschert

Considering that oil and gas have been flowing from under the North Sea for the best part of half a century, it is perhaps surprising that more writers have not taken the uncompromising conditions that are experienced in this area – which extends from the north of Scotland to the coasts of Norway and Germany – for the setting of a novel. James Boschert's latest redresses the balance.

The book takes its title from the name of an area regularly referred to in the legendary BBC Shipping Forecast, one which experiences some of the worst weather conditions around the British Isles. It is a fast-paced story which smacks of authenticity in every line. A world of hard men, hard liquor, hard drugs and cold-blooded murder. The reality of the setting and the characters, ex-military men from both sides of the Atlantic, crooked wheeler-dealers, and Danish detectives, male and female, are all in on the action.

This is not story telling akin to a latter day Bulldog Drummond, nor a James Bond, but simply a snortingly good yarn which will jangle the nerve ends, fill your nose with the smell of salt and diesel oil, your ears with the deafening sound of machinery aboard a monster pipe-dredging ship and, above all, make you remember never to underestimate the power of the sea.

–Roger Paine, former Commander, Royal Navy.

PENMORE PRESS
www.penmorepress.com

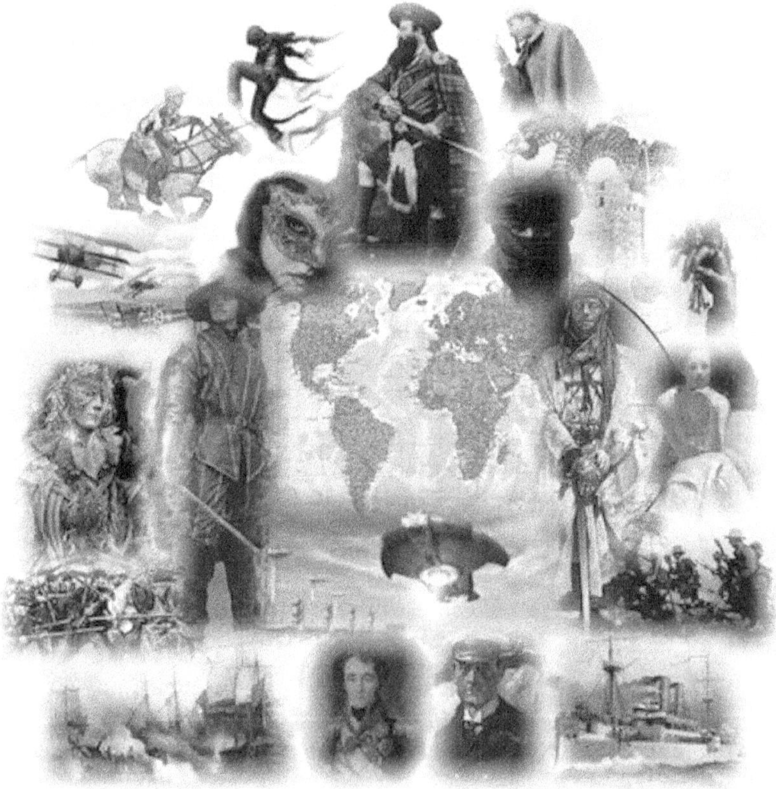

Penmore Press

Challenging, Intriguing, Adventurous, Historical and Imaginative

www.penmorepress.com